# THE ENEMY OF TIME

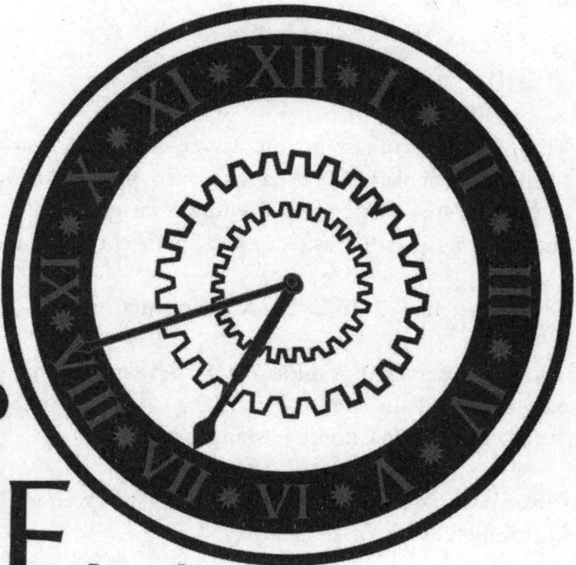

HALEY-GRACE MCCORMICK

This book is a work of fiction. Any references to historical events, real people, or real places are used fictitiously. Other names, characters, places, and events are products of the author's imagination, and any resemblance to actual events, places, names, or persons, is entirely coincidental.

Text copyright © 2026 by Haley Grace McCormick

All rights reserved. For information regarding reproduction in total or in part, contact Rising Action Publishing Co. at:
http://www.risingactionpublishingco.com

Cover Illustration and interior designs © Haley Grace McCormick
Distributed by Simon & Schuster

ISBN: 978-1-998672-16-5
Ebook: 978-1-998672-17-2

FIC027240 FICTION / Romance / New Adult
FIC043000 FICTION / Coming of Age
FIC071000 FICTION / Friendship

#TheEnemyofTime

Follow Rising Action on our socials!
Twitter: @RAPubCollective
Instagram: @risingactionpublishingco
Tiktok: @risingactionpublishingco

*To my dad, who read my words aloud every night, thank you for lending me your voice when I was still finding my own.*

*To my mom, who pushed me forward on the days I dug in my heels, thank you for challenging me when I doubted myself.*

*To my grandparents, whose gentle, steady love has always been my soft place to land.*

*To my godparents, whose kindness and guidance added a light to my life that I will carry always.*

*And to the ones who were told their dreams were too big or their voice too small, This story is for you.*

THE
ENEMY
OF TIME

# CHAPTER 1

You don't have to love to be loved.
You don't have to live to be alive.
You don't have to die to be a ghost.

**3:00 p.m.**

Dante once wrote, "There is no greater sorrow than to recall happiness in times of misery." But the worst part isn't remembering—it's knowing you can't go back.

Today is May 4, 2022. Five years had passed since I escaped my hometown in Massachusetts and moved away to college—five years since I stepped foot in my mother's car, and now here I am, driving back to my childhood home.

"The brakes need fixing," my mom said as we pulled into the cracked driveway after a high-pitched squeal cut the silence between us. The house looked the same. The yellow shutters were still barely holding on by silver nails, the front door remained an alarming firetruck red, and the front lawn overflowed with too many plants and flowers, causing the house to disappear into a tiny jungle. Everything appeared to be precisely the same.

Pulling my worn purple suitcase out of the rusted trunk, I struggled to drag the wobbly wheels over the cobblestone path leading to the porch steps, which desperately needed replacement.

My mother touched my shoulder. "Alex, why don't you head upstairs and get some rest before dinner? It's been a long day, and tomorrow won't be any easier."

All I could manage was a nod; words wouldn't form. As I reached for the doorknob, my hands began to shake. Damn. How hard is it to turn a freaking handle? I cursed myself, feeling like a foolish, emotional child ruled more by my heart than my head. That's what this house did to me, what this town did to me, and it's why I promised never to return. But promises are just empty words, as fragile as a house of cards.

An icy dread seeped into my veins as I twisted the gold handle and opened the door. It felt like ripping a bandage off my skin. I cautiously stepped over the threshold, entering the house like a five-year-old intent on sneaking a cookie from the kitchen, my red pumps barely making a sound on the heavily scratched wood floors. The house was just as I had left it: small and overcrowded with furniture and trinkets.

The loud clatter of my suitcase against the stairs filled the silence as I wrestled it towards the top. Our house wasn't grand, but the stairs certainly were. My mom and I had moved in with her new husband, Julian, and his son, Lucas, when I was five years old. His wife had passed away three years earlier; Julian had been living alone, and it showed.

The walls were covered in garish yellow wallpaper, and the wooden floors were hidden beneath a layer of green shag carpet. Mismatched chairs in the living room were held together with duct tape, and random pizza stains tainted the fraying brown rug. Although the house dated back to the 1870s, it was clear that a 1970s renovation, with its bold colors and lava lamps, had obscured its Victorian charm.

My mom wasted no time restoring the home to its original craftsmanship. On the day we moved in, she tackled the staircase, which was covered in the same green shag carpet that plagued the rest of the house. My mom immediately grabbed a box cutter and slashed the carpet off the steps, pulling it away with such force that Lucas and I became covered in fluffy shreds of decade-old material, making us look like characters from The Muppets.

Next, she sanded down the old, chipped paint from the original banister, leaving a thick layer of powdery dust throughout the house. It took six days to strip the staircase of an unappealing brownish-green paint down to its original beauty, but it was all worth it when my mom applied the first coat of stain to the mahogany wood. From the delicate carvings on the banister to the intricate molding on the wall, every element of the staircase gleamed as if it were thanking us for bringing it back to life.

Memories flooded back with each step I took. The way light filtered through the stained-glass window at the top of the stairs, broken four times throughout my childhood; the creaky step that woke mom up when I was fifteen and trying to sneak home in the middle of the night; the way the baseboard still smelled of nail polish from when I splintered the wood and covered it up. Each step felt like swimming through the past, my eyes dancing over the familiar field of memories displayed on the wall. Photos of family, friends, and cherished moments from my childhood were mounted in thick, ornate frames. They ascended the stairs like a picturesque timeline, a mismatched storm of bad haircuts and braces. For most families, the kitchen was the heart of the home, but in this house, it was the staircase. Somehow, this pile of carved wood brought our two broken families together and created a home for us.

One picture, mounted in a gaudy gold frame hanging six steps up, immediately drew my attention. It was of Lucas and me on his seventh birthday; I've always hated that he was older by just a few months. The party was pirate-themed, which he still denied was my idea, even years later. We had been bickering since sunrise, a common occurrence back then, but it escalated to unprecedented heights on that particular day.

Competitions against each other were constant: best grades, the highest score on Mario Kart, who could run fastest from the car to the front door—trivial stuff. On the morning of his birthday, we had a teeth-brushing competition, and Lucas won, putting me in a bad mood for the entire day and ramping up my competitiveness to level 10. An intense relay race occurred just before our parents cut the cake, which I won by 1/10 of a second. Lucas refused to accept the loss and called a foul, blaming me for his trip right before the finish line. I was furious at his accusation, even though he was entirely correct.

That morning, I applied a layer of super glue to the soles of his shoes to make them extra slick. What Lucas called cheating, I called competitive ingenuity. As Lucas was about to blow out his candles, Mom was prepared to take the picture, but he grabbed a chunk of the cake and threw it at me, painting blue frosting all over my white shirt. I retaliated by blowing out his candles and smashing his face into the cake. The result? The infamous family food fight photo.

That picture of two kids covered in the aftermath of sibling rivalry had always been my favorite. Back then, Lucas and I couldn't go five minutes without talking to each other, but five years of silence had passed because of one decision: one moment, one stupid fight, one second that altered the course of our entire lives. How insignificant a single second seemed until it became the last.

As I reached the top of the stairs, I could feel the weight of adolescent mistakes piling on my shoulders like boulders trying to bury me in a mountain of regret. Yet, there was a weird sense of comfort and peace, knowing my childhood would always be preserved on that wall, a time capsule forever hanging right there, a speck of proof that life was once pure. That peaceful feeling died quickly upon seeing a photo that stopped me dead in my tracks.

It was him.

Jamie and I met about a year after we moved in with Lucas and his dad. He became my first and only friend despite my mom's failed attempts to force me to socialize.

It was an agonizingly hot day in July—the kind that turned the playground, made of 40% plastic and 60% metal, into a blistering barbecue upon which you could cook a child's leg. I had the burn marks to prove it. My mom, hoping for some sibling bonding, had taken Lucas and me to the park. Lucas and I had been at each other's throats ever since I moved in, and not just with typical sibling bickering; I mean, full-on barbarian head-bashing attacks. Once, when Lucas tried to steal my pink unicorn eraser, I stabbed him in the hand with a pencil—no regrets.

Laughter had filled the air at the park, but none of it had

been mine. I'd never been the giggly type, and once Lucas saw my mom's attention drift to the other parents, he abandoned me for the other six-year-old boys, leaving me alone on the teeter-totter. As I sat there, my bare thighs sizzling on the searing metal, a blonde, blue-eyed girl approached. I thought maybe I'd have some company, but then I recognized her—Bethany. Our moms had forced us into playdates a few times, the last ending with me spilling watercolor paints all over her puffy princess dress. Her tiny feet rushed toward me, and without a word, she threw a muddy rock at my head, knocking me off the teeter-totter and into the wood chips.

When I opened my eyes, four girls surrounded me, with Bethany clearly in charge. She grabbed my hair like a grizzly bear clutching a dead fish while another girl beside her menacingly snipping pink scissors. The instant I felt the tension released from my scalp, I knew she had taken a crucial chunk of my hair. I was still convinced those Barbie bitches worked for the devil, and I was meant to be their human sacrifice.

A blur of movement caught my eye as a boy about my age with black hair darted in front of me. Bethany folded her arms across her chest and stepped forward, clearly ready to confront him. As she moved, the boy stuck out his foot, sending her tumbling forward, crashing into the wood chips below. The sunlight caught on the glittery sandals of her friends as they gasped and scattered in a flurry, racing back toward their mothers. Bethany scrambled to her feet, little sticks clinging to her knees, and shot me a venomous glare. 'You'll pay for this!' she yelled before stomping off after them.

The boy helped me up, then grabbed the fallen scissors,

turning them in his hand for a moment. Without a word, he snipped a chunk of his hair, mirroring my missing lock.

"I needed a haircut anyway," he said with a smile that lit up his face.

That was the moment I knew this messy-haired boy was my favorite person in the world. When I met Jamie, my entire life flipped on its axis and lost all direction. That moment changed my life forever. If only I had known then just how much.

A few minutes passed before my mother finally noticed the chaos and rushed over to Jamie and me. After examining my new scrapes and the uneven haircut, to my surprise, she didn't yell or scream. Instead, she looked at us with the biggest smile. Her greatest wish had finally come true: I had made a friend. She quickly pulled out the disposable camera she always kept in her purse and snapped the first picture ever taken of Jamie and me.

"Why the hell hadn't Mom removed this picture?" I muttered to myself as I squinted at the old photograph, feeling a pang in my chest as I traced the edges of our smiling faces.

I tore my eyes away from the photo.

"Keep moving," I whispered, a plea to my feet, urging them to take me toward my old bedroom. I opened the door and found the room half-filled with boxes—my parents had finally decided to turn it into a puzzle and craft space. I couldn't blame them. After all these years, why not? But standing there, seeing everything packed away, it felt like walking through a graveyard.

The walls were the same soft purple, but the paint was now faded and chipped beneath the yellowing crown molding. My bed was still pushed against the far wall, but my once-black comforter had been replaced with a vibrant pink one featuring yellow watercolor daisies along the edges. The desk I used to do homework on was gone, and a long craft table cluttered with old papers and books stood in its place.

I walked over to the window and looked outside at the backyard, which used to have a trampoline and swing set before Lucas broke them both. Apparently, playground equipment couldn't handle a lightsaber battle between my six-foot brother and Jamie. Laughter had once filled this room, but now emptiness echoed through these ghostly walls.

As I wandered around, a small, faded black door in the corner caught my attention. A smile spread across my face. It was my old hiding spot—my imaginary castle as a child and dungeon as a teenager. Mom let Jamie and me turn it into our secret clubhouse, where we discussed important things such as the best pizza toppings and what was better, Star Wars or Star Trek.

Kneeling at the door, I pushed it open to reveal a small, cramped space that had once seemed massive. Crawling inside, an overwhelming scent of forgotten youth—A.K.A. the Justin Bieber perfume phase—smacked my nose. Everything remained exactly as I had left it: vibrant tapestries draped the walls, stacks of magazines and comic books littered the blue carpet Jamie had picked out, and two five-year-old Coke cans rested on the wobbly shelf we used as a table.

I'd like to think my cleaning skills had improved since childhood, but one look at my Boston apartment said otherwise.
Top of Form

I sank into the old beanbag chair only to get jabbed in the spine by a pointy edge, most likely something I'd hidden from Lucas, or a fossilized slice of pizza Jamie had stashed away. After unzipping the bean bag chair's cover, my fingers brushed against a rigid rectangle covered in soft leather. I swiftly pulled the object from the chair's grasp, revealing a thick, well-worn journal—my high school diary.

Flipping through the musty pages revealed secrets and stories that had been kept hidden from everyone, even myself. The taste of salt passed my lips as tears trailed down my cheeks, and my chest heaved with a mourning cry. The diary held memories in its pages, memories I didn't want to remember yet desperately wanted to hold onto. Memories of Jamie, my first friend, my first kiss, my first love, my first heartbreak.

I wanted to leave the diary right where it was, to let it sit in the chair as nothing more than a forgotten artifact. Burying it back into the silence of the room felt easier than facing the pain it had promised, but the harder I tried to ignore it, the louder it screamed. Crawling out of that little room of forgotten happiness, dashing down the stairs of memorialized youth, and running as fast as my legs could carry me out of that town filled with flashbacks wouldn't erase the past, no matter how far I tried to escape.

I had already tried that once, and five years later, I was a twenty-three-year-old woman just as broken and terrified as the day she left. The thing about the past was that no matter how far I ran from it, it always followed me like a somber shadow, a stalking ghost, a wound that would never heal.

So, instead of burning the journal and watching every particle of the past go up in flames like I had wanted, I opened the diary to the first page.

Less than twenty-four hours remained until I had to

confront the stark reality of who I was. In just twenty-four hours, the past and present would collide in a morbid dance at our high school reunion. Twenty-four hours before my eyes would meet Jamie's for one last time.

# CHAPTER 2

You don't know love until it hurts.
You don't miss happiness until sadness strikes.
And you don't appreciate a moment until it becomes a memory.

**5:30 p.m.**

"Alex!"

The deafening sound of my mother's voice pierced my right ear like a needle. Rubbing my watering eyes with the back of my hand, I slowly peeked my eyelids open, allowing tiny bits of light to filter back into my corneas. I was huddled in a ball, my knees firmly touching beneath my chin and my face pleasantly smushed on my pillowcase. Piled on me, the crumpled bed cover created the perfect mountain of cushiony solitude.

"Come help me with dinner!" my mom called, the canals of my ears vibrating as she pronounced each syllable.

"No, thank you. I don't feel like seeing the fire department today."

"Don't worry, I'm not making you use the stove after last

time … I need your help with chopping."

"I can't. I don't have medical insurance, and I like all my fingers attached."

"You don't have medical insurance!?" Judgment bounced off the four walls of my room; my safe place was compromised.

Flinging my comforter off my limp body, I physically grabbed my legs to throw them over the side of the bed. My heels smacked the floor as I used the edge of my side table to force my body upwards. Everything around me blurred as if windshield wipers had washed my eyes, and my mind spun faster than the teacup ride at Disneyland.

Once my vision and brain rejoined reality, the blood slowly rushed back to my head, allowing me to move one foot in front of the other. How can the most straightforward task of getting out of bed feel as taxing as running a marathon?

Stumbling like a drunk down each step of the staircase, my bare toes finally hit the old wooden floor, filling the room with a familiar crackling sound that echoed through the hall. I shifted my weight from one leg to the other, hoping to hear that magical high-pitched squeak once again. I thought about how many times I had listened to those rusty nails move up and down during my childhood, but I never stopped to appreciate it, to value the history and memories that had been pounded into these old wooden floors. Then again, I hadn't appreciated a lot of the things I'd had.

Walking down the hallway past the living room and dining room into the kitchen, my nose was met with a surprisingly mouthwatering fragrance. It wasn't that my mom was a bad cook by any means; she didn't enjoy cooking unless it was breakfast. So typically, when it was her night to make dinner, she'd hand Lucas and me six takeout menus, and we could pick out whatever we wanted if we could agree on something, which usually ended in a very violent game of rock-paper-scissors and one time a hospital trip for a broken finger.

Lucas's dad, Julian, made most of the meals in the household. Food was his passion; he even studied in Europe during his twenties, but when his dad passed away, he took over the family hardware store. Julian passed down his love of cooking to Lucas when he was finally old enough to hold a knife, and like everything else in life, Lucas excelled.

As soon as my foot hit the transition between the hallway's wood floor and the kitchen's black hexagon tile, it was clear that the miraculous smell was not my mother's Lean Cuisine in the microwave. My brother, hovering over the stove, stood like an obnoxiously perfect Greek statue.

"How did he somehow get taller?" I murmured under my breath as I shuffled my feet to the kitchen island. I propped my elbows on the surface, allowing my chin to find the perfect resting position on the palms of my hands. I couldn't tell if it was the concrete counters or the icy chill of unspoken words that sent a wave of shivers through me.

"I didn't know you were coming," I said, the words coming out more jagged than intended. Exhaustion could be blamed, but truthfully, being in a room with Lucas felt like being in a room with your principal; you know you're getting detention, but you're not ready to admit you did anything wrong.

"Five years. After five years of freezing me out, that's the first thing you say to me?" His voice was deeper than I remembered. Ever since middle school, he had sounded like a captivating audiobook—mesmerizing and enduring. Now, it sounded rough and removed like a wind blowing through a hollow canyon.

"I don't know what you want me to say." After chewing on the inside of my cheek like a piece of bubble gum, I continued, "Mom yelled for me to come down and help her with dinner." I looked around the kitchen to find any trace of my mother's whereabouts, "But obviously, I've been tricked."

Lucas chuckled, still keeping his eyes locked on the boiling water. "Yeah, I figured she was up to something. Same old Monica. Remember when she locked us in that shed outside when you blamed me for breaking your toy?"

"You did break my toy!"

Lucas flipped around, meeting me stare for stare, his arms crossed over his massive chest and his eyebrows raised. "No, I accidentally stepped on your transformer, barely bending its leg, and you retaliated by smashing it into my head."

"Yeah, and your big-ass head broke it in half!"

"I had a black eye in my first-grade yearbook photo."

"Karma's a bitch."

"Then you must be related."

Biting my lip to keep from grinning, I refused to give him the satisfaction of winning an argument. "You better keep an eye on your water before it burns."

"The only person in the world capable of burning water is you," Lucas smirked as he picked the wooden spoon back up.

"That only happened once, and it was your fault for leaving a child unsupervised with a gas stove."

"You were sixteen." His thick eyebrow raised at me.

"Which still legally constitutes a child!"

"Is that your same argument for the cookie disaster of 2015?"

"If the baking industry didn't want kitchens to be burned down, then they shouldn't make parchment paper and wax paper look the same!"

A subtle twitch of Lucas's facial muscles betrayed his soldier boy exterior. Despite his best efforts, his eyes crinkled at the corners, hinting at the light joy bubbling beneath the surface; then, almost like a sneeze, a flicker of surprised laughter escaped. His posture stiffened as if the action physically pained him.

"I miss this," he said under his breath. I'm not sure if he was speaking to me or himself, but those three words hit like a ruler slapping against my skin.

"I'm sorry." My voice came out as a rattle. Lucas's big eyes locked with mine, and for the first time in five years, I felt like I was home.

"I know." A silent understanding passed between us. "Here, why don't you help me with the dessert?"

"Are you sure that's a good idea?" I grimaced.

"No. But if this mushy gushy moment continues, I'm going to turn into you, and that's a fate worse than death."

"Ha, ha! Very funny, soldier boy."

"Ouch! Haven't been called that since high school."

"Looks like the shoe still fits."

"Careful now; if you don't behave, I'll call Monica back in here to supervise you."

Throwing my hands in the air, I surrendered to his threat. "Okay, so what exactly do I do with this?" I glared at the sliced apples and cinnamon.

"Everything is pretty much done; you just have to put it all together." My puzzled expression must have been evident, because Lucas walked over and began explaining the baking process, as if teaching a second grader to spell. "It's simple. First, put some flour on the counter and roll the pastry dough large enough to cover the pie dish. I already prepared the apple filling, so all you have to do is assemble the pie. Pour the apple filling into the pie dish, then roll out another portion of pastry dough and create a lattice pattern by cutting thin strips and weaving them together. Lastly, place the crust over the filling, seal the edges, and place the pie in the oven."

"That sounded like another language!" I stood there dumbfounded.

"Lord knows Spanish was never your strong suit."

"One time! I asked you to do my Spanish homework once, and you've never let me forget it!"

Lucas rolled his eyes. "Just yell for me if you get stuck." He returned to add the noodles to the pot.

Next to the water was a large saucer with sautéed minced garlic and chopped onions surrounding hot dog chunks and tomato sauce. "It needs more banana ketchup," he grumbled, tasting the Filipino spaghetti sauce from the wooden spoon. "I haven't made this in ages."

"Really?" I questioned as I rolled out the pastry dough on the floured counter. "I would have thought you'd want to cook all the time for that new girlfriend of yours. Mom wouldn't stop sending me pictures of you two last year."

"That was last year." His shoulders deflated. "We broke up a few months back. She wanted a boyfriend who lived in the same country as her."

"Life as a foreign correspondent must be pretty lonely," I pried, pouring the apple filling into the pie dish and splattering tiny bits of apple juice on my shirt.

"It's not without its challenges …" Lucas's eyes narrowed as if there was more to his sentence. "So, what about you? Still sleeping with your boss?"

I choked on air. "Dude! Gross! No—it wasn't like that. He wasn't my boss, and neither are we still dating, nor am I still employed."

"You got fired! Mom is going to kill you! Please let me tell her!" He was almost jumping up and down.

"Quiet! Keep your voice down!" I hissed. "I wasn't fired. I quit … after Mark threatened to fire me."

"So, he was your boss." I wanted to smack that boyish grin right off his annoyingly perfect face.

Surrendering to his accusations, I threw the mangled dough on top of the filling. "Fine. Yeah, he was my boss."

"God. I couldn't believe it when Jamie told me you were banging your boss—"

"You talked to Jamie?" My heart fell to my feet. The sound of his name in the air made a ball of nerves gather in my throat.

Lucas looked like a kid caught sneaking out of the house past curfew. "I called him last month." He spoke to his shoes. "After he saw you in Boston."

Boston. The memory overwhelmed my senses: skin on skin, lips crashing into each other in desperation, the feeling of his body intertwined with mine, heat rising in my face.

Then reality came rushing back. I couldn't catch my breath, my lungs playing tug of war with my heart. Collapsing right where I stood felt like a real possibility. My face twitched involuntarily as I searched for words that didn't exist.

"Hey, guys," a familiar squeaky voice poisoned the air around me.

Not possible. I clenched my jaw so tightly I could hear my back tooth squeak against my top molar. She wouldn't dare. I slowly turned my head to the right, holding my breath while I decided which kitchen utensil would be my weapon. Butcher knives were always a solid choice, but reminded me a little too much of Scream, the horror movie, for my liking. The meat tenderizing mallet, though? That had potential.

"Your mother invited me." She fiddled with the hem of her sleeve, her fingernails baby pink. Kayla looked the same as if five years had been five minutes, except now she seemed unsteady.

She rocked on her heels. "You're imagining how to kill me with the blender, aren't you …"

"Meat mallet, actually."

# CHAPTER 3

You can't always get what you want
But you don't always know what you want until it's gone.

**August 16, 2012**

Life gives and takes, but we only notice when it steals what it's provided. Maybe this is the curse of being human—we're bound to stumble through life with eyes closed, only opening them when something is gone. My awakening to this harsh reality began in eighth grade. If only I had opened my eyes sooner.

It was the dreaded first day of eighth grade, the day I had to bid farewell to summer memories and begin another torturous year of school. My insides churned like acid as my mother drove up to the front of the carpool line. The red bricks of the school building loomed, taunting my every breath. My heart pounded in my chest like it was plotting an escape.

"Hey, Ms. M," Jamie asked my mom from the back seat. "If Jinx passes out at gym class again, can I ride with you guys to the hospital this time?" Jamie found endless amusement in my last name, Jinx—a fitting metaphor for the afflictions my father seemed to bestow upon my life. He was the kind of man who lit a match to see what burned, then wondered why the smoke never cleared. He walked out when I was too young to remember much—my earliest memories of him faint, like shadows cast by a dying light. Yet his absence still shaped my life like the lingering echo of a storm that never fully passed.

I smacked Jamie's arm. "Thanks for the support. Truly, I'm lucky to have such a caring best friend." My voice dripped with sarcasm. "And for the record, that gym thing was one time!"

"You passed out because a ball almost hit you," Jamie countered, barely holding back a snicker.

Lucas chimed in from the front seat, turning his body to face us, his eyes gleaming with mocking taunts. "You do realize it's our duty never to let you live that down, right?"

I jabbed my finger at Lucas's slightly crooked nose. "First of all, that ball was an inch from my cheek. Second, I told that meathead PE teacher that sports and I are mortal enemies. She didn't listen, and her punishment was paying my hospital bill."

My mother chuckled from the driver's seat. "After you threatened to sue her for child endangerment."

I leaned forward, positioning my elbows on my knees. "Attorney911.com specifically told me I had a case. I'm just saying."

"Okay, miss hotshot lawyer, get your debating butt into class before I get called into the principal's office on the first day again."

I shrugged and flashed a sassy grin. "Hey, you're the one who said you wanted more family traditions."

Her blue eyes met mine in the rearview mirror, disapproval etched in her gaze. "Yes, but I'd prefer traditions that don't end with me picking you up from detention."

"Take it or leave it."

The school cafeteria buzzed with the usual chaos of hormonal teenagers playing a game of Russian roulette with their seating choices. Every year was the same: students nervously paced the cafeteria floor, waiting to be granted a seat in the clique of their choice. Parents liked to think their taxpayer money paid for the enrichment of their children's minds, but eighth grade was a cesspool of hormonal preteens clawing at the chance of fleeting popularity.

I couldn't care less about "who sat with whom," but that wasn't up to me. Middle school was a ferocious jungle filled with training bras and eyeliner. Consequently, a set of laws and a hierarchy system kept the ecosystem protected. The prized spot was reserved for the jocks, who plagued the corner table with tales of touchdowns and slam dunks. The preps, with trust funds bigger than their vacation homes, occupied the tables near the exit. Artists and musicians, bless their tortured souls, sat nearby. Goths and emos claimed the dimly lit center table while gamers battled digital dragons by the vending machines. The bookworms, immersed in their novels, sat in the corner by the window. Drama kids, ever theatrical, sat on the floor against the blue cinderblock wall. Lastly, the nerds, geeks, and science whizzes solved the mysteries of the universe over by the teacher's table.

We were the wildcards, the social pariahs who didn't conform to a table. Lucas should have sat with the jocks, Jamie with the artists, and I should have eaten in the counselor's office. Instead, we chose social suicide and made our home at the community table—the island of misfit toys, where conspiracy theorists, Minecraft builders, and dry-erase sniffers gathered.

We were perfectly unnoticeable, and I loved it. No one bothered us, and we flew under the radar until today.

"Hey, give me your lunch." Lucas grabbed at my brown sack like a heathen.

"No way, I'm not eating your nasty chicken salad sandwich."

Lucas pouted like a baby. "Come on, please, this thing smells like wet dog."

I raised the bag high. "How much is it worth to you?"

"No!" Lucas shouted, his face reddening. "I'm not paying you any more money. I'll need a job because of you!" He shook the offending sandwich in my face, its smell assaulting my nose.

"Or you could stop making dumb decisions that put you in debt to me."

"You're unbelievable." Lucas glared at Jamie, who was enjoying the show. "Are you going to let her extort me like this?"

Jamie shrugged, taking a bite of his PB&J. "Sorry, dude, I'd help, but I owe her like thirty bucks."

"Fine!" Lucas grumbled, digging through his pocket for a crumpled pile of five one-dollar bills and fifty cents. "Here." He shoved the wad in my face.

"Nice doing business with you." I took the money, my grin enraging Lucas further.

My mood had lifted considerably. What had started as a dreaded day was turning into a profitable one. But I should have known it wouldn't last. The cafeteria doors swung open, and in she came—wild, black curls bouncing, thigh-high red snakeskin boots clicking against the linoleum like a warning shot. Heads turned, and conversations faltered. She was impossible to miss, and that was exactly the problem.

She strode down the aisle like she owned it, each step bringing her closer to our table. My stomach twisted. This table wasn't supposed to be seen. That's why we sat here, tucked away, invisible, just how we liked it. If she sat with us, all of that would change.

I ducked my head, willing her to stop, to turn, to sit anywhere else. But the sound of those boots grew louder and closer until she stopped right beside us.

Lucas, oblivious to my internal meltdown, grinned and leaned back in his chair. "Hey, you must be new. I'm Lucas. Need a place to sit?" He patted the seat beside him. "I wouldn't want such a pretty face to eat alone."

The girl blushed and batted her eyes as if something was caught in her lashes. I quivered at the flirtation in front of me. I was forced to share a bathroom with Lucas; thus, the concept of him having any appeal to the opposite sex was utterly lost upon me.

"Thanks." The girl smiled back. "I'm Kayla." She slid onto the bench beside Lucas, who beamed like a child with a new toy.

Jamie took a swig of his Gatorade. "I'm Jamie," he said, scanning Kayla briefly.

Jealousy twisted inside me. "I'm Alex," I spat, my words sharp.

Lucas leaned towards Kayla. "So, where'd you move from? Heaven?"

Kayla matched his grin. "I just moved from LA. My grandma's not doing well, so my dad thought we should move to help."

Tap! Tap! Tap! The sound of pink pumps against the cafeteria floor signaled trouble. I wearily tilted my head up—great, the preps. The queen bee, Bethany, stood before our table, arms crossed, her designer tank top wrinkling.

"You should be more careful, new girl. It's your first day, and you've already made a stupid mistake," Bethany hissed.

Kayla's eyes narrowed. "And what would that be?"

Bethany's smirk grew. "Fraternizing with the freaks."

I stood up, my short frame barely reaching Bethany's chest. "Back off, Bethany."

Bethany cupped her ear. "Did you hear that? Sounds like a little mouse in need of another haircut."

My blood boiled. Bethany had been tormenting me since we were kids. She was the bitch who mangled my hair when I was six, a little demon brat who had grown into the devil. Before I could react, Kayla grabbed Lucas's lonely chicken salad sandwich, leaped in front of me, and squished the mayonnaise-filled lunch against Bethany's hot pink beaded top with a satisfying squelch. The absurdity of it all transformed my previous jealousy into pure amusement, and I couldn't help but laugh. The sound reverberated throughout the room, drawing shocked attention from nearby students. Bethany let out a high-pitched shriek, piercing the air like a fire alarm.

Alerted by the commotion, a teacher approached swiftly.

Ms. Martin's footsteps smacked the tile like the gavel of a judge, and her voice was stern, instantly silencing the crowd. "What on earth is going on here?"

Still in shock and covered in mushed chicken, Bethany pointed a trembling finger at Kayla. "She did this to me! She ruined my top!"

I delivered a pleased grin. "I don't see it that way. Kayla was embellishing an already nauseating attire. She was making it smell as bad as it looked."

Kayla faced the teacher calmly, her words measured and composed like lyrics. "Exactly. I was trying to help the poor girl out."

Ms. Martin's eyes looked seconds from popping out of her skull. "This is not the way to handle conflicts." Her stare locked onto mine, her irises matching the pulsing vein on her forehead. "I expect this sort of shenanigans from you, Ms. Jinx." She turned to Kayla, risking knocking the tight bun off her head. "But Ms. Jones! I hope you'll reevaluate your choice of friends after this little incident."

I scoffed at her insinuation. "Always the freak's fault, never the preps," I grumbled. For a millisecond, I considered the repercussions of my words, but that never stopped my mouth from moving. "Tell me, what's it like peaking in high school?"

Her face contorted in shock and offense. Her eyebrows shot up, and her nose flared. "That's it!" she yelled through gritted teeth. "Alex, Kayla, you're coming to the principal's office with me."

"You owe me ten bucks!" Lucas shot up from his seat like an outraged toddler. "You too, Jamie. Cough it up."

Jamie bugged his eyes at me. "You couldn't have waited another day to get sent to the principal's office? I had my bet on Tuesday."

"Sorry to disappoint."

As we walked down the hallway toward the principal's office, I knew I should've been nervous—but I couldn't help striding along with a ridiculous sense of glee. I hadn't seen Bethany squeal like that since Jamie tripped her in third grade—and honestly, it was beautiful.

Kayla and I sat outside the principal's office, waiting for our turn to be reprimanded, when she finally broke the silence. "I hope I didn't get you into too much trouble," she whispered.

"Nah, it was worth it. Seriously, I feel like I should be throwing you a parade."

Kayla's eyes widened. "Good! So, are we okay then? Like friends?"

I pondered this. I had been the only girl in our trio since day one, and honestly, we needed more estrogen to break up all that testosterone. "Sure, why not?"

There was a brief pause, a moment of mutual tolerance during which I entertained the idea that I might not mind this reckless girl's company. That was until Kayla spoke up again, her words tinged with a hint of embarrassment. "By the way, Alex, I hope you don't think I'm into Jamie."

I choked on her words, my throat tightening from the insinuation. "I don't care." My voice was high-pitched. "Jamie and I are just friends."

Kayla rolled her eyes. "Really?" She raised a single judgmental brow at me. "Is that why you looked at me like you were gonna take my head off when I sat at your table? Because you're 'just friends?'"

I gasped. "I truly have no idea what you could be insinuating."

"Whatever you say, Ms. Denial."

I had never thought of Jamie as anything more than just a friend—my best friend, my other half, the person I had no doubt I would spend the rest of my life with. But when I saw him look at Kayla with that flicker of intrigue, that gleam of curiosity, I realized I wanted Jamie to look at me that way.

I didn't know what I wanted until I couldn't have it.

# CHAPTER 4

Memories are not always facts.
Facts are not always true.
So, what is real?
What is fake?
True and false don't give; they take.

**6:00 p.m.**

Lucas stood frozen like a victim of Medusa, his eyes scanning Kayla as if he thought words were forming on his lips. Their relationship was more complicated than untangling a box of Christmas lights, but I had no interest in delving into that mess. I refused to waste another second contemplating Kayla's questionable life choices.

The rapid scuff of shoes hurried toward us, stopping abruptly where the kitchen tile met the hallway's wooden floor. My mom's eyes darted between our trio: Kayla, looking like a child being punished; Lucas, wearing a giant W of confusion; and me, no doubt turning a shade of red that could rival the apple peelings in the pie before us.

"Kayla, dear." My mom's voice wavered as she painted on a smile. "I didn't hear you come in."

"I hope I'm not too early." Kayla sounded as nervous as she looked.

The clinking of silverware against pots and pans played like a discordant symphony as Lucas fidgeted with his dishes. His face was flushed, possibly from the stove's heat or the burning tension in the room. "You're never too early. I'm just finishing up." His black eyes always seemed brighter when they met Kayla's. What used to be sweet had turned sad. "Why don't you help Alex set the table?"

Leaning against the kitchen island, I locked eyes with Kayla, who stood on the opposite side of the counter—a safety barrier between my nails and her eyes. I spoke at her, not to her, as if she were nothing more than an obstruction. "Are we just going to ignore the backstabbing bitch in the room?"

My mother gasped. "Alexandria!"

"Oh, I'm sorry. Was that rude of me?" I feigned shock. "I thought 'bitch' was the nicest word I could use. Want me to try again? Jackass Judas, serpent slut, heretic whore?"

Lucas threw a dish towel over his shoulder and crossed his arms. "How biblical of you."

Why was he protecting her? Kayla had screwed him over as badly as she had screwed me. Yet, he still shielded her like a loyal guard dog.

Kayla's voice broke my glare at Lucas. "At least that English degree is paying off for you, Alex."

"I spent $45,000 a year. I'd have to write The Hobbit for it to pay off." I scoffed.

Lucas snorted. "Nerd."

Kayla took two steps towards Lucas, mimicking his crossed-armed stance. "Says the grown man with a Star Wars action figure collection."

He gasped. "How'd you know I still have that?"

Kayla smirked. "Because you just admitted it."

"Nicely played." I nodded at Kayla, swiping my finger across the sticky sugar residue on the pie bowl.

"I learned from the best."

I licked the pie guts off my finger. "True. I was an excellent Obi-Wan Kenobi."

"See this!" My mom pointed between us. "This is why I invited Kayla! You guys need this!"

I pushed off the counter and stomped my foot, trying to assert dominance, but I likely ended up looking like a toddler in a tantrum. "The pleasantries were a reflex. I don't need her in my life."

My mother matched my stomps, her hair flicking behind her. "What life? You don't have a life."

I readied a response, but the truth of her words silenced me.

Lucas cupped his mouth. "Ouch, burned by Monica. That's gotta sting."

Mom turned her piercing gaze to him. "And when was the last time you talked to anyone who wasn't from work?"

"HA!" I spat. "She got you, too."

Lucas narrowed his eyes at me, his lip twitching. He wouldn't dare. "Alex got fired."

Mom whipped around to face me. "You what?"

"Lucas's girlfriend broke up with him!"

She turned back to him. "Another one?"

"Kayla quit college!" Lucas fumbled.

Mom's head flipped to her. "Again?"

Kayla gritted her teeth. "Why did you bring me into this?"

Lucas fiddled with the kitchen towel that hung from his shoulder. "I panicked."

Mom smacked her palms on the counter, sending a shockwave through the pie. "Now, do you believe me? You all screwed up the moment you split. Your group was codependent in high school, and without each other, you've regressed into children."

I rolled my eyes. "Bull—"

"You might be twenty-three, Alexandria Darra Jinx, but don't think for a second I won't ground your ass." My mom's tone was sharp, and even though she had no real authority to ground me, I wasn't eager to test her resolve.

"Yes, ma'am." I backed away as if I were a reluctant bride at the altar.

"Now, set the dinner table before I ground every one of you." Mom's jaw clenched so tight I could almost hear her back molar crack.

"Geez, okay! I'll grab the silverware," I said.

Kayla darted to the cabinet below the sink. "I'll get the

placemats."

Lucas, gripping the pot of boiling noodles, hurried to the sink, nearly colliding with Kayla. "I'll start dishing up the plates."

Fumbling with the silverware in the drawer, I grabbed a thick stack of forks and knives. The drawer slammed shut, nearly catching my pinky in the process. As I scurried to the dining room, Kayla was right behind me.

"She wouldn't ground us, right?" Kayla placed the cream placemats on the cherry wood table, her wide eyes meeting mine.

"Remember the morning after prom?" I asked, setting a fork and knife on the worn placemat.

"Yikes … hide the spatula!"

As we finally settled around the table for dinner, I couldn't shake the feeling of déjà vu—like I'd stepped into a time machine, Marty McFly-style, and landed straight in the past. We sat there, napkins on our laps, each of us in our assigned seats, unchanged since we first formed our little group of misfits. My parents occupied their usual spots, my mother at the head of the table, and Julian at the foot. Kayla sat closest to the living room, her chair's leather cushion showing signs of wear. Lucas was to her right, and I sat directly in front of her.

It felt like nothing had changed, as if the past five years were just a bad dream, but as I glanced to the left, I snapped back to the present. Jamie's seat sat empty, a haunting reminder of where his warmth once filled the room, now replaced by the cold grip of solitude.

Silence encased the table like a thick fog, the tension as palpable as the steam rising from the plates of Filipino spaghetti before us. Lucas's mother, who arrived in America from Mindanao at eighteen, had introduced Julian to this dish on their first date. He hated it but was desperate to impress her, so he ate the noodles covered in hot dog slices and sweet tomato sauce with a smile. After they married, she made it for every occasion, even Christmas. When she passed away, Julian continued the tradition with Lucas. This dish reminded me that even when something is gone, it's not truly lost.

Julian broke the silence, his voice a beacon in the night. He turned to Kayla, his fork tracing patterns on his plate. "So, Kayla, what have you been doing since you moved to Atlanta?"

Kayla twirled a strand of spaghetti on her fork, her eyes fixed on her plate. "I moved back home last week."

The room filled with the soft clinking of silverware, a symphony playing tug of war between silence and crescendo.

"That would be your third college, right?" I asked, not because I didn't know the answer, but because I wanted to see her squirm just a little.

Kayla's reply was hesitant, still coaxing a strand of spaghetti with her fork. "Fourth. It wasn't the school; I've learned college isn't for me."

Julian took a deep swig of red wine. "What are your plans now?"

Kayla's shoulders were hunched inward. "I'm not sure yet. That's why I'm staying with my dad until I figure out the life I want to live." Kayla resembled a Chihuahua in a thunderstorm, shaking and tiny.

The conversation was painfully awkward, yet the urge to pierce the silence was irresistible.

"Don't worry, I'm sure you'll just steal somebody else's," I quipped, twirling my pasta like a cat playing with a ball of yarn.

Lucas's palms slapped the table, making the plates rattle and the glasses quiver. "Can't you let the past die?"

"No." The wine glass pressed to my lips, the sour grapes mirroring the bitterness in the room. "I don't make amends with boyfriend thieves."

Kayla threw her napkin on the table. "I didn't steal him from you! You don't even know the whole story!" Her voice reached a new, annoying pitch.

A scoff and a smile played on my lips. "I think seeing you naked on his bed painted a good picture."

"We should let them talk about this." Julian motioned for my mom to follow him out of the dining room, but not without first grabbing his plate of food. My mom shook her head at us one last time before following him.

With her face turning red, either from embarrassment or anger, Kayla clenched her fork tightly. "Fine, you think you know everything? Stop pretending you're innocent! You could have fought for him, but instead, you cut us all out. You lost Jamie. That's on you! But you'll never admit you were wrong because you can't admit when you've screwed up! Stop playing the victim!"

Lucas tried to mediate, waving his hands like a conductor calming an unruly orchestra. "Kayla—"

I catapulted from my chair, sending it crashing into the china cabinet behind me. "Me? I'm playing the victim? Name one time I ever did anything to you!" My voice sliced the air.

Kayla's breath quickened, her eyes searching for the next jab, her lips nervous with tension. "You stole my first kiss!"

Not to throw myself under the bus, but there were several things she could have jabbed back at me. This was absurd. "What?"

Kayla huffed. "The summer before high school at the town carnival."

Lucas turned in his chair, angling his shoulders at Kayla, his face just as confused as mine. "That's what you're arguing? The freshman carnival? There are so many better options. Like when Alex—"

"Don't help her!" I snapped at him, my voice octaves higher than intended.

Kayla stabbed her fork into her spaghetti, sending bits of tomato sauce flying onto the placemats.

"You grabbed Brandon and kissed him right after he won me that stuffed bear!" Kayla said.

"Okay? So, I kissed a boy. What's the big deal? You didn't even like him."

"Yes, I did! And you would have known that if you hadn't gotten jealous when you saw Jamie kiss Meghan Townsend and stole my date to get back at him."

Memories started to flood back, but I wasn't ready to

admit defeat. "First, I wasn't jealous; second, he wasn't your date!"

"Yes, he was! That night, we all paired up: Lucas with his annoying girlfriend, Meghan with Carter Hitch, you with Jamie, and I with Brandon. But when Carter got sick on the Ferris wheel, Meghan snatched Jamie, and you retaliated by kissing Brandon."

My brain spun like a hamster on a wheel, getting nowhere. Technically, Kayla was right, but not factually. "You're delusional! You're twisting the story. You're the boyfriend stealer here, not me!"

Kayla's face flushed with anger. In a split second, she plunged her hand into the tomato-covered pasta, gripped the slippery noodles, and flung them at my head.

A faint whistle punctuated by a wet thud echoed as the food slapped my cheek, noodles sliding down my face. Kayla's eyes widened, likely in shock at her actions. After five years apart, this was her attempt at making amends. My hands dug into my meal, the noodles feeling like worms between my fingers. I launched the spaghetti at her, sauce splattering across the table. Half the noodles landed on Kayla's face, the rest ricocheting onto Lucas's shoulder.

Lucas flicked a piece of hot dog off his chest, his initial shock giving way to a mischievous glint. He grabbed a handful of butter and flung it in my direction. Lukewarm dairy smacked my neck and slid down my shirt like a slug on a slip-and-slide. Perhaps Mom was right—we had indeed regressed to toddlers.

My mom screamed as she entered the dining room. "You three are cleaning this up!"

I had thought about that carnival night a thousand times—my first kiss, my first heartbreak—but never through Kayla's eyes. How could two people see the same night so differently? Who was right? Who was wrong? I guess it doesn't matter. In the end, memories are only true for the one who lived them.

# CHAPTER 5

Your eyes can lie to you.
Your mouth can curse you.
Your heart can betray you.
Your brain can fool you.

**August 4th, 2013**

I came to understand that moments are like reflections on water—disturb them too soon, and the truth vanishes in the ripples. Looking back, I should've waited for the surface to settle. Instead, I threw a stone and watched the image slip away.

The first Sunday of August 2013 marked the final day of our town's two-month-long carnival. I had managed to avoid that forsaken funhouse for over a month, dodging Kayla's and Lucas's pleas and Jamie's smooth attempts to drag me there. I hated loud noises, screaming children, sticky cotton candy, and flashy carnival games. The funnel cake, however, was the only redeeming quality.

I had been as skillful as a spy in my attempts to dodge this year's carnival, but when August fourth came, my efforts crumbled. Jamie had spent every night at my house the week leading up to that dreaded evening. My parents no longer allowed sleepovers after we turned thirteen due to "hormones," but Jamie needed an escape from his house. Jamie's home life was never a Leave It to Beaver reality, but on the days his dad was living at the bottom of a bottle, it was safer for Jamie to be elsewhere.

I never understood why his mom stayed in that house of horrors. She moved from a Hopi Reservation in northeastern Arizona to Massachusetts with some girlfriends when she was eighteen. She was a very kind woman, always smiling and baking cookies for school events. On the surface, she seemed perfect: hair meticulously curled, nails glossy red, dress ironed to a crisp. You would never know she lived with an abusive, drug-dealing alcoholic in Raymond Hills trailer park.

The week before the carnival closed, Jamie's dad reached a new level of jackass. One of his errand runners split with a "package," costing him the rent money. Instead of getting a job, Jamie's dad did what he always did: participated in nightly bar fights and screamed at Jamie's mom for not working more shifts. Jamie learned at a young age not to intervene, though it took four black eyes and a gash from a broken beer bottle for the lesson to sink in. By thirteen, he had stopped trying to protect someone he couldn't save.

Jamie was always a restless sleeper, kicking and elbowing in his sleep. But that week, the kicking stopped, replaced by something far worse. He screamed and cried in the dead of night, his voice raw with pain. When I finally got him to open up, his words broke me. Every night, he said, a new terror gripped him, each one ending the same way—with the image of his mom's lifeless body. He told me this with tears in his eyes, like he was still there, trapped in the nightmare, unable to wake up.

The sun hung low, casting a golden hue over the carnival grounds. Laughter and chatter filled the air, mingling with the scent of overcooked popcorn and candy-coated caramel apples, creating a sweet and slightly burnt aroma. The carnival lights blazed, casting a neon glow over the scene. I walked between Kayla and Jamie, their chatter blending with the chaos around us. The Ferris wheel loomed in the distance, its rotating lights mesmerizing as carnival music boomed.

Jamie punched his elbow into my shoulder. "Ready to puke your guts out on the Tilt-A-Whirl?"

I replied with a smirk. "Oh yes, it's everything I've ever dreamed of. Thanks for forcing me into this child-polluted loony bin." Our feet shuffled on the muddy grass as we continued ahead.

"You're welcome." Jamie's self-enjoyment was palpable. He lowered his head to mine, which just six months ago was at my same level—damn teenage boy growth hormones. "Technically, you're a child too." He chuckled.

"I prefer 'underdeveloped short person,'" I quipped back.

Jamie's eyes scanned my body, landing just below my chin and above my ribs. With a cocky raise of one eyebrow and a curl to his lips, he tilted his head. "Not so underdeveloped now ..."

I slapped his chest. "Perv! You're sleeping on the floor tonight."

"Oh, please." He rolled his eyes. "You love me in your bed."

My heart quickened, my tongue-tied, and my stomach flipped. Jamie and I always talked like this—flirting, fighting, finishing each other's sentences. We were an old married couple without sex. But that summer, his smug smiles were besting me, sending butterflies dancing in my stomach and making my heart flutter.

Kayla's heels dug into the mud beside me, coming to a screeching halt. "I'd love to continue this episode of One Tree Hill, but we should probably find Lucas." She crossed her arms over her baby blue tank. Kayla appeared less excited about today than I was. Lucas had invited his new girlfriend, Becky, and her friends, which was likely what was causing a permanent scowl to stain Kayla's face.

Jamie shoved his fingers in his jeans' pockets. "He said he'd meet us at the pretzel stand."

Kayla rolled her eyes. "We've been here, what, five minutes? And I've already seen seven pretzel stands." Her hands shot to her hips after flicking her blanket of braided hair over her shoulder. "This is why the girls plan the outings; boy brains can't handle fundamental details!"

I glared around the crowd. "Just listen for the sound of air leaving somebody's head."

Jamie's eyes scrunched up. "What? Why?"

"Oh, there you silly geese are!" An ear-piercing voice cut through the crowd like a manic baby bird. Becky's red curls bounced as she skipped over, her fingers intertwined with Lucas's.

"That's why," I said to Jamie.

"What does silly geese mean?" he whispered. The brush of his lips against my ear sent shivers down my spine.

"It means she flunked English." I chuckled.

"At least I'm not the only one."

Jamie could take apart a truck engine and rebuild it in an afternoon, but when it came to school, he was a fish out of water.

"You didn't fail. You got a D. There's a difference."

Jamie's mouth was dangerously close to mine. "I only got a D because I sat next to you."

I turned slightly closer to him, the heat of his breath gracing my face. "And you were smart enough to cheat. That qualifies you for at least a C."

Kayla stepped forward to meet Becky. "Hey, glad you made it too." Her voice was sweet yet carried a bite.

Becky's porcelain face twitched like a smiling robot short-circuiting. "Oh, hey, Kayla. Lucas didn't mention you were coming." Yes, he did. I heard them arguing about it on the phone last night.

Kayla's cheeks flushed. "It's Kayla, actually," she snapped. "Really?" Becky tilted her head. "It sounds like a misprint."

My spine stiffened. "Hey Becky, I like the new red hair color." I turned my attention to my brother. "I didn't know you had a thing for Woody Woodpecker, Lucas."

Lucas flinched. "Alex. Be nice."

Jamie almost choked on his laugh. "That's a tall order. Lower your request."

Lucas's jaw clenched. "How about being less hostile?"

I shook my head in response. "You know I can't make any promises regarding bodily harm."

Lucas stepped toward me, but Becky laid her hand on his chest. "It's all good, Lucas. Us girls are just joking around."

"Oh yeah, I'm a real Heath Ledger," I mocked.

Lucas wrapped his arm around Becky's waist. "Let's go meet everyone else before the hair-pulling starts."

Becky's group, the theatre kids, awaited us. They were loud, obnoxious, drama-possessed, and believed every day was a play and they were the stars. Thanks to my lovesick brother, I had to spend the night with them.

As we followed Lucas through the carnival, lights flashed, music pounded, and children giggled. Finally, we reached a row of tents featuring stuffed animals and games.

The aroma of sugary funnel cakes and motor oil from the bumper cars filled the air. Becky's group stood by the Dunk Tank, imprisoning a depressed-looking clown: Brandon was a quiet guy with blonde curls and freckles, while Carter resembled a pocket-sized Peter Parker. Then there was Meghan, the drama teacher's daughter, who always landed the lead role and the lead guy.

We scattered into mini-groups, each drawn to a game. Lucas and Becky headed to the Balloon Pop, while Carter and Meghan went to the Basketball Toss. Kayla dashed off with Brandon to the Water Gun Race. I chose to hide by the Whack-a-Mole. The solid grip of the mallet in my hand, combined with the tuneful thud of plastic mole-beating, created a unique blend of delight.

"Remind me never to let you own a bat." Jamie chuckled. "I'm gonna grab some food. Want anything?"

"Funnel cake!" I grinned like a possessed doll as I bounced the mallet from target to target.

Jamie grinned. "I told you you'd have fun."

I pointed the mallet at him. "Careful, boy, I'm armed."

Jamie laughed. "Those are two words that should never come out of your mouth." He backed away, disappearing into the crowd.

I continued smashing moles until a tap on my shoulder made me swing around, mallet in hand.

"Whoa, careful," Megan squealed, jumping back.

I put the mallet down. "Do you need something?" Politeness was wasted on Megan.

"Are you and Jamie a thing?"

I couldn't stop my eyes from widening. "No."

Megan leaned against the Whack-a-Mole machine. "Are you sure? You two are always together. Everyone assumes."

Every school has a girl who talks in backstabbing riddles. Megan was that girl.

"Tell anyone who cares that Jamie and I are the poster children for Platonic Friendships."

"Oh, good," Megan perked up. "I think Jamie's cute. I was going to ask him out, but didn't want to step on toes." Her breath hung on mine as if my discomfort were a drug to her.

I imagined Megan's head as a plastic mole. "Aren't you dating Carter?"

"At the moment, yes. But I was thinking about Jamie for

after."

Just as my anger erupted, Jamie reappeared with funnel cakes.

"Alex, let's go do the ring toss?" Jamie glanced at Megan. "Oh, hey, you can come too."

I pushed between them. "Let's ride the Ferris wheel."

Jamie frowned. "But you hate heights."

Meghan chimed in. "I love heights! I can go with Jamie."

"That's a nice offer, but I'm fine," I said, matching her fake smile.

Jamie finally noticed the tension. "Why don't we all go? I'll get Lucas and Kayla. Meghan, you grab Carter and Brandon."

Annoyance flickered in Meghan's eyes as she stomped away.

Jamie handed me my funnel cake. "What was that about?"

I stuffed a chunk in my mouth. "Nothing."

Everyone gathered in line for the Ferris wheel, and apparently, I wasn't the only person uncomfortable. I watched as Lucas stood stiffly near Becky, but his attention was entirely elsewhere. His eyes darted to Kayla and Brandon, his fists clenching every time they talked. When the operator called for the first pair, Lucas and Becky climbed into the swinging bucket seat. Even as the bar locked them in, Lucas's gaze lingered on Kayla and Brandon, his stare almost daring Brandon to look back.

Kayla had gone out with plenty of boys over the summer, always keeping things quick and casual, treating dating like a game she was always sure to win. She would flirt, have her fun, and move on without a second thought—always in control, always unbothered. But something about Brandon was different. I could see it in the way her laughter lingered just a little too long or how her cheeks flushed when he spoke. It was almost like, for the first time, the rules of her game didn't quite apply.

Lucas noticed, too. He kept cutting into their conversations, making sarcastic remarks, or physically stepping between them like an overzealous bodyguard. Jealousy was an understatement when it came to Lucas and Kayla.

Finally, it was Jamie's and my turn. The operator seated us and locked the lap bar. I gripped it tightly.

"Are you sure about this?" Jamie asked.

"Yeah, what's not to be sure about? It's just two tons of metal moved from town to town. Totally safe."

The ride jolted forward, and I tensed, gripping the seat so tightly my nails chipped the red paint covering the metal bar.

"Hey, it's okay," Jamie comforted, covering my hand. "You're safe. This ride's been spinning all day. There's nothing to fear."

"Murphy's law ..." I choked out.

"What?" Jamie chuckled.

"Murphy's law. Anything that can go wrong will go wrong."

Jamie squeezed my hand. "You know all that anxiety will give you a heart attack one day."

"Or an aneurysm. Fifty/fifty chance."

I opened one eye and gasped.

Jamie turned my face to his. "Just look at me."

For a brief second, I was transfixed by his eyes, the way they gleamed into mine so effortlessly and longingly. His cheeks blushed a deep red.

My heart raced, but not from fear. I didn't intend to move forward, but somehow, I did. He did too. We stopped just short of each other, close enough that the space between us seemed to vanish.

I gave the tiniest nod, and Jamie responded to my silent request. His lips brushed against mine, gentle and unsure at first. Then, with a bit more certainty, he kissed me again. I could barely breathe. His hand caressed my neck before sliding into my hair, drawing me closer, as if we were something delicate and secret.

And just like that, he pulled back, his eyes wide as he searched mine, as if he wasn't sure it had really happened either.

"I'm sorry," he said. "I wanted to do that tonight."

My head was dizzy. "Why?"

"I wanted to be the first. High school starts in a week, and life will move fast. It'll be like blinking, and when we open our eyes, it'll be graduation, and everyone will leave. You'll leave. I might not have you forever, but now I can be your first forever. That counts for something, right?"

Jamie seemed frozen, waiting for my response.

"Everything," I said. "It counts for everything."

As if my words were mouth to mouth, he sucked in a breath and smiled.

If only the night had ended there. When we got off the Ferris wheel, Carter had gotten sick, and I offered to wait with him until his mom came to pick him up. Then I went back to find the others. They were gathered around the High-Striker game. Jamie hit the mallet as I approached, causing a bell to shriek and lights to start flashing. Meghan wrapped her arms around Jamie's neck and pulled him in, shoving her mouth against his, but he didn't pull away.

I should've walked away. I should've swallowed the humiliation, turned on my heel, and left without another glance. But instead, I stood there, watching, the pain throbbing in my chest like a wound I couldn't stop poking. Jamie kissed her back as if nothing that had happened between us mattered.

My legs moved before I could stop them, carrying me towards the group. Jamie's lips were still on hers, but his eyes flicked up when I approached. For a split second, our gaze met. His expression twisted, shock, maybe guilt, or panic, but I didn't wait for him to speak or explain.

Instead, I snapped. I didn't think. I couldn't think. I reached out and grabbed the nearest body. The boy's startled expression barely registered before I pressed my lips to his. The kiss was messy and rushed, his lips tasting of hot dogs and cheap mustard. I wanted to scream, to cry, to run, but mostly, I wanted to make Jamie feel the same ache.

I pulled away quickly, my heart racing. The air felt heavy, and everyone was staring. Kayla's face swam into focus, her mouth slightly open, her expression between shock and betrayal. When I looked at Jamie, expecting hurt or anger, there was nothing. No emotion, no reaction. His face was unreadable, his eyes cold and unyielding. And somehow, that was worse.

Back then, I thought I knew what heartbreak was. But I was wrong. True heartbreak is when your legs betray your body, and you're left lying on the floor. When your lungs shrivel to sand, and you're left gasping for breath. When your brain melts to nothing, and you are left without a word. True heartbreak is when every second of every day feels like an eternity lost in the dark.

I would trade everything and anything for the simple sting of a fourteen-year-old's heartbreak.

# CHAPTER 6

Growing old doesn't mean you've grown up.
Growing up doesn't mean you've grown old.

**6:50 p.m.**

The top of my skull smacked the rusty faucet as I leaned my head under the running tap. Cold water drenched my hair as I attempted to wash away the remaining spaghetti and butter that coated my roots after the food fight moments ago. Maybe I should consider therapy ...

Kayla, who had been unusually quiet, stood beside me at the double sink vanity. Her guilt-filled eyes met mine as I turned off the faucet. I was aware that fifty percent of the incident downstairs was my fault. I provoked the situation and thus received a spaghetti-filled eardrum, but I didn't throw the first noodle. Hell, I wasn't the one who cheated! I admit I played a part in ruining Kayla's first kiss, but a peck on the wrong lips is far different from walking in on your best friend naked on your boyfriend's bed.

"Are you just going to keep staring at me, or are you going to open your big mouth and apologize?" I asked Kayla, then yanked a green towel next to the shower off its hook.

Kayla gathered her bundle of tiny braids to one side and squeezed them tightly. A cascade of dirty water and hot dog particles flowed from the tips of her hair into the sink, her eyes glued to the water instead of mine. "I'm sorry for throwing food at you."

"And ...?" My voice gritted.

Kayla smacked her hands on the counter, her acrylic nails almost chipping from the force. "What do you want me to say?"

"Are you genuinely asking? Or have you lost brain cells in the last five years?"

Kayla folded her arms over her sauce-stained shirt. "I've been apologizing to you nonstop over what happened with Jamie. I've called you a hundred times, written you dozens of letters, and even showed up at your dorm room, but still, you won't forgive me. I don't know what else to say or do to make you understand how much I wish I could take that day back." Water coated the corners of Kayla's eyes. I expected this to fill me with pleasure, but instead, my intestines twisted.

"If you want to make amends so bad, then tell me the truth!" I stepped forward like a lawyer defending my position to a jury. "You've apologized, but neither you nor Jamie has ever told me what happened that night."

Kayla chewed on her glossy lips and picked fiercely at her cuticles with every word I spat.

"Tell me, why did the two of you throw Lucas and me away like we were a fucking pair of old shoes you were tired of?"

I stepped forward again, placing my face in front of hers, which was painted with a thick line of running mascara. "What was more important than us? Sex? Were you in love or just fucking bored that day!?" Unwelcome tears welled up in my eyes and slowly trickled down my cheeks. "Please!" My voice cracked. "Please just tell me why, so I can move on." Begging for a flicker of truth, I searched her eyes.

Kayla opened her mouth as if imprisoned words had broken free, trying to escape. But then she sealed her lips and caged her voice.

"I can't, Alex, I promised Jamie I wouldn't," she finally confessed.

"But why—"

The door slammed as Lucas entered the room. He glanced at Kayla and me, both with tear-filled eyes. "Sorry to interrupt." The best thing about Lucas was that he didn't pry; he took in the situation and moved on. "Here." He handed Kayla a large black T-shirt and neon green running shorts that were undoubtedly an old pair of Mom's.

"Thanks." Kayla took the clothes from Lucas.

Kayla rubbed the shirt's heavy material with her thumb as her burgundy lips rose slightly. "You always did like me in your clothes," she teased Lucas.

Their flirtatious exchange made me cringe, and I decided it was high time to leave. I pushed past Lucas and exited the bathroom, marching to my room to change. The soft fabric of the hoodie against my skin provided comfort, a welcome retreat from the whirlwind of emotions and secrets. I stared at my closed bedroom door and contemplated my next steps. I knew the adult thing to do was to go downstairs and apologize to my parents for painting their white walls orange with spaghetti sauce. But everything in my trembling nervous system told me to unlock my bedroom window, push its wooden latch open, and escape. Then again, that was Jamie's specialty, not mine. Climbing up wasn't a problem, but climbing down was an adventure that typically ended with a split lip and a golfball-sized lump on my head.

I reluctantly took a deep breath and wrapped my fingers around the doorknob. Its cold metal stung my hand, acting like a red warning sign urging me to rethink my life's choices. I twisted the handle and forced my right leg through the door frame, then my left. As I stepped into the hallway, Kayla emerged from the bathroom. Then, a heavy-footed Lucas came out of the room straight ahead of me. His eyes widened drastically when he gazed upon Kayla in his clothes. The two stood frozen, facing each other like mannequins.

Walking towards the stairs, I positioned my body directly between them. "Are you two going to move or just continue this weird staring contest?"

Lucas blushed and quickly looked away from Kayla. Meanwhile, Kayla responded with a bashful grin, crossing her arms over her chest. "What? Something on my face?" she asked Lucas with a mischievous smirk playing on her lips.

Lucas shook his head. "No, it's just … feels like déjà vu."

Kayla stepped a little closer. "Yeah, I guess I did use to steal your clothes a lot. But technically, you gave me your shirt the first time—at that party, freshman year."

Lucas let out a soft laugh. "God, that night was a mess."

Kayla smiled. "And just like then, I'm still not a princess

in need of saving."

Lucas rubbed the back of his neck; his expression caught somewhere between a smile and a wince. "Wow, you're never going to let that comment go, are you? And for the record, you did need help that night." His eyes held onto hers as if she were an angel shining just for him. But then his demeanor stiffened. He looked so tired, as if the weight of all the unspoken words between them was finally crushing him. "You never needed saving. I just thought you deserved someone who stayed." His voice didn't rise, but the next part cut deeper. "But you made sure I couldn't."

She flinched; her voice came quieter than before. "When are you going to stop punishing me?"

He let out a slow breath. Not quite a sigh, not a full pause. Just tired. "I'm not punishing you." He met her eyes. "I'm just telling the truth."

Kayla froze. Arms crossed. Shoulders tense. One breath, two. Then she inhaled. "So, one mistake and I'm the bad guy forever? Just because I didn't play the part you wanted me to. You think you're so much better because you're the hero, and I became the villain. Newsflash, Lucas: there are no heroes and villains, just misunderstood stories with unwritten endings."

Lucas's face contorted with pain and submission. "Maybe. Or maybe it was easier to be the villain than risk finding happily ever after."

Sensing the rising tension, I broke their exchange. "Okay, enough, both of you. We've got bigger problems right now." I moved between them. "Can we please get through this night without any more drama?"

Kayla rolled her eyes at me. "Oh, please, you're the queen

of drama."

"I beg both of you: no more fairytale references; this night is getting way too Once Upon a Time for my liking."

I ignored both of their rebuttals and moved my bare feet quickly onto the cold stairs, the scent of our failed dinner lingering in the air as I descended. On the ninth step, I froze, my gaze fixated on the scene unfolding before me. My parents stood side by side, facing the front door. My mother slipped her jacket on, and Julian fumbled with his keys.

Perplexed, I blurted out, "And where do you two think you're going?"

That was mistake #1: never address your parents like a parent.

My mother's clenched face turned to me, her expression a mix of annoyance and an eerie calm. "Alex." She shifted her weight to her back foot as her hands flew to the sides of her hips. "You had a food fight in my dining room and shielded your face with my grandmother's china!"

I huffed at my dramatic mother and wrapped my hand tightly around the banister.

That was mistake #2: never let your parents see your disobedience.

The octaves in my mother's voice rose. "This fight between you three has gone on way too long, and I, for one, cannot handle seeing you kids act so childishly any longer." She wrapped a scarf around her neck. "Your father and I are going out to eat, and then we are going to stay at the Chesher Cat Inn for the night."

A wave of disbelief swept through me as the word sank

in. I couldn't believe what I was hearing. My gaze reflexively darted back to Lucas and Kayla, capturing the shared astonishment in their exchange glances, mirroring my shock.

My mother continued, "When we come home tomorrow, I expect to see that dining room and kitchen spotless!"

Julian's mediating voice cut through the argument like a poorly timed sitcom interruption. "We ordered you kids pizza. Maybe this time, try eating it instead of throwing it."

From behind me, Lucas's voice piped up. "You didn't have to do that."

Julian raised an eyebrow, completely unfazed. "If you're all going to act like children, then I'm going to treat you like children. It's high time you had a time-out to sort out your problems. And no one—and I mean no one—can stay mad while eating pizza. It's a grease-filled, cheesy peace treaty." He paused, then shrugged, "Besides, I didn't pay for it. Make sure to leave a good tip."

Without another word, Mom and Julian headed out the open front door like they hadn't dropped a verbal grenade into the middle of the group.

I stared after them, then swung my head toward Lucas and Kayla, blinking in disbelief. "Did we get … grounded?"

Kayla shrugged. "I mean, technically, we're unsupervised with pizza, so … I call it a win."

"I call it trapped."

# CHAPTER 7

Life starts when you're not looking
And ends when you stop looking

**August 10, 2013**

Lucas and Kayla always fought, but not the kind of fighting that ended in screaming matches or tears. To the outside world, it looked more like the beginning of a rom-com—or, honestly, the intro to a poorly written porno. It was flirty, playful, and always led by Kayla. But that's just how she was with everyone. Kayla could walk into any room and grab the attention of every man, woman, and probably even a few inanimate objects. That was Kayla, and she loved it that way.

Looking back, I should've noticed that there was something deeper to her actions: her need for attention and perfection. However, when I was fourteen, the whole world revolved around me and my emotions, like all teenagers. I forgot to stop and realize that everyone around me was the main character of their own story, with their own plots, their own heroes, and their own villains. Maybe I was the savior in someone's story, or maybe I was the evil queen. The truth is, I was probably both, just like Kayla was both a hero and a villain in mine.

Kayla was one of us—the fourth Musketeer in our odd little group of misfits. But she didn't like talking about her past or childhood, and none of us pried. Jamie and I had the Cliff Notes, but we never delved deeper into her chapters. Lucas, though, was different. He committed every detail about her to memory, as if each aspect were a riddle he had been quietly solving his entire life. He knew the exact cadence of her laugh, how her voice softened when she was sad, and the way she always tucked her hair behind her ear when she was nervous. He could anticipate her mood before she even said a word.

The truth was, Lucas understood Kayla in a silent, unshakable way that only someone who completely loved another could. When Kayla acted out, Lucas was the only one who truly understood why. He didn't shy away from her temper or her sharp words; instead, he handled her in a way that seemed effortless. Lucas understood Kayla like no one else could. He always had.

On August 10, 2013, while Jamie and I were caught up in our own storylines, Lucas had been the only one looking out for Kayla's happy ending.

It was the last weekend before our first day of school. The entire month before freshman year felt like an unhinged teen TV series in its final season—constant drama crashing into our lives left and right. The latest blowout had been Jamie's and my carnival fiasco, and after all that, I just wanted to stay home, curled up in a blanket, eating a pan of undercooked brownies, and watching Gossip Girl. But Kayla decided we all needed to hit the reset button, and she was determined not to let us start high school in the middle of a fight.

Instead, she thought it was a great idea to cozy up to one of the senior football jocks and get us an invitation to the first party of the year. As soon as we stepped inside the house, the music hit us like a wall, and the deep bass vibrated through my chest as if it had been trying to dislodge my heart. Kayla was in full-on Kayla mode, practically dragging us into chaos like this party was some life-altering experience. Spoiler alert: it wasn't. But try telling that to Kayla. Once she set her mind on something, it was more solid than the concrete holding the Pentagon together.

"This is going to be the best night of our lives! The start of our high school social status! We have to do this right!" She snatched two tiny plastic cups off a round platter at the front of the door and jettisoned one at me. It was a weird, green substance, half liquid and half underdeveloped Jell-O.

"I agreed to come to the party; I did not agree to get plastered." I shot back at her.

"No! No Debbie Downer tonight! We are all going to have fun." She jabbed a pointy finger into Lucas's chest. "That includes you, too, Mr." She handed him her green goop.

I glanced at Jamie, who had been doing an awe-inspiring job of pretending I hadn't existed since the carnival mess. Lucky me. If I had a dollar for every time he eyed me with that stupid mix of guilt and hurt, I could afford a trip to the Bahamas.

I refocused my attention on Kayla. "Tonight is the worst idea you've ever had," I stated more to myself than to her. "But what the hell, we're about to be high schoolers. Time to act like it, I guess." I raised my green cup to my brother and we toasted, then quickly downed the contents. The strange texture slithered down my throat like sour mucus.

Kayla jumped up and down like a kangaroo on coke. "Yes! Now that's what I'm talking about!"

She dashed into the crowd, dragging Lucas along. He wasn't resisting much, though, probably because he had no energy left after the breakup. It had only been two days since he and his girlfriend split, and he'd been in a mood ever since. I, however, could not be more thrilled that his summer romance was over. Ding dong, the witch is gone.

Jamie trailed behind me, silent but radiating discomfort. The night had "disaster" written all over it, but we were already in too deep. We followed Kayla into the lion's den. What else could we do? Be sensible? That ship sailed the moment we agreed to come.

The house was packed, mostly with seniors who wouldn't look at us twice if it weren't for Kayla. I scanned the room, my eyes landing on the scattered red solo cups, a stained couch sinking under the weight of too many people, and a flickering lightbulb overhead. The mingled scents of sweat and cheap beer hit me a second later, making me briefly wonder if we could make a quick escape. However, Kayla had other plans. She was already in full force, working the room with her effortless charm. Lucas watched her from a distance. His expression was tight, and tension pulsed from him like radiation.

"Lucas, you sure you want to be here?" I asked.

He barely spared me a glance, his eyes never leaving Kayla. "Do I have a choice?"

His stare narrowed as Kayla started chatting with the guy who had invited us. He leaned against the wall, all cool and cocky, eyes fixed on her like she was his prize for the night.

Jamie hung back, quiet as ever. This wasn't his scene, and it wasn't mine. But here we were.

As Kayla laughed at something the guy said, my gaze drifted to his friends standing just a few feet away. I hadn't noticed the one guy initially, but how his eyes lingered on me made my stomach tense. His hair, slicked back with too much gel, caught the light as he pushed a hand through it, his smile stretching a little too wide when he realized I had noticed him.

He took a step closer, and the overpowering scent of his cologne reached me before he did. "So." He leaned in as if we were already in the middle of a conversation. "What's a nice girl like you doing at a party like this?"

Is he flirting?

I let out a surprised chuckle, partly out of embarrassment but mostly out of shock. "I um … wow, is that your best pick-up line?"

"Did it work?" He flashed his white teeth at me.

A strange shiver rippled through my chest. "Maybe. Or maybe that weird green goo is going to my head."

"Hey, I made that green goo. I'm very proud of my artistry."

"Oh yeah, you're a real Picasso."

The guy chuckled. "I'm Nicholas. What's your name, Miss Drink Critic?"

I bit my lower lip, contemplating whether or not to give this older boy my real name. "… Alex."

He took my hand in his. "Well, Alex, would you like to dance?"

I was going to say no. I had no intention of being a piece of freshman meat to a hungry senior boy. But when I felt Jamie's presence looming behind me, I glanced back. He stood just a few feet away, staring in my direction, though pretending not to. His jaw was tight; his shoulders squared like he was bracing for something. Before I could answer, Jamie's fingers twitched at his sides, his eyes hard as they flicked between the guy and me.

"I don't think so," Jamie's voice cut through the air like a blade.

I turned to him, my eyebrows raised. "Excuse me?"

"Seems like I need to keep you from making poor choices tonight."

Heat rose in my cheeks. "What? Like letting you talk to me?"

Jamie's lips twitched, but he didn't smile. "No, like entertaining this guy," he shot back, "Or maybe you're just turned on by swapping spit with random strangers. Wouldn't be the first time this month."

I blinked, caught off guard by how much that stung. I turned back to Nicholas. "So, uh ... that dance?" I said, letting my smile linger a little too long, feeling Jamie's eyes burning into my back.

"I thought you would never ask," Nicholas said, taking a step closer and offering me his hand. But before anything else could happen, Kayla emerged suddenly, seizing my arm with uncontainable excitement.

"Oh my god, yes! Let's dance!" Kayla's voice cut through the pounding bass as she tugged me—and Nicholas—into the center of the room.

The crowd surrounded us, the heat rising as bodies pressed against each other. The floor drummed beneath my feet, each pulse of the bass vibrating through my legs. Kayla was already in motion, spinning wildly, her hair whipping around as she threw her arms into the air. Nicholas slid beside me, a grin tugging at the corner of his mouth as he easily matched my movements. I laughed, breathless, as Nicholas playfully twirled me again and again, the world around us blurring into lights and motion.

Now dancing with the senior boy, Kayla swirled through the crowd, her laughter bright and sharp. She reached for another drink, tossing it back as she stumbled, her hand brushing my shoulder before she caught herself with a breathless giggle. She grabbed another shot off a passing tray, downing it in one fluid motion, then snatched one more and shoved it into my hand. "Your turn!" she yelled over the music, her eyes gleaming with mischief. Without thinking, I tilted my head back, letting the liquid burn its way down my throat.

Nicholas pulled me closer, his grin widening as the song picked up speed. I couldn't remember the last time I felt so free. There was no awkward tension with Jamie, no worrying about Lucas brooding in the corner: just Kayla, me, this random hot-as-hell boy, and terrible music. I let out a loud laugh as Kayla grabbed another drink, her hand trembling slightly as she lifted it to her lips.

I watched her for a second, my steps slowing as concern began to creep in. She nearly tripped, catching herself on the senior's arm, her eyes glazed with the alcohol she'd been tossing back so easily. Something wasn't quite right. Kayla's laughter was a little too loud, and her steps a little too wobbly.

"Kayla, maybe—" I began, but my words were drowned out by someone yelling from the other side of the room.

"Spin the Bottle upstairs! Let's go!"

Kayla's eyes lit up like fireworks. "I love that game!" she squealed, grabbing my arm tightly. Her fingers dug into my skin as she yanked me toward the staircase, her pace quick, almost frantic.

"Wait, Kayla, maybe we should—" I tried again, but she was already pulling me through the crowd.

Kayla flew up the stairs, the senior boy trailing behind her as she darted to the top. Nicholas eagerly followed behind, urging me to come along. But something didn't feel right about this whole thing.

"Kayla, hold on!" I called after her, but she was already halfway up, not bothering to look back. Her hair swayed as she dodged people, determined to get to whatever madness was waiting upstairs.

Lucas, standing near the foot of the stairs, groaned, rubbing the back of his neck. "Is she serious right now?"

Jamie appeared next to me. Everything was happening so fast that I couldn't keep up with the shifting world. My head was spinning from too much heat and too much cheap liquor.

Jamie shifted next to me, his eyebrows raised as he stared at Kayla disappearing up the stairs. "What's her deal tonight? She's acting like it's her last night on earth."

Lucas sighed heavily, eyes still on the top of the staircase. "Something is going on. Did she say anything to either of you guys?"

I shook my head. "No, but I haven't talked to her much this past week."

I looked up and saw Kayla leaning over the banister, waving us up. "Come on, Alex!"

Jamie ran a worried hand through his hair. "We can't leave her alone up there. Can we?"

"No," Lucas spat, already heading up the stairs.

Jamie rolled his eyes but followed Lucas, shooting me a glance. "Guess we're all going, then."

I sighed because, of course, I had to follow. "Lead the way, boys," I said dryly, dragging my feet as I made my way up after them.

The hallway at the top of the staircase felt narrow, packed with bodies moving in and out of rooms. I followed closely behind Jamie and Lucas, my shoes scuffing on the steps. The closer we got to the top, the louder Kayla's giggles became.

"Finally! Took you guys long enough." Kayla bounced on her toes impatiently.

Lucas gave her a flat look. "This is dumb, you know that, right?"

She rolled her eyes. "Loosen up, Lucas. It's just a game."

"Yeah, a game everyone gets mono from," he muttered.

We moved to sit in a circle with people we barely knew, who were much older than the three of us. On one side of me was Jamie, practically radiating annoyance, and on the other was Nicholas, grinning from ear to ear. His attention was flattering, but right now, I was more concerned about Kayla, who was walking a tight line between fun drunk and the kind where your insides somersault out your nose. Yet, she was still acting like everything was fine.

She bounced around the room like a pinball, kissing

anyone the bottle landed on, boys, girls—it was all the same to her. Most of the others were laughing and encouraging her, but Lucas, sitting next to Jamie, looked like he was about to turn into a knight in shining armor. Soldier boy mode activated.

"Damn, she's going to regret this tomorrow." I grimaced.

"I'm just trying to figure out when to step in," Lucas answered.

"Now would be good," I said a little louder as Kayla leaned in to kiss a girl with a pixie cut. She was laughing, but in a manner that made me wonder if she was trying too hard.

It was now Nicholas's turn, which he speedily took. The bottle spun again, its glass scraping against the wood floor with a sharp pitch. It landed directly in front of me, the little bit of Coke still trapped in the glass sparkling as it came to a stop.

Nicholas leaned in slightly, the corners of his mouth curling into a teasing smirk. I caught Jamie moving out of the corner of my eye. His hand flexed, his fingers curling into a fist. There was a tightness in his posture, a barely restrained tension that made me want to push him just a little harder.

I leaned in and gave Nicholas a quick kiss. It was over in a second. When I pulled away, Nicholas was still grinning, and I gave him a polite smile, resisting the urge to taunt Jamie with a glance.

Next, it was my turn to spin, and just my luck, it landed on some random guy I barely knew. I shifted forward, preparing my mouth for the attack, when a hand grabbed my wrist, yanking me back. My heart jumped into my throat as Jamie pulled me toward him.

"Hey—" I began, but my words disappeared the second

his lips crashed into mine.

He kissed me—no warning, no build-up—a quick, unexpected press of his lips against mine that left me completely flustered. My heart hammered in my chest, and my hands found the fabric of his shirt, clutching it as if to steady myself.

After a dizzying few seconds, Jamie broke the kiss, but he didn't move far. His forehead pressed against mine, his breath warm against me, and for a moment, neither of us said anything.

"I'm done watching you kiss other guys." His words brushed against my skin.

I blinked, trying to process what had just happened. I opened my mouth to respond, but before I could, Kayla's voice cut through the moment like a knife. "My turn!" she yelled, oblivious to the emotional storm in my mind.

Jamie hesitated, his hand loosening around me, but he didn't move away. His eyes lingered on mine for a moment longer before he finally let go, leaning back into his spot.

I tried to catch my breath, but it was hopeless. I was hopeless. We were hopeless.

God, I'm screwed, I thought as I watched Kayla spin the bottle.

Her hands trembled slightly, and her eyes looked dazed as the bottle landed on the senior boy for the second time. According to the game rules, this meant that a simple peck on the lips wouldn't suffice. Kayla and the boy stumbled toward the closet, just a few feet away from where we were sitting, to conduct their awkward Seven Minutes in Heaven.

For 420 seconds, Lucas's knees bounced a hundred times as he stared at the closet door, seconds away from tearing it off its hinges. He shook his head, his voice tight. "I can't just sit here and watch her do this."

The closet door opened before I could say anything, and the senior boy poked his head out with a smirk. "We may need another seven minutes." He laughed as if it were all a big joke.

Kayla stumbled out, her shirt gone, her hair a tangled mess. She swayed forward, one hand clutching the frame for support. Before she could take another step, the boy's arm shot out, gripping her wrist, yanking her backward. She stumbled, her body collapsing into the clothes hanging behind her, a low, mumbled plea slipping from her lips. "Let me out ..." Her words were slurred and soft, but the boy didn't listen. Instead, he shoved her further inside, the door snapping shut behind them.

That was all Lucas needed. He was on his feet in an instant, his body taut, his eyes dark with rage. He crossed the room in two long strides, every muscle in his frame coiled like a spring about to snap. Some random guy, lounging by the door like a self-appointed guard, reached out to stop him. Lucas barely acknowledged him—one shove and the guy flew backward, crashing to the ground, landing flat on his ass with a grunt.

Lucas reached the closet in seconds, yanking the door open so hard the hinges groaned. His hand shot out and grabbed the senior by the collar. Without hesitation, he ripped him away from Kayla and slammed him against the doorframe, pinning his neck to the wood.

"Lucas, what the hell?" Kayla's voice trembled as she attempted to pull Lucas back, but her efforts were weak and did nothing to stop him. "Stop it!" Kayla shrieked.

Lucas didn't even register her plea. His chest was heaving as he pushed his forearm into the senior's neck, crushing his throat. "If you ever touch her again, I'll break your fingers." Lucas leaned closer, his weight pressing on the guy, who was squirming helplessly. "And you can kiss any football scholarship goodbye. You hear me?"

The guy stammered something incoherent, his face pale with panic. "Yes! Yes, okay! Just get off me!" he finally yelled, his voice cracking.

Lucas stayed there for another second, his gaze lethal, before releasing the boy. He turned to Kayla, who looked eager for an argument until she glanced down momentarily at her half-naked chest. Kayla's hands flew up to cover herself. She looked completely lost, her whole body trembling.

Lucas acted so quickly that it almost startled me. He slipped off his flannel, wrapped it gently around Kayla's body like a blanket, and pulled her close, his arm circling her protectively as though nothing else mattered. He guided her toward the door, leaving the guy crumpled on the ground, still gasping for air.

"We're leaving," he commanded Jamie and me.

Jamie's hand slipped into mine, his fingers firm and steady. "It's okay," he whispered. I hadn't even realized my breath had caught in my throat, but his thumb brushed against my palm, grounding me. "She's alright."

I felt his other hand against my cheek, gently wiping away a tear I didn't even realize had escaped. I didn't even know why I was crying. Everything happened so quickly; only seconds ago, we were all joking around, and then, in the blink of an eye, everything spiraled out of control. What would have happened if Lucas hadn't been there? Would anyone else have helped Kayla?

Would she have made it out of that closet? Or would the party have continued uninterrupted, with everyone silently witnessing this assault?

My heart pounded in my ears, but the noise of the room was distant, as if I were underwater. Jamie's hand stayed warm on my face. "Come on. Let's get out of here."

He kept his arm around me as we followed Lucas, my legs shaking beneath me, the adrenaline pumping. We moved through the house, the party fading into the background like some distant nightmare, until the cool night air hit me, sharp and sobering.

Kayla wiggled out of Lucas's hold, her bare feet stumbling on the grass as she turned her body to face the three of us. We didn't say a thing. Six hundred thousand words in the dictionary, and not one of them seemed right.

"Stop looking at me like that! I'm not some damsel in distress."

Lucas stepped closer to her. "Then stop acting like a spoiled princess in need of saving!"

Kayla froze at the intensity in his voice.

He lowered his tone, which was barely audible over the breeze that stirred the trees around us. "Kayla, what's going on?" His hands came up, gently resting on her shoulders. She flinched at the contact but didn't pull away. Her eyes flickered up to his, tears clinging to her lashes, tracing silent paths down her cheeks.

Her lips parted, but no words came out. She closed her mouth, swallowed hard, and stared at the ground as if it held the answers she couldn't find. Her hands fidgeted at her sides, fingers curling and uncurling around the hem of Lucas's flannel.

Lucas waited, his gaze steady, never leaving her face. His grip on her shoulders tightened just slightly, a wordless reassurance, a silent I'm here.

Finally, she looked up, her eyes red-rimmed and glassy. Her voice cracked, barely more than a whisper. "She should've been here, Lucas … my mom … she should've been here." Kayla's face crumpled. "She should've been here to see my first day of high school."

Lucas's brow furrowed, and for a moment, it was like watching all the pieces of a puzzle click into place behind his eyes. Without saying anything, he stepped forward and pulled her into his chest. Kayla collapsed against him, her arms wrapping around his waist, her body trembling with silent sobs. Her shoulders shook violently as she clung to the front of his shirt, fingers gripping the fabric as though it were the only thing keeping her upright. Lucas's arms circled her fully, pulling her closer, his hand rubbing slow, soothing circles across her back. He didn't speak—he didn't need to. He just held her, his chin resting on the top of her head, grounding her as her tears soaked into his shirt.

It made sense now, the reason she'd been spinning through the night like a hurricane. I only knew fragments of the story. Kayla's dad needed to move back home to take care of his elderly mother, but Kayla's mom refused to uproot her life and follow. That was the story they told everyone. However, one night during a sleepover at Kayla's place, I overheard him telling his mother that Kayla's mom had left because of another man.

I watched Lucas hold Kayla as she cried, feeling completely useless. This wasn't just Kayla being a wild teenager or acting out for attention. This was simply a young girl who missed her mom. A young girl who had built her new life around pretending not to care that her mother wasn't there, and now that façade was cracking, falling apart under the weight of what she wanted—her mom to care enough to show up.

Jamie moved beside me, his arm sliding around my waist. He didn't say anything, but the way his hand rested on my side, the way his body leaned into mine, made me feel anchored. He tugged me forward, pulling me into a hug, and before I knew it, all four of us were there, wrapped together in this tangled mess of arms and emotions. I felt Kayla's shaky breaths against my shoulder, Lucas's hand still moving rhythmically along her back, and Jamie's warmth pressing into my side, steady and reassuring.

Jamie glanced down at me. "Truce?" he asked, his voice barely a whisper.

"Truce," I whispered back.

For a moment, none of the tension or fights from earlier mattered. It was just the four of us, and somehow, that was enough.

# CHAPTER 8

The past doesn't stop hurting.
The present won't stop ticking.
The future can't stop looming.
So, what's the worst of the three?
The person who can't let them be.

**8:00 p.m.**

I was armed with a damp cloth as I wiped every last trace of spaghetti and hot-dog pieces off the walls. The cold, slimy remnants stained the paint worse than spilled wine on a cotton shirt. I needed a fake ID, a thousand dollars in cash, and a fast car to escape my mother's wrath.

Kayla meticulously stacked the plates and cutlery as she cleared the dining table. Awkward silences were her kryptonite, and currently, all three of us were held captive by the emptiness of words. The only sound came from the clinking of glass and china, orchestrated by Lucas as he scrubbed the dishes clean.

Five years had passed since we graduated high

school—only five years, yet it was painfully apparent that time had hardened us. We had become strangers to each other, like three walking corpses: the same features, same hair, same eyes, but lifeless and cold. How could three people, who had once known every intimate detail about each other, now feel so detached?

The absence of sound stung like acid, eroding my bones, but it was still better than speaking words I didn't believe and better than hearing ones I didn't want to. However, what I wanted and what I got never seemed to align. Kayla was the first to attempt to break the ice. She carried a stack of forks, knives, and plates into the kitchen and placed them next to the rest of the piled dishes.

Lucas's eyes widened at the mess of china, which continued to multiply before his eyes. "This is worse than when I worked at Grannie's as a dishwasher sophomore year," he grumbled as he grabbed a dirty dish from the middle of the pile and plunged it into the scalding water.

Kayla hopped onto the counter, her heels bouncing off the cabinet as she slid back into a seated position. "Hey, you can't claim all the misery. We all worked at Grannie's that year."

Lucas continued to scrub dish after dish. "You get no sympathy from me. You spent the entire year flirting with every customer from age fifteen to thirty. Grannie had to warn the basketball team about you."

A subtle smirk of mischief painted Kayla's lips, "Then it's a good thing I only had eyes for the football team."

Ouch … I knew Kayla was trying to make conversation, and her way of breaking bread was usually accomplished by breaking boundaries. But right now, her flirtatious anecdotes were the last thing Lucas needed. He was the wide receiver for our team and had spent his entire high school life pining after Kayla, only for the love of his life to cheat on him with his best friend after they finally got together. Lucas had faced the same situation I had, but he seemed to handle it better. It was as if his mind functioned like a giant filing system, with a folder for every betrayal neatly tucked away—always present but never reopened.

Lucas dropped the plate he was scrubbing into the hot, soapy water and stared into the cloudy liquid as though it were a crystal ball.

"Don't," he whispered to the submerged plates. "Please just don't do that." His voice stopped as if his own words hurt him. "I used to love hearing my name dance off your lips." His big eyes met Kayla's shocked ones. "But now it just hurts too much."

Kayla's voice was so low I could barely hear her words. "I'm sorry, I'm so sorry—" Kayla moved her hand to his cheek, but he flinched like her skin burned.

"I don't want you to be sorry. I don't want to hurt you." His gaze softened. "But I can't allow myself to feel even a fraction of what I felt for you in the past." He tucked a single braid behind her ear. "When you speak to me as if we are still sixteen, my heart forgets what my brain will always remember, and I don't deserve that pain."

If I weren't harboring my own resentment for Kayla, I would have yelled, Kiss her, you big idiot at my brother. But I didn't. I stayed silent and pretended I didn't just hear their heartbreaking conversation.

Kayla opened her mouth to respond, but as she hesitated, the doorbell rang, its chime cutting through the heavy atmosphere like a bolt of lightning.

"Saved by the bell." I put my damp cloth on the dining table.

I bolted to the front door, partly to escape the second-hand embarrassment but mostly because I was starving. If there was any luck in this world, that doorbell would have been the announcement of freshly baked pizza, ready to whisk me away with its cheesy bliss. I yanked open the door, hoping to be greeted with the sinful smell of grease and pepperoni, but instead, I was met by the beady green eyes of an unexpected visitor holding my dinner hostage.

A sly grin spread across my face as a strange mix of amusement and delight filled my cells. "Look, Kayla!" I yelled down the hall to the kitchen, "Your past has literally come knocking."

"What?!" Kayla yelled back. She marched down the hallway to see what all the fuss was about.

I stepped aside, giving Kayla a perfect view of our guest. Her reaction was instant, eyes wide, shoulders snapping back, one hand darting to her hair, smoothing it down like it might save her. She plastered on a smile that looked about as stable as a wet napkin. I had to bite the inside of my cheek to keep from grinning.

"Annalise …" Kayla choked out in a light squeak as if her larynx was being squeezed by an invisible hand. Kayla approached the door, her still-wet hair lightly dripping down the back of Lucas's baggy T-shirt, which hung tent-like on her wiry figure.

Annalise eyed her disheveled ex-girlfriend up and down.

"Hey, Kayla, it's nice to see you. Are you in town because of Saturday?"

Of course, she's here for Saturday. What a ridiculous question, I thought as I lingered close behind Kayla, not wanting to miss any of the show before me.

Kayla replied, "Partially, yes, and also because I just moved back home …"

Annalise's eyebrows furrowed, but there was a slight upturn at the corners of her lips. "Oh, I'm sorry."

Kayla cut her off, "It's fine. I mean, you get it." She gestured to Annalise's pizza delivery uniform. "Adulting isn't as glamorous as it was advertised to be, am I right?" Her voice wavered between defensive and self-deprecating.

Annalise shifted the extra-large pizza box in her hands to the side, resting it on her bony hip. "I own Mikey's Pizzeria now. And the movie theater and the bowling alley next door."

Kayla's face turned a deep shade of burgundy, her embarrassment bringing a sting to even my eyes.

I contemplated allowing Kayla to continue standing, mortified and wordless, but my better instincts took over. Damn, my conscience can't let me have anything. Cursing at myself for not allowing Kayla to die of self-loathing, I stepped forward to grab the pizza from Annalise. "I would say it was nice to see you, but we both know that's not true." I began to close the door.

Annalise huffed. "What, no tip?"

Through a four-inch gap in the door, I said, "Sure, here's one: If you have to brag about your life to feel superior, then maybe it's not as great as you think." Before I could hear the gasp from Annalisa's mouth, I slammed the door and quickly locked it behind me.

Kayla wrapped her long arms around my shoulders like I was the last lifejacket on the Titanic. "Thanks, Alex."

I felt my arm hug her back, a reflex I refused to believe was anything more than muscle memory. I broke from Kayla's grasp. "Don't get all sappy on me. It's not like I gave you a kidney."

Kayla's face drooped.

"You're welcome," I said to break her wounded puppy expression. "But honestly, that was the most fun I've had all month. I hated Annalise in high school." I shuddered.

"I second that," Lucas said from down the hallway, leaning against the kitchen's archway.

I brought the pizza into the living room, Lucas and Kayla following, and laid it on the coffee table. "You only hated her 'cause she dated Kayla before you did."

Lucas gasped, two red circles forming over his tanned cheeks. "Everyone dated Kayla before I did!" he shot back.

Kayla slapped his massive shoulder, eliciting a booming laugh from Lucas that I hadn't heard in years. "What is this? Gang up on Kayla day?!" she said through a whimper.

I opened the pizza box and snatched a pepperoni-covered slice, shoveling its greasy end into my mouth. "Can we make that a national holiday?" I said with a marinara-covered smile.

A piercing yelp blasted from Lucas's phone. He swiftly dug it out of his pocket, probably worried it was a text from work, but it was unfortunately not a job crisis. Lucas's eyes shot at Kayla's face. "Annalise posted to the alumnae's Facebook page …" He gulped.

"What did she post?" I swear I could see Kayla's heart racing through her shirt.

Heavy tension filled the space as we gathered around Lucas, who promptly pulled his phone close to his chest, obscuring the image from our eyes.

"Lucas, let me see," Kayla barked.

"Don't overreact. Annalise is just being her normal viper self. It doesn't matter. She doesn't matter." Lucas's voice switched to his soldier boy tone. Damn, it must have been bad; he only sounded like that when he needed to talk Kayla down from a ledge.

"Lucas Adonis Drakos, show me that post right now!" Kayla pulled out the middle name … this meant war.

Lucas slowly unclenched his hands, his breath still paused in suspense. "Just please don't throw my phone when you see it."

Kayla ripped the phone from his grasp. "Oh my god!" Kayla's hand swiftly slapped her mouth as she sucked in a gasp of mortification.

I snatched the phone from her clammy hands to see the damage. "Oh my god …" I echoed Kayla's breath. "When did she even take that photo?"

The post was a meme made from a picture of Kayla talking, her mouth wide open, her wet braids dripping over Lucas's tattered shirt, next to a photo of Annalise on a yacht drinking a fancy drink with a frilly tiny umbrella, embellished with the caption: "When you run into your ex, and they're living with their parent, but your bank account is six figures."

The post had already gotten 200 likes, all from former classmates and even some teachers. I didn't dare open the comments section. There was already a 70/30 chance Kayla was going to have an aneurysm from the photo; I didn't want to risk the odds of her seeing the biting words of teenage-brained adults who didn't have anything better to do than mock a former classmate.

Kayla hastily flung herself onto the couch, burying her face in her hands. Through pillow-muffled cries, she screamed, "Oh, God, please let the floor swallow me whole!"

I tried to offer some comfort. "Come on, Kayla, you've survived worse. Remember the time you forgot to wear underwear to the homecoming dance? I'm pretty sure you twirling around in that ridiculous tulle dress, commando, is worse than a little post."

Kayla turned her head, still fused to the couch cushion, to glare at me. "Thank you for reminding me about that. I feel so much better now."

I said, tried. I tried to offer comfort. But comfort was not my job in this friend group.

"Lucas." I tagged him into the ring.

"Yeah, yeah, I got her." He went to the couch and gently lifted Kayla's head off the cushion before softly placing his body where her face used to be. Then, as swiftly as a ballroom dance, he returned her head to his lap, and his long arm wrapped around her. Lucas moved so effortlessly around Kayla that it seemed his body responded before his brain reacted to pull away. Kayla didn't flinch or acknowledge his presence; she exhaled slowly and quietly, as if his touch had steadied something fragile within her. They seemed to be on autopilot, programmed to respond to each other's touch.

I bit the crust off my pizza violently. "We need alcohol."

I dragged my weary body up and walked over to the locked cabinet next to the fireplace. Squatting down, I reached under the cabinet door, running my fingers over the slightly splintered wood until they found a piece of tape holding a metal key. I quickly removed it and pulled it out from under the furniture. "It's been fourteen years, and they still haven't changed their hiding spot." I inserted the key into the cold brass lock and turned it clockwise until I heard the familiar click. I opened the doors and took out the vodka.

"Monica and Dad are going to kill you." Lucas rolled his eyes.

"Why? We're old now. This is the first time I've broken into this cabinet when I've been legal."

Lucas's eyebrows rose, and his mouth parted, ready to rebut my statement, but then he stopped and nodded slightly. "You're right."

What did he say? I can one hundred percent guarantee that my jaw hit the floor. "Could you say that a bit louder, please?" I pressed my hand to my ear, urging him to inflate my ego further.

"Just hand me that before I change my mind." Lucas reached out for the bottle, which I handed him with glee. He opened it and took a huge gulp. "Here." He lowered the bottle to Kayla, who was still resting her head on his lap. "You need this more than me."

Leaning up slightly, Kayla chugged the clear liquid, gulping it down like water out of a fountain. Then she passed the now backwash-infested drink to me and sighed. "High school was like five years ago; why does it feel like I'm fourteen again?"

I wiped the spit off the bottle's rim before sucking the

liquid down, the burning sensation causing my chest to heat like a pressure cooker. "Because high school was a battlefield of hormonal social climbers clawing and killing each other to fit in." I swigged the stinging liquid again. "And now we all have PTSD."

Lucas reached for the largest slice of pizza in the box. "What did you all want to be before the world told you who to become?" he asked as his fingers ripped a slice of burnt pepperoni off the cheese.

Kayla was the first to answer. "Travel Photographer." A little smile turned her lips up, but it wasn't happy—it was almost pitiful. "That's what I wanted." She gazed at the ceiling. "I wanted to see the world and for the world to see me."

Lucas gazed down at Kayla, his eyes holding hers as if they were the only two people on earth. "Why didn't you do that after high school?"

"Because my dad always said a degree was the only way to succeed. I guess I didn't want to let him down."

I almost hacked on the vodka, burning my tongue. "Your dad must be really proud of me. I have an English degree, and the only job that answered my resume was from an adult toy store looking for a D-cup sales lady."

Lucas choked on the cheese of his pizza. "Please tell me you didn't interview for that."

"I'm on their schedule for Wednesday." The absurdity of the situation caused me to topple over in a heap of self-deprecating laughter, which was quickly joined by everyone else. "What about you, Lucas? What did the little soldier boy want to be growing up?" I asked, hoping not to be the only loser in the room.

"I wanted to be a foreign correspondent."

Kayla shook her head. "What child dreams about that?" She chuckled.

"I'm not sure if I ever dreamed it. It just seemed like a smart, logical job that would pay well and allow me to travel. It was practical." He paused, reflecting. "But now that I look back, I wonder what I would have wanted to be if I had allowed myself to dream."

The vulnerability in Lucas's voice was sobering. He never doubted his decisions, and honestly, I never doubted him. He wasn't a rock, he was a boulder—a forever solid, unmovable force, yet right now, he looked like a little boy, the same little boy I met for the first time after his mom died, and we had moved in. I suppose even those who seem to have it all figured out are just as lost as those who wander.

In trying to divert the spotlight from himself, Lucas spoke again before we could respond, "So, before the adult toy store, what was your childhood dream, Alex?"

"I didn't really have one," I whispered to the floor. "Jamie was the one who pushed me into writing after he stole my journal that first day of freshman year." A wistful smile crossed my face. But then, my expression fell, and I admitted, "Obviously, it was a pipe dream because the only thing I've written in the last year was a bad review of my Uber Eats driver."

Kayla's eyes locked onto mine, and at that moment, I knew she would ask a question I didn't want to answer. "What are you going to do when you see him?"

Pain. That's all I felt. In my chest. In my lungs. In every cell that made my body function. Pain was the only sensation. "I don't know." I stared blankly through the hole of the glass bottle before me. "I guess I've been trying not to think too much about it."

That was a lie. All I could do was think about it. How was I supposed to look at the boy I loved all my life in the eyes, knowing our fate was sealed? I traced the cold glass with the tip of my index finger. "Jamie was my compass, and without him, I can't find my way home anymore."

Lucas let out a soft, sorrowful sigh, "Maybe it is time to be your own map."

"Thanks for the advice, Magellan." I huffed.

But Lucas didn't stop. "You know forgiveness doesn't mean admitting defeat. It means you're finally setting yourself free."

"Maybe I don't want to be."

# CHAPTER 9

A single choice
Becomes a story
Retold a thousand times

## August 12, 2013: PART 1

The second Monday in August marked the day all kids either eagerly awaited or earnestly sought to avoid: freshman year. Our grade was split into two groups: group one, comprised of those popular in middle school who eagerly counted down the days until freshman year, their moment to assume their rightful place among the other privileged souls and commence their reign of torment over the less fortunate; and group two: the freaks and geeks, the kids who trembled in fear as Monday approached.

Jamie and I found ourselves on opposing sides that fateful day. Personally, I was thrilled. High school's arrival meant I was one step closer to executing my life's master plan: packing my belongings into a giant trash bag and making a swift exit from this small town. Of course, I had no clue where I was headed; I just knew it had to be anywhere but here. Jamie, however, was dreading the first day of school. To him, it marked the beginning of the end. It was the day we'd all be split into different classes: Lucas would try out for the football team, Kayla would run for student body president, despite being too young. And in Jamie's anxiety-clouded eyes, this was the day I'd realize I was too good for him. The first time he vocalized this fear, I had to grab the back of the doorframe I was leaning against to keep my body stable as knee-shaking laughter erupted from my lungs, reverberating through the room with a force that no stand-up comedian could replicate with a joke.

Don't get me wrong, I wasn't laughing at Jamie, and I genuinely wasn't attempting to downplay his emotions. But the concept seemed comical to me; the notion that I could ever consider myself too good for him was ridiculous. In reality, Jamie was the one who was too good for me, too good for anyone. I wish I could have made him realize that.

I stood at the foot of my bed, hands on my hips, staring at the long-haired, tangled mass of overgrown limbs submerged under my comforters, which refused to roll off my mattress.

"Jamie!" I yelled. "Please get your lazy ass out of my bed before my mom walks up here and sees you wrapped in my sheets!"

Jamie gripped the sides of my flattened pillow and squeezed the edges over his ears. "Scared she'll think we're doing it?" he grumbled.

"Gross, dude!" I slapped his blanket-covered foot. "Besides, you're fully clothed; it's not like we could have been doing anything R-rated anyway."

Jamie flung his body to the side, propping up his head with his elbow. "Wanna test the theory?" I didn't know if his boyish grin made me want to throw myself on top of him or to slap him.

"Your hormones are rotting your brain, you know that." I rolled my eyes at him, not entirely out of annoyance, but because since our kiss at the carnival, I couldn't meet his gaze and maintain our flirtatious banter without my body feeling like my atoms were melting.

"Yup." Jamie propped himself into a sitting position, my comforter bunching around his waist. "And you love it." I thought his summer glow-up was going to his head. But damn, if he grew taller or his hair grew any longer, he was going to have to start sleeping on the floor.

"Get up, please." I tried to reason with him.

Jamie crossed his newly defined arms over his way-too-sculpted chest. "Make me."

I cocked my head at his smugness. "Fine."

Just as Jamie was about to inch further into my sheets, I sprang into the bed, the mattress bouncing beneath me. If there was one thing in this world that Jamie hated the most, it was being tickled. It was his very own personal self-destruct button I could hit anytime.

As I landed, fingers ready for their mission, I ran them up the sides of his torso, causing him to screech, "Please! Please!" His limbs flailed about like fish out of water. "Okay! OKAY! I'll get up! Please, no more."

He skillfully caught my arms with one swift move.

I could feel the steam of his breath on my neck and the

beat of his heart against my chest. He released my hands. His eyes didn't meet mine as if he was scared to join my gaze.

His lips parted lightly. "Or maybe … we could just stay here. Like this."

"Is that what you want?"

"It's what I always want."

I should have kissed him right there, right then. But I didn't. Instead, I did what I always did: I ruined the moment.

"What about Meghan? Don't you have a date with her this Friday?"

Jamie pulled his eyes away from me and shot them to the ceiling. "You told me to say yes."

I didn't. Not technically, anyway. The day after the party, Megan texted Jamie to ask if he wanted to see a movie. And some dumb part of me thought that after Jamie kissed me for the second time, it meant he wouldn't be going on dates with other girls. I was wrong. "No, I told you to say yes if you wanted."

Jamie propped his body up with his hand, his chest almost leaning on top of mine. "And how is that different?"

I pleaded for my mouth to stop moving. "I said if you wanted to. Not that you should." My pleas went unheard.

The shriek of my bedroom door opening jolted me upright, the sudden intrusion sending my heart into a panicked rhythm. I met my mother's eyes, which were wide and darting back and forth between Jamie, sprawled happily on my bed, and my guilt-ridden, ghost-white face.

Her lips pushed together as if a bee had stung her gums. "You know we do have a front door, Jamie."

Jamie reclined deeper into the bed, his hands casually

interlocking behind his head, his elbows dramatically stretched out as if this humiliating moment had been simply a lovely conversation in a coffee shop, instead of a nightmare plaguing his day at 6:30 a.m.

"Oops, my bad. I keep forgetting about that." He grinned, revealing his overly white teeth, at my mom.

"We weren't doing anything," I stammered, my eyes darting nervously towards Jamie, who graced me with an eye roll and a smirk. "I swear! He just needed a place to sleep last night."

My mother's freckled arms folded over her yellow tank top. "And every other day this week?"

I stepped forward and lowered my head. "Come on, Mom, you know how his dad is right now."

My mom sucked in a thick breath and her eyes pinched inward; I could tell she was contemplating which emotion would win: pity or discipline. "Yes, unfortunately, I do." She released the breath she was holding. "Could you two maybe meet me halfway and have Jamie sleep in Lucas's room from now on?"

I stomped my foot. "That's not fair—"

"Yes, I can do that," Jamie interrupted, standing up from the bed and moving to my side. "Thank you, Monica." He elbowed me in the side, urging me to stay quiet and, for once, let this battle die.

My mom gave her signature nod and thin-lipped smile to both of us—a gesture I knew all too well, one which acknowledged her victory. "Now get ready and run downstairs before Lucas eats all the breakfast. I swear if that boy grows anymore, I'll need to have the door frames heightened."

Honestly, I was lucky that my mother didn't lock me in a tower and behead Jamie with her hedging shears the second she caught him in my bed. Yet I found myself testing the strength of the line she drew, waiting for Jamie to stop fixing his messy black hair in the bathroom.

"If all the bacon is gone by the time we get downstairs because you've decided to care more about styling your hair than my need for over-salted pig fat, I'm going to kill you and bury your remains at school so your ghost will forever dwell in math class ... do you understand me!" I yelled as I confiscated Lucas's hair gel from Jamie's hands. The clear gunk smothered on the bottle cap stuck to my palms like hair-covered playdough.

Jamie's eyes lowered to mine. "Excuse me, Miss Time Warden, but if you're gonna drag me to school, I might as well look half decent." He smoothed the sides of his hair with his palms, his wavy strands held hostage by too much product.

"You do realize it's 2013, and you're not a greaser, right?

"First, you love John Travolta. Don't deny it. And second, if you would stop yelling at me, I would already be done."

Ten minutes later, the bathroom was still rumbling with our argument. It wasn't until I took Jamie's comb that he finally stormed out of the room to chase me down the hall and stairs. I raced forward, skipping three steps at a time, the heels of my boots slamming against the ground and leaving permanent imprints of my soles on the wood floor.

I dashed down the hallway to the kitchen and pivoted my

body toward the stove like a racecar approaching the finish line. I could see the over-greased pan of happiness. As I reached my fingertips toward the lightly burnt bacon, an evil force snatched away my joy and shoved it into his big mouth.

"Sorry, sis, you snooze, you lose." Lucas licked the remnants of shiny bacon grease off his fingertips.

My face scrunched towards my nose, and my jaw bit down on my back molars, causing my masseter muscle to make a concerning crack and then an ear-ringing pop. Faint footsteps clattered behind me. I turned, quick and sharp, toward the figure lingering at my back.

"Now I'm stuck with oatmeal. Are you happy?" I grumbled at Jamie as I stole a lightly chipped bowl from the counter and scooped in a heap of mushy oats into the porcelain.

Jamie tiptoed next to me and grabbed his own bowl, which he filled with Lucky Charms. "Can I be cremated instead of buried?"

"Nope, I plan on dismembering you and burying your pieces around the school in the shape of a pentagram so that not even a priest can set you free."

In the dining room, Julian put his morning paper down with what had to be deliberate rustling. "Your knowledge of occultism is concerning. I don't know if I should call a therapist or an exorcist."

Lucas stole a piece of bread from the middle of the dining table. "I think an all-girls Catholic school would do the trick. I have pamphlets upstairs if you want to see them." He smiled through toast-covered teeth.

Jamie and I sat in our typical seats. His eyes traced me

from head to boot. "I wouldn't mind seeing you in one of those uniforms."

Before I could match Jamie flirt for flirt, Julian interrupted, "So, Jamie, sleep well?" He raised his brows so high I was worried they would fly off his forehead.

Jamie swallowed a baseball-sized lump of Lucky Charms as his cheeks flushed pink. "Sorry, Mr. D, we were watching a movie, and it was really late. I fell asleep."

"Yeah, and I didn't want to wake him," I added.

Julian folded his morning paper into a long rectangle. "That's understandable." The table stayed silent as if the placemats and silverware were betting on the severity of my punishment. "It's lucky, though," Julian continued.

"What's lucky?" I immediately regretted my question.

"That you had fresh clothes for Jamie in your room," he said, eyeing the newly washed black flannel and worn-out jeans hanging on Jamie like two oversized blankets.

Busted. Jamie had stashed his things all over my room this past summer. It was easier than him constantly stealing Lucas's shirts.

"Uh, yeah, they're from over the summer. He got something on them, so I washed them, and he forgot to take them back home," I stammered, trying to find the perfect lie.

Julian put a piece of salty ham on his plate and neatly placed the bite into his mouth. "That makes sense. Very responsible of you." He paused, putting his fork back on the table. "Just one more thing, Alex. How do you turn the washing machine on?"

Yep, I'm dead. I was a quick liar, truly a skilled manipulator, but Julian could call bull on even my best performances. He was a human lie detector, a fourteen-year-old girl's worst nightmare. I shoved a chunk of oatmeal in my mouth, my feeble attempt to muffle my fib.

"The on button ..." I choked out.

"Where would that button be located exactly?" An amused grin tugged at Julian's thin lips.

I glanced at Jamie for help.

"Don't look at me. My mom takes everything to the laundromat."

Just as my mouth opened to dig my hole an extra two feet deeper, the front door burst open, sending a shrill squeak from the rusty hinges across the interrogation room.

"You guys started breakfast without me!" Kayla whined at us as she stomped into the dining room and took her place beside Lucas.

Julian leaned in towards me. "Saved by the door. Again. I think you two planned that sometimes."

Kayla placed a napkin on her lap and turned her attention to my mother, who sat adjacent to Julian at the other end of the table. "Make any pancakes today?" She grinned with an expression that begged for sugar.

My mother raised a brow back at Kayla. "What is this? Waffle House?"

Kayla snatched a piece of toast from the bread plate. "Your hash browns could definitely use some improvement, but you're almost there!"

"I appreciate the almost compliment, Kayla, but you kids should start walking to school, or you'll be late."

"But I didn't get any bacon yet!" Kayla bellowed.

Lucas grabbed his backpack, which rested on the floor, leaning against his leg. "Here, I saved this for you." He pulled out a grease-soaked rolled-up wad of paper towels and swiftly unwrapped them, revealing the last three pieces of bacon—let me rephrase that ... my last three pieces of bacon!

"Breakfast stealer!" I yelled at my brother.

My mother rose from her chair, "Nope, no fighting. Get up and get out."

After a few more yells and screams, we left the table. I slung my tattered purple backpack over my shoulder, the sheer weight of it sending me almost flying on my ass. Damn, I really have to empty this thing, I thought as I exited the door. Jamie never carried a backpack, so I always packed two of everything, even though there was no chance that he was ever going to crack open a book or take any notes in class, but just in case, I always had everything he might need.

My foot barely hit the sidewalk when Jamie said he forgot something. His eyes darted around like a criminal stalking a bank, but before I could pry, he dashed back into the house.

Jamie's middle name was "self-destruction." Perhaps if I hadn't been so preoccupied with the excitement of my first day of freshman year, I might have given more thought to his actions and realized something wasn't right. But I didn't think anything of how his hands shook when he grabbed his bowl or the rapid beating of his heart when we were lying on my bed together. I simply didn't consider it, at least not until he managed to wreck his first day of high school, earning himself the reputation that would haunt him like a lurking ghost.

If I could go back in time, I would have run into that house and given in to his pleas to ditch school. I would have given him one day where he didn't have to think about reading in front of a class or a teacher calling on him without his permission. I would have given him one day where school was an afterthought and not a nightmare.

But I didn't.

Instead, I waited for him to exit the front door, his fingers gripping a plastic water bottle firmly to his side. The bottle would later become a nuclear bomb, evaporating any possibility of happiness we may have had. I know that sounds dramatic, but life is like dominoes: one wrong move and everything comes crashing down.

# CHAPTER 10

Knives might slice you
Words might cut you
Lies might stab you
But a rumor will stay with you.

**August 12, 2013: PART 2**

As we stepped into the halls of adolescent chaos, the four of us were instantly separated. I was forced to endure boring lectures and lessons without the companionship of Jamie's snores as he dozed on his desk or the obnoxious flinches of Lucas's hand, which would raise high with every question the teacher posed. I even missed the smacking noise of Kayla's pen dancing on her college-lined notebook paper as she doodled cartoon characters of our other classmates.

So, there I was, forced to endure my morning classes surrounded by peers whose names I either barely knew or didn't plan to learn.

Jamie and I only had one class together—math, thank God—because he would've failed eighth-grade algebra without our brilliant cheating system. One tap on the desk meant A, two meant B, and so on. It worked flawlessly … until our math teacher, Ms. Snitch, suggested to my parents that I get tested for ADHD because of my "fidgeting problem."

Finally, after four hours down, the passing seconds whispered the promise of lunchtime ahead—the only escape from the monotony of what supposedly were my educational hours. I stared at the clock with glazed eyes. Whoever dreamed up the brilliant idea of confining 400 unbalanced teenagers to a concrete building must have been indulging in something more substantial than Jamie's dad's stash. I leaned to the side in my desk chair, accidentally overhearing the latest gossip from two guys with matching mullets. Eric Perez dated Laura Simmons over the summer until a party at Danny Leatherman's house, when Eric and Laura's stepsister treated the partygoers to a nude show in the hot tub—earth-shaking news. I rolled my eyes—American tax dollars well spent. Now I know who Biffy's bopping this week; I'm going to make an excellent doctor or scientist now.

The sound of glorious angels—the lunch bell!—pierced the suffocating air around my desk. I dashed out of my seat and flung my bag across my back. The crushing weight of books inside slammed into the pointy part of my shoulder bone, causing my joint to make a concerning pop and crack. I ignored the sudden sharp pain as I ran down the mud-speckled tile that lined the hallway of happiness leading to the best room in high school: the cafeteria.

My toes made a high-pitched squeal as they halted in place three feet from the door's threshold. I swiveled my head back and forth, searching for the weather tower that was my brother. My eyes locked onto the sight of his black hair, neatly aligned against the blue-painted wall, as he waited in the lunch line. I dashed to his side, cutting in front of the students behind him, causing a roar of yells and hollers. But I paid them no attention; instead, I noticed the one missing voice in the crowd.

"Where's Jamie?" I asked Kayla, who stood next to Lucas, wearing an almost guilty expression. Her eyes flickered to Lucas and then back to mine as if debating who should break the news.

Lucas lowered his head slightly to mine. "The last I heard, he skipped English with the Donahue brothers . . ." His Adam's apple bobbled as he swallowed a deep gulp.

A burning sensation radiated from my chest to my stomach. If one thing was for sure in this world, it was that associating with the Donahues was as bright as putting your finger in a light socket. Dallas, the oldest brother, was eighteen and still a junior—not because he couldn't graduate, but because high schoolers were convenient, gullible targets who spent their parents' money on brain-numbing substances and fake IDs. The Donahue family dealt in everything from liquor to crack, and anyone treading these halls with them was expected to follow suit. They were our town's sorry excuse for a gang, and at the head of the useless pack of mutts was their father, Jack Donahue—Jamie's dad's best friend and business partner.

Jamie's dad wasn't always scum on the bottom of my shoe. He was rumored to have been a kind boy, working at the local bowling alley to support his sick mother. That was until Jack Donahue offered to bring him along on a job, and just like that, the blood-soaked history was etched.

"Why the hell would you two not stop him?" I yelled,

forgetting we were standing in line with fifty other students.

Lucas's fists clenched. "What did you want me to do? Ditch class to save his ass again?"

"Yes!" I growled.

Lucas straightened his posture like a drill sergeant, readying his voice to scold a shoe-shining soldier. "If Jamie wants to throw his life away following those worthless thugs, then that's on him. He didn't even make it through the first class before skipping off with them."

I wanted to scream, stomp my feet, and smash my brother's head into the undercooked meatloaf the lunch ladies were shoveling onto flimsy plastic trays. But as I opened my big mouth to protest, I caught the hurt lingering in Lucas's eyes. It was the same look I had when Jamie kissed Maghen. That bitter, jealous ache that burned a hole in my stomach faster than acid. Lucas wasn't mad at Jamie; he was jealous. Jamie chose the Donahue brothers over the only class Lucas and Jamie had together: English.

I rolled my eyes. "Boys," I muttered.

Kayla slapped Lucas's arm and nodded in the direction of the door. Standing in the black-painted frame was the wobbling silhouette of the boy I was about to kill. He stumbled and swayed as he staggered through the cafeteria, bumping into tables and students with every step.

"Damn, I thought the line would have moved faster," Jamie slurred as he proceeded to cut in line next to me.

The sound of crinkling plastic filled my ears as Jamie unscrewed the white cap of his not-so-water bottle. My fingers fumbled over his in a feeble attempt to lower the bottle out of the lingering sight of lurking teachers.

"Are you crazy!" I then backtracked my words faster than I had spoken them. "Of course, you're fucking crazy! You're crossfaded at 12:30 in the afternoon!"

Lucas glared at me. "Language!" He gritted his overly white teeth at me as his black eyes darted around, likely praying no teachers overheard us.

I spun my chin to face his big head. "Is this the time for an etiquette lesson, Captain America?"

The line launched forward, causing my hand to act faster than my brain. Swiftly, I stuffed Jamie's detention-begging bottle into my bag, its plastic cracking just loud enough to make my heart jump into my throat.

As we inched forward, the rattle and clatter of dingy red trays matched that of my pulse. I cannot get expelled on my first day. I shuddered at the thought as the eighty-year-old lunch lady slopped a thick slice of mushy meatloaf on my tray. I was used to getting in trouble. I had a big mouth, and I liked to use it. But this was different.

I reached for an overripe banana wedged between what I guessed was applesauce and what I hoped was refried beans. As my fingers brushed the browning surface, Jamie's fingers crashed into mine.

"Oh, sorry." Jamie used his palm to rub his bloodshot eyes.

I didn't respond or move forward when the line raced before me. "What's going on with you?" I asked, attempting to avoid sounding like an authoritarian mother.

Jamie's eyes were unfocused as he gazed at me. He remained silent and seemed to be barely even breathing, trapped in an internal tug-of-war between apology and argument.

"Nothing," he said in a singular breath.

"Bullshit," I spat back.

The people at the back of the line began shouting at us to move forward. The cafeteria could have approached me with pitchforks and torches, and I wouldn't have moved an inch. Jamie, on the other hand, shifted his eyes nervously toward the hollering students.

"Why don't you just stay out of my business for once?"

I stumbled back as if shot. "Wow, only one morning of hanging out with garbage, and you're already acting like trash."

The muscles of Jamie's jaw twitched as he sucked in a breath. "You do realize the people you call 'garbage' are my neighbors, right?"

"Don't give me the 'poor me' speech. You're better than that, and you know it."

Jamie charged forward, his body now closing the gap between us. The air hung thick with an unspoken fury that also flashed in his black eyes. There was nobody in this world I felt safer with than Jamie, but in that moment, it was as if the person I knew and the person staring back at me were separate entities, two halves of the same whole, but this half was darker and scarier than the one I thought I knew.

"You're not my girlfriend. Stop acting like it." His demand struck me like a slap across my cheek.

And that's when I felt it. Hot, sticky liquid traveled down my cheeks, likely accompanied by dripping mascara. I knew it was probably in my head, but it felt like the whole cafeteria had paused its thunderous conversations and turned into the most humiliating moment of my life.

My attempt to breathe felt futile, the air replaced by an emptiness that clawed at my insides. The silence was deafening, and every effort to articulate a response felt like grappling with an invisible force.

So, in a heated second, I decided that words were not going to be my weapon of choice in this battle. With trembling fingers, I pushed him backward … I didn't even remember doing it. One second, my cheeks were painted with tears, and the next, my palms were firmly thrusting against Jamie's chest.

He tumbled backward, colliding with Lucas behind him. The domino effect rippled through the helpless line of students. A cascade of bodies and trays crashed to the floor, creating a cacophony of clattering dishes and startled shouts. The once orderly line morphed into a messy scene of tangled limbs and scattered lunches.

A lump of guilt formed in my throat as I looked down at the pile of bodies: Jamie sprawled across Lucas, who was half-crushed on top of Kayla. All three of them were stacked like a human sandwich, and judging by the groan she let out, they were definitely going to need to check that poor girl for a concussion.

Jamie glanced back at me with a mix of hurt and embarrassment. As he pushed himself off the ground, a shadow suddenly loomed over us: Mr. Johnson, his expression as dry as a stale biscuit.

"What in the world is going on here?" Mr. Johnson demanded, his voice cutting through the chaos.

I had made it through half the day without receiving a

threatening glare from a teacher. I believed I deserved some credit …

I tilted my head toward Jamie. "Nothing, sir; Jamie just slipped and collided with Lucas."

There was a four-second pause where I could see the wheels turning in Mr. Johnson's brain, likely contemplating whether he wanted to waste his time dealing with our teenage drama. "I think the two of you could benefit from some time at the counselor's office. Why don't you follow me there now?"

Jamie rolled his eyes at me as if somehow all of it was my fault. Okay, maybe fifty percent of it is, but I do not take credit for the full one hundred.

As we rounded the corner and headed towards the lunchroom doors, my rebellious backpack snagged the side of a passing table. My heart sank as my backpack made an unpleasant ripping sound. My mind was racing with disbelief. Why me? Why today? I took a deep breath and slowly turned my head to assess the damage. A chaotic dance of paper covered the floor tiles as my pencils bounced on their erasers across the cafeteria. My notebooks sprawled open and slid in all directions, but that wasn't the worst part: Jamie's cursed water bottle fell to the floor. The lid must not have been screwed on properly because the vodka inside soaked all my belongings, filling the air with the scent of impending doom.

Mr. Johnson's lips parted, his eyebrows furrowed, and his chest heaved. Before he could utter a word, I swiftly raised my hand in the air, cutting him off mid-sentence.

"Principal's office, yeah, I know."

I didn't say a single word during the walk down to the

offices. Jamie and I sat in two rusty metal chairs, waiting for the principal to expel us, no doubt. Sometimes, there were simply no words. There were no letters that could equal the thoughts that rattled and ricocheted through my mind like a pinball machine. And no sentences that could express the ache that burned in my chest after my best friend practically poured acid on my heart. Instead of wasting worthless verbs and adjectives and screaming at Jamie for being an inconsiderate ass, I just sat there, silent and still.

I fused my eyes to the door, my pulse matching the ticking of the clock as the seconds passed with the speed of a snail on morphine.

Fumbling with the buttons of my calculator, I juggled all my belongings, clutched in my arms. There were forty teachers and faculty members in the area. Yet, not a single one offered me a garbage bag to help manage the mess of my scattered belongings after the zipper on my backpack was broken by a loose nail on the cafeteria table. Jamie attempted to help by gathering as many of my notebooks and textbooks as possible from the lunchroom floor, but they had turned into a soggy mess of alcohol-soaked cardboard and paper.

There was a faint sound of flipping pages that prompted me to flick my head towards Jamie. That journal stealer is reading my diary!

"Give that back to me!" My anger escaped in a sharp scream that quickly became a whisper as I noticed the receptionist's hostile gaze fixated on us from behind her plastic IKEA desk.

Jamie wiggled his thick eyebrows at me with an evil little grin. "You should thank me for picking it up off the floor before a stranger found it and learned all your dirty little secrets."

"First of all, I don't write my secrets in there, and second, my journal wouldn't have been on the floor if you hadn't pissed me off!" I hissed.

Jamie continued flipping through the pages of my journal as if it were a treasure map to a lost fortune. "Oh, you absolutely have a few secrets in here …"

His eyes creased inward as they passed by sentences meant to be private. "You know, these little poem things you write aren't half bad. Maybe you should become a writer after high school."

I snatched my journal back from Jamie's grasp. "They're just dumb words on paper. Nothing I can do anything with." I lowered my head to my lap and chewed on my lip.

A long, drawn-out breath exhaled from Jamie's lungs as he drifted his eyes to the ceiling, "At least you have something you're good at."

"You're fourteen, not fifty. You don't have to figure that out yet." I was still furious at Jamie, but I wasn't going to let him talk that way, even if I wanted to hit him with a frying pan.

Jamie placed his head against the cold center block wall behind him. "Then why does it feel like everybody else has?"

"Because we're friends with Lucas and Kayla and they're superhuman freaks who make the rest of us normal folk look dumb in comparison."

"I think we both know there's nothing normal about you."

I snorted out a chuckle. Jamie's smile liquified my icy glare like a hot August day melting a popsicle.

"I knew I'd get a smile out of you." He turned to face my flushed cheeks. The ends of his black hair rested over his eye as he stared at me with a half-apology and half-flirtation. "So, you don't hate me?"

"No," I confessed begrudgingly. "But I don't understand what's going on with you right now." I shifted my body closer to his. "You don't talk to me anymore."

He shrugged me off. "I talk to you."

"Not like you used to, not about important stuff."

Jamie's eyes left mine and moved to his palm, his fingers picking at his nails. He always avoided eye contact when he didn't want to talk about something, like maybe if he couldn't see me, then possibly I couldn't see him.

"What happened with you today? You've always said hanging out with the Donahue brothers was like signing your prison sentence. And I mean, sure, we've snuck beer from your dad's fridge before, but you broke into my parents' liquor cabinet without even talking to me about it."

Jamie still wouldn't look at me. "I just really didn't want to deal with today."

"I know school's not your thing—"

"Not my thing?" His hot breath scoffed. He pulled back, and he narrowed his black eyes like a Jaguar preparing to strike. "You think I don't like school because it's 'not my thing?'" His glare shot to mine. "I can't do the work, Alex! And it's not about concentrating harder or studying more. No matter what I do, I just don't get it. Words swirl around the page like a cyclone, numbers collide like two trucks on a highway, and nothing I do ever straightens them out!"

"So, instead of asking for help, you thought it'd be better to get shitfaced?"

"I'd rather be the drunk kid than the dumb kid."

I finally understood all the irrational stuff he had done over the summer, every fight he got into, every night he spent passing out on my floor, and every troubling rumor he'd been part of over the months. Jamie wasn't being reckless for the fun of it; he was building a persona, a mask that could hide what he thought were failures.

Jamie was never able to shake that first day of high school. It followed him around like a somber shadow. And as the rumor of Jamie's day with the Donahues infected the school like a perilous plague, the tighter Jamie's mask became. From that day on, he spent half his time with us and half his time with them—split between two worlds.

If you wear a mask long enough, it becomes a part of your face.

# CHAPTER 11

It's easy to forgive,
It's impossible to forget.

**10:20 p.m.**

Images of Anne Hathaway and Julie Andrews twirling in tiaras and ball gowns flashed across the screen, slapping my retinas like some royal fever dream. Lucas, Kayla, and I were sprawled out in the living room watching the first Princess Diaries—because isn't watching a movie what everybody does after an emotional breakdown after five years of not speaking to each other?

"I can't believe you two talked me into watching this," Lucas complained from the couch in front of the TV.

I lifted my head off the ground, which I had draped with various pillows and blankets. "Hey, it's your fault for not convincing Mom and Dad to get Netflix." My parents had an aversion to technology and refused to convert their DVD collection to anything stored on a server.

I staggered to the TV and bent down to the console,

which held a vast collection of movies and VHS tapes. My parents also had not upgraded half of their collection from its original publication format.

"No!" Lucas bellowed with a cry, "I beg you, don't make me watch the next one." He flipped his head to Kayla, trying to appeal to the more reasonable one of us.

Kayla pouted at him. "But the next movie has Prince Nicholas! His witty banter with Mia launched an entire generation of girls' unhealthy obsession with enemies-to-lovers!"

Lucas crooked his head back at her. "Is that supposed to be your sales pitch?" He turned back to me. "Come on, Alex. There has to be something else we can do."

"Well, your hair isn't long enough to braid, so I don't know." I shrugged, only to be met with a stern glare. "Dude, it's 11:30 p.m. in Nowheresville, Massachusetts. The only thing open is the movie theater, which reeks of thirty-year-old burnt butter."

Kayla stretched her arms in the air and let out a deep yawn before placing her palms on the armchair's edge. "We could play truth or dare..."

"No!" I bellowed.

"Why not?" Kayla protested. "Not like we have anything else to do, and if I have to sit through any more awkward silences, I'm going to start painting Lucas's nails like we used to do."

Lucas leaped up from the couch and crossed his big arms over his puffed-out chest. "That was one time."

The corner of Kayla's mouth rose with way too much joy. "Three times, actually. I vividly remember a purple, pink, and red incident."

"It was green, not red. And I second Alex. Last time you

made me play truth or dare, I ended up naked in Lovers' Lake, floating on an inflatable yellow duck wearing sunglasses."

Kayla pushed herself off the armchair and matched Lucas's stance; fighting was foreplay to those two. "First of all, that was the best night of your life." She poked him in the bicep, driving her point forward while simultaneously making me gag as I was forced to watch yet another rerun episode of their flirtation. "And second, I only dared you to take your shirt off. You were the one who went to second base butt naked with a duck."

Lucas stepped forward, no doubt close enough for Kayla to feel his breath on her cheeks. "After you dared me to shoot seven shots of tequila off your stomach!"

Kayla slid her teeth along her lip. "You didn't exactly complain about it at the moment, did you?"

"No … I mean … I …" Lucas stumbled over words.

Kayla padded the edge of Lucas's shoulder. "That's what I thought, big guy."

I leaped from the floor to interrupt the scene before me. "I still think it's hilarious that a six-foot-four giant can't hold his liquor."

Lucas gasped as he looked back at me. "Excuse me, but I was an athlete. I didn't pollute my body with toxins like you two alchys and stoners."

"Hey, watch your facts." Kayla shifted her weight to her back foot. "I was simply a social delight at parties, who occasionally indulged in a few margaritas. Alex and Jamie were the stoners."

Okay, so that was technically true ... but I was not going to give anyone the satisfaction of being right. "Hey, don't bring me into this. Jamie was a stoner; I merely took advantage of the stash he hid in my bedroom."

Kayla's face lit up with a blanket of mischief that sent a shiver of caution down my legs. I swear, between her and Jamie, I'm not sure how we lived past high school. That look meant a plan, and not just any plan, a Kayla plan, which typically involved breaking the law and waking up dressed in somebody else's clothes in the middle of a park.

Lucas jabbed his finger at Kayla like a parent scolding a child. "Stop that."

"What?" Kayla questioned back with a knowing grin.

"That look! Stop with that look!"

"I don't have a look." She chuckled through her protest.

"Yes, you do! Your cheeks rise, and your eyes lower. You look like Harley Quinn plotting revenge against the Joker."

I raised my judging eye at my dork of a brother. "Wow, you can take the boy out of the comic store, but you can't take the comic store out of the boy."

A scowl painted Lucas's face, giving me just enough satisfaction to smile back.

Kayla flipped her head towards me. "Where exactly did Jamie hide his stash?"

"In the clubhouse, why—" Ohhhh, now I get it … "I'm on it!" I ran up the stairs; Kayla followed close behind, with a whining Lucas next to her.

"My clothes are staying on this time!" he notified Kayla as we entered my bedroom.

"We'll see about that." She winked.

I wrinkled my nose. "Gross, dude, that's my brother."

I crouched to the ground before the clubhouse's tiny door, dragging my knees forward into the cove of forgotten friends and lost loves. I stopped once I heard the familiar echo of the high-pitched squeak from beneath my leg. I plunged my fingernails into the curves where the two pieces of dingy wood met, then pushed them up until the wood popped freely off the ground. I stabbed my fingers into the dark hole beneath and fumbled my nails over the surface below. About an inch towards the right, my index finger brushed against the corner of something with a distinct crinkling sound.

"Bingo." I snatched the bag out of the hole and shuffled my way back out of the tiny room, cracking my neck back and forth as I stood. "Damn, I don't remember my bones making so many crunching noises coming in and out of that thing."

Lucas leaned against my desk, his weight making the wood yelp. "Why are you holding a Cheeto bag?"

I placed both of my thumbs on the inside of the bag and opened it dramatically. "Because inside this five-year-old sack of preservatives and orange food coloring is the cure to our night's boredom."

"There's no way that stuff is safe." His face twisted with a cross of disgust and trepidation.

Kayla rolled her eyes at Lucas. "It's weed, Grandma, not meth."

He angled his body toward Kayla's. "It's a five-year-old joint that's been kept in a Cheeto bag under musty floorboards since senior year."

I hopped on my bed, landing with my legs firmly criss-crossed underneath. "Still not seeing the problem?"

"You do realize we are adults now? Not rebellious teenagers."

I hacked out a laugh before my brain could devise a witty comeback. "You were never a rebellious teenager. You were an unwilling accomplice to our idiocy but never a rebel."

I reached my hand into the Cheeto bag, orange dust leaving a residue on my fingertips as I pulled out the horribly rolled joint. "Okay, Boy Scout, toss me the lighter I know you keep in your back pocket."

The heel of Lucas's shoe dug into the wood beneath as he placed all his weight on his back leg and crossed his big arms. "I don't have a lighter."

"Yes, you do." I jabbed my voice back. "You haven't left home without a lighter, pocketknife, and a matchbox since you were thirteen."

"Why do you carry both a lighter and a match? Isn't that redundant?" Kayla hopped on the bed next to me, the springs squeaking slightly as she bounced her legs.

Lucas huffed. "Because a lighter can break or run out of fluid. You know what? You two will thank me if we're ever on a plane together and it crashes, leaving us stranded atop a mountain."

"Wow …" Kayla glanced at me with shock and a hint of concern.

"Oh, that's nothing. In sophomore year, he made us practice earthquake drills every weekend after California had that 7.4 scare."

Her eyes flicked back to Lucas. "You do realize we live in Massachusetts, right?

"Sue me for being prepared." Lucas let out a frustrated breath.

I shifted my hands back and forth as if they were plates of a scale, "Prepared ... paranoid—"

"Fine!" Lucas cut the end of my word off as he plunged his fingers into his pocket and smacked the warm metal lighter onto the palm of my hand. "Here, you can have it if it will finally shut you up."

I stretched my smile from ear to ear. "Oh, we both know I can't make that promise."

I patted the edge of the bed. "Come on, live a little before you die."

Lucas let out a long exhale as he clenched his teeth and shifted his eyes, looking like a child trying to decide which path to take in a haunted house. No matter which way he went, he knew there would be a zombie with a chainsaw waiting for him behind one of the doors.

"Nope."

"Your loss." I shook my head as I twirled the joint in my fingers. Not that Lucas would ever have admitted it, but that boy was lucky to have me as a sister. Without my somewhat questionable influence, he would have stayed home every Friday night, playing with his action figures and going to bed by 8:30 p.m.

I turned to Kayla and handed her the key to sweet, sweet bliss. "Want to do the honors?"

She took the rolled-up paper out of my hand. "I thought you'd never ask."

The flick of the lighter echoed as the flame cast a muted glow over Kayla's lips. The sizzle of the crackle accompanied the deep, sour aroma of the weed as wisps of smoke cut the air. Kayla exhaled in a long, drawn-out breath. She stared at Lucas, who still refused to sit on the bed. His towering presence stared down at us like a judgmental parent.

"Okay, Lucas, you're first, Truth or Dare."

"Do we have to do this?" he whined.

I leaned my weight on the back of my palms. "Yup." I showed him my teeth with glee. "Your choice: Truth, Dare, or Smoke?"

"Fine, Truth," he said, finally admitting defeat. He shuffled over to the side of the bed before sitting down, causing my poor mattress to dip and sway underneath. I could have sworn I heard the bed frame cry for help.

"Of course you picked Truth." I scoffed.

"Are you Truth or Dare shaming me?"

"Yes. Yes, I am." Kayla passed the joint back to me. I pinched the end and brought it to my lips. The warm inhale of dead plants strangled by white paper filled my lungs like a hot air balloon, lifting me into the sky and parting the clouds. Just as the musty, skunk-like smell penetrated my nose and scratched at my eyes, the perfect Truth lit up my brain like a dingy lightbulb.

Lucas didn't have secrets. No, let me rephrase that. Lucas couldn't have secrets. They burned a hole in his stomach like acid and physically made him sick. One time, we had to take him to the hospital with a 104 fever after I begged him not to tell Mom and Dad that Kayla and I skipped school to go to the mall.

My lips curled into a sly grin, the kind that only appeared when I knew I was about to make Lucas squirm. "I got a truth." I locked my eyes with my brother's concerned ones. "Why don't you tell Kayla what happened that Christmas when you made dinner for everyone in our sophomore year?"

Lucas's eyes widened in pure panic, his pupils dilating like a deer caught in the headlights. His hands clenched my comforter as a nervous quiver danced across his bottom lip. "Alex, please don't."

Kayla sat up, curiosity lighting up her face. "Wait, what happened? I think I buried that night in my memory."

Lucas's face turned crimson. "It's not a big deal."

I shot him a knowing smile. "Oh, it's a big deal. Go ahead, Lucas. Tell her how you almost set her hair on fire."

Kayla gasped, her eyes darting between us. "What?!"

Lucas groaned and rubbed his face. "It wasn't like that—"

"Oh, it was exactly like that." I cut him off with a laugh.

"Lucas winced. "Jamie put it out before you noticed."

Kayla threw her hands up. "Unbelievable. Yet another reason that dinner was a disaster."

I leaned forward with a sly smile at Lucas, holding the blunt in my hand again. "So … Truth, Dare, or Smoke?"

"I answered a Truth! And you realize this is peer pressure, right?" Lucas ran his fingers through his hair, lightly gripping the strands as they reached the nape of his neck.

"That doesn't count." I shook him off. What's it going to be?"

Lucas's brows knitted together, his eyes fixating on the choice in front of him. A distinct frown formed on his face, and his inner tension was evident in the lines across his forehead. His fingers drummed nervously on the edge of my bed until they finally jetted forward.

"Give me that before my better senses kick me in the brain."

"Attaboy." I grinned.

It's funny. I hadn't thought about that Christmas Day in years. Though it was funny now, Kayla would never have let Lucas live that incident down if she'd known in the moment. Some secrets are better kept between siblings and friends who casually save you from going up in flames.

Sometimes, it's safer to stay in the dark.

# CHAPTER 12

Sometimes love is the antidote,
And sometimes it's the poison.

**December 24, 2014**

It was the best and worst Christmas of my life. We were in our sophomore year of high school. Jamie and I were still best friends. Kayla and Lucas were still obsessive overachievers who profusely denied their feelings for each other, and all of us still spent a codependent amount of time together. On the surface, everything was exactly as it had always been, but beneath all the late-night study dates and movie marathons lay a silent tear, a muscle strained past its limits, a constant ache reminding me that something just wasn't quite right.

Since that first day of freshman year, Jamie earned the title of 'brooding burnout.' Everything had changed. He spent half the day high and the other half getting wasted with the Donahue brothers. He still always made sure to stay somewhat coherent when he was with us, but you can't live in two worlds without crumbling.

No matter how many times I tried saving Jamie, every day would start and end the same, with him breaking and my heart shattering.

Freshman year was tough, but nothing could have prepared me for sophomore year. Jamie skipped all his classes and vanished without a trace during the first week. When he returned, I was livid and yelled so hard that I scratched my vocal cords, leaving me sounding like an elderly smoker for a week. I wasn't angry that he left; I was hurt that he didn't take me with him. Aiden and Dallas needed his help with a delivery to New Hampshire. Jamie may have hung with the Donahues, but he wasn't one of them until that night, and I didn't know if Jamie, my Jamie, would ever return.

That was, until Christmas Eve.

It was 5:00 p.m., and I had undercooked, overcooked, and lit three batches of Christmas cookies on fire in under thirty minutes. All the while, Lucas and Kayla meticulously prepared gluttonous amounts of food. Lucas had spent over a week preparing and prepping after convincing Mom to let him take over cooking that year. He mumbled something about responsibilities and wanted to help out more, but I knew that was a pretty little lie wrapped in a tongue-tied bow. The truth was that Lucas was a perfectionist, and he couldn't stand the thought of another year with Mom's dry-ass turkey and burnt stuffing.

"Why are there chunks of carrots in this batch?" Lucas questioned as he inspected the graveyard of cookie corpses to my right.

"Because you cut carrots for your satanic stuffing on the

same counter I rolled my dough out on!" I barked back.

He cocked his head at me. "How is it my fault you didn't wipe the counter? And my stuffing is heavenly, thank you very much."

Kayla stirred an excessive amount of brown gravy in a lightly tarnished pot. "I second that. You're stuffing is a religious experience."

"Dude!" I threw my flour-covered hands to my hips. "Don't inflate his already enormous ego!"

Kayla tossed her palms in the air in defense. "Sorry, sorry."

I locked my eyes back on Lucas. "The carrots for your stuffing poisoned my only batch of cookies that didn't burn or turn into mush, so yes, it will forever be satanic stuffing in my mind, and I will hold a grudge against that mushy bread until I am six feet under."

Lucas moved to pick up a knife so big it could fillet a fish and an arm. "Issues. You have issues!" He waved the knife at me with each syllable.

Down the hall came shuffling footsteps.

"Hey," Jamie said, leaning against the arch that bridged the hallway and kitchen.

He looked good—really good. And not in an "OMG, he's so dreamy" kind of way, but like a functioning human being. His hair was actually washed and combed, his clothes matched—from the oversized leather jacket to his favorite worn-in boots—and his eyes were open and bright, like he'd just woken up from a Disney sleeping spell.

I dashed from the counter and lunged at him, throwing

my arms around him and squeezing until he let out a strained laugh. God, he smells good. Over the last two months, he had started shaving, claiming it was needed despite having exactly two hairs that occasionally poked through his tanned skin. But the best part about Jamie's need to be a man was the aftershave. Julian got it for him after Jamie's first attempt at shaving left him with a face full of little dots of dried blood. It smelled better than freshly brewed coffee on a fall day.

"What's all this affection for?" My hair muffled Jamie's chuckle as I squished the air out of his lungs.

"You look good," I whispered into the collar of his black button-down shirt. "I miss this."

He lightly pulled away, his hands traveling down my sides and landing on my hips. "Oh, come on, with these cheekbones, we both know I look good daily." His smile was cocky, but his cheeks were flushed red.

"You know what I mean," I said back. "You look … I don't know … sober?" He lowered his head and bit his lip as if I had embarrassed him. I placed my finger under his chin and tilted his gaze back to mine. "I just like seeing you like this. That's all."

Jamie pulled me closer, oblivious to Lucas and Kayla's eavesdropping.

"I figured your parents wouldn't appreciate me slurring my words through dinner." His dark eyes locked with mine as the corners of his lips morphed into a cheesy smile that sent butterflies from my chest to my toes. "And I know that Christmas Eve is your favorite day of the year." He tucked a piece of hair behind my ear. "I guess I just didn't want to miss any part of it." His eyes moved to my cheek and then my chin before stopping on my neck. "Why do you look like you lost a fight with a baker?"

I had completely forgotten that I was covered in flour and egg. "Lucas is forcing me to bake the cookies this year."

Jamie grimaced at Lucas as he retracted his hands from my waist and put them in his pockets. "Lucas, I thought you said you wanted this dinner to be perfect?"

I gasped. "Hey!"

Lucas removed the turkey from the oven and sucked up a substantial amount of dark liquid from the roasting pan into a syringe before inserting it into the turkey's thigh. "I am trying to cook Christmas Eve dinner for six notoriously picky eaters. The potatoes are not boiling, the stuffing isn't crisping, the sweet potatoes that Kayla insisted on are not sweet enough, apparently, and Dad's loaded French Fries are not cheesy enough, according to him. I am making four different kinds of potatoes for you tyrants!" He sucked up another syringe of over-salted turkey water and plunged it into the bird's other leg. "All I asked was for Alex to take over the cookies so that I could concentrate on the main course while Kayla worked on the sides, but no, that was apparently too much responsibility, and thus, now I'm left with babysitting a cookie killer!" The volume of his voice grew with each word as the tone heightened to a pitch I swear only dogs could hear.

"Okay, okay, dude, I hear you. I'll help Alex with the cookies. But you need to breathe before that vein on your forehead explodes."

Jamie followed me to my slaughter table and began pouring new flour into a giant blue bowl. "You do realize that cookies are only like four ingredients? How in the world did you manage to burn through three dozen?" His eyes glazed over the mounds of misshapen sugar.

I lightly pushed his shoulder. "Less judging, more working."

"Yes, ma'am. Or should I call you Betty Crocker since you're such an expert at this?" His cheeks were decorated with a slap-worthy grin.

"You think you're so cute, don't you?" I playfully rolled my eyes as I retrieved the eggs from the fridge.

"I think I'm adorable," Jamie corrected.

Ignoring Jamie's remarks, I lifted the egg to the rim of the blue bowl, feeling the cold shell against my fingertips. I tapped the egg on the side and peered inward to watch as the yolk slid out of the shell and landed in the flour. Jamie reached over and grabbed the tin measuring cup filled with white sugar, and with a quick flick of the wrist, he dumped it into our mixture. The sweet aroma filled the air as he poured in milk and a dash of vanilla extract.

"Time for mixing." I rolled up my sleeves.

Jamie moved his arm over the bowl to stop me. "Wait, you have to add baking powder."

"Why?"

There was a loud gasp behind me that sounded like my overdramatic brother, "You weren't adding baking powder to the cookies!?"

"Why would I need baking powder? What even is that?" This is just one of many examples as to why Lucas should never have put me in charge!

Lucas threw down the baster he was using to coat the potatoes in a thick layer of melted butter. "You are the reason I have migraines."

I gave him a thumbs up covered in flour. "Love you too, bro." It wouldn't be Christmas Eve without it ending with Lucas wanting to kill me.

Jamie poured a tablespoon of baking powder into the mixture and plunged his hands into the unmixed dough, combining all the ingredients until it formed a single, giant ball of ooey, gooey cookie dough.

"Grab a baking sheet and butter the surface so the dough doesn't stick."

"Aye, aye, captain."

He glanced at me over his shoulder as he crouched to the lowest cabinet on the left; smiling sweetly, he quickly darted his face back to the bowl when he noticed I caught him staring. I unwrapped the giant stick of butter and smeared it all over the pan's surface. Jamie began to roll the dough into small balls and placed them onto the pan's surface. Each ball was the perfect size, one and a half inches, convincing me he had some magic cookie-dough ruler built into him. Once he had arranged them perfectly in six rows and three columns, Jamie placed the pan into the oven below where the turkey was cooking. He then twisted the round, white timer, which was resting near Kayla, who was opening a can of green beans.

"What are you doing?" Lucas barked at Kayla.

"I am helping you make your dinner. Thank you very much, Gordon Ramsay." Kayla waved the can opener at him.

Lucas grasped the handle of the potato masher in his left hand. "Why are there canned green beans in my kitchen?"

"Because three days ago, you told me not to forget the

green beans on my way over here, so I didn't forget the green beans!" The red ribbons tied to the ends of her two boxer braids bounced as she jabbed her finger into my brother's chest.

"I didn't mean canned green beans, I meant fresh green beans from the vegetable aisle!"

"And there's a difference?" she taunted him.

"Yes!"

"Well, it's too late now. Looks like it's a canned green bean Christmas."

Lucas chewed on his back molars. "Over my dead body."

Jamie hopped in the middle of the two of them. "You guys are fighting over a waxy vegetable that nobody likes unless smothered in heavy cream." He looked at Lucas. "Alex and I are done with the cookies; if you guys can take them out when the timer goes off, we can drive to the grocery store and get some green beans."

"Fine." Lucas released the breath he had been holding. He marched over to the fridge and opened it wide to pull out the ham that Julian wanted instead of the turkey. "Alex, where's the ham?" He shot his head back at me.

"It's in the freezer."

"Why would the cooked ham be in the freezer?!?"

I slipped my right arm into my jacket, readying myself for a quick exit. "Because it's not cooked …"

Yep, that vein on his forehead is going to explode. "What do you mean, it's not cooked?"

"You told me to go to the store and get a ham, so I got a ham from the frozen meats department."

His mouth opened and closed as his right hand clenched

his chest as if he were having a heart attack. "No, I told you to get a cooked ham from the deli! I have a turkey cooking in one oven and everything else cooking in the second. We don't own a third oven, and thus, I needed an already-cooked ham!" He slammed the refrigerator door and began pacing like an alcoholic outside a closed liquor store.

Jamie hopped in front of Lucas and placed his hands on Lucas's shoulders. "Dude, breathe, we're going to the store. We will get the ham and the green beans; everything is going to be okay."

Lucas began taking slow and controlled breaths. "Just make sure you take her with you because I cannot guarantee her safety when you return."

"Completely understood."

Jamie grabbed the car keys off the counter and gestured for me to follow. I glanced at Lucas, who was standing there with a Crème Brulé torch, looking like he was about to declare war on the sweet potatoes. "You good, or should we get you a fire extinguisher?"

Lucas muttered something about marshmallows and perfection, still determined to give them that "extra crisp."

I swung my eyes to Kayla, who was at the sink, humming to herself as she worked on shaping the dinner rolls, her hair swaying dangerously close to Lucas and his culinary torch.

"Are you sure you know what you're doing with that thing?" I asked Lucas, my tone flat. "Because I'm about ten seconds away from calling the fire department."

Lucas didn't even glance up, too busy perfecting his marshmallow masterpiece. "Relax, Alex. I'm not the one in this family who lights dinner on fire." He absentmindedly waved the torch a little too close to Kayla's hair as he spoke.

"Lucas!" I gasped.

Jamie's eyes widened as he saw the flame hit the end of Kayla's braids. Without missing a beat, he grabbed a dish towel, dampened it at the sink, and quietly, almost casually, patted the flame out before Kayla had a clue what was happening.

Kayla, still focused on making the dinner rolls and oblivious to what we were all screaming about, shot her head back at Jamie. "What are you doing?"

"Uh, just admiring all the work you put into these tiny braids," Jamie said, completely deadpan, as if a teenage boy talking about female hairstyles was normal.

Kayla, still blissfully unaware of the near disaster, rolled her eyes. "You guys are so weird today."

I glanced at Jamie as we headed for the door. "Think we should tell her?"

Jamie grinned, shaking his head. "I think we should take this one to the grave." He glanced back at Lucas before exiting. "Hey, dude, at least you got the marshmallows crispy."

The car stereo blasted my favorite song as Jamie drummed his fingers on the wheel, his voice rising high above the music. The car shook with each thump of the bass, but Jamie didn't seem to care. We were driving down to the market, and as I watched Jamie, I couldn't help but smile at his childlike glee. It felt as though I hadn't seen that smile all year, but finally, here it was, shining brighter than ever.

As we approached a red light, the cars around us honked

their horns and glared at us disapprovingly, partly annoyed by the disruption we were causing to the traffic and partly because Jamie's voice, when mixed with mine, sounded worse than nails on a chalkboard. But we didn't care. Singing to terrible music at the top of my lungs was the best ten minutes of my life. Six hundred seconds where nothing else mattered, no parental problems, no school drama, no fighting with friends; it was 600 seconds of pure, uninterrupted happiness with my favorite person on the planet.

Everyone has a memory that warms their stomach and makes their cheeks burn with bliss—a memory that can forever put a smile on their face and melt sadness from their heart. This was my magical moment.

When we strolled into the grocery store, I reached down to grab a small green shopping basket, but Jamie's warm hand pressed on top of mine. I looked up at him to see a sneaky little grin dance over his lips.

"We are going to need a bigger cart." He practically skipped over to the line of blue shopping carts and pulled one from the row. "Get in."

I knitted my eyebrows together. "What?"

"Get. In." He punctuated each word like a grand sentence from a Shakespearean play.

"You're crazy, you know that."

He pushed the cart closer to me and rested on the handrail. "Absolutely. That's why I'm so irresistible."

I rolled my eyes and snickered. "Ohh, whatever."

I gripped the sides of the shopping cart and contemplated my choices. A: Refuse to go along with Jamie's childish antics, which would probably save me a concussion and a trip to the store manager. Or B: say screw it and most likely have my photo on the wall of band customers for eternity …

Let's be honest, there was no other choice. I threw my left leg into the basket and then my right before plopping down into the metal cage that seemed much roomier when I was a child.

"That's my girl."

"Your girl?"

"Forever, and always."

My heart jumped into my ears. I knew he didn't mean it the way I took it, but what's life without a bit of delusion?

Jamie drove the shopping cart up and down the aisles, creating a rumbling thump and clunk as the wheels moved over the grocery store's dirty tile floors. Our screams and laughter muffled the sound as he bumped me into chip bags and stacks of water. I felt my ribs contracting and expanding with the best pain I've ever felt as my chuckles turned into full-blown body cackles and snorts.

As we rushed through the crowded aisles of frantic last-minute Christmas shoppers, I scanned the premade food shelves, searching for the ham Lucas so badly wanted. Only a few options were left, including some pre-made lamb shanks, a variety of sides such as mashed potatoes and creamed corn, and approximately two dozen turkeys. Finally, through the piles of animal carcasses, my eyes locked on the one and only ham in the mix. Its glossy exterior looked like the perfect amount of disgusting to be wonderful.

Jamie pushed the cart forward so I could get a better angle to reach for the ham. I stretched out my fingers, ready to grab it, but before I could, another hand materialized from out of nowhere and snatched the ham away with lightning speed. My breath caught in my throat, and my pulse quickened as I watched the ham slip from my grasp. My jaw tightened, and my heart retreated into my stomach as I looked up to see Ms. Bragg, our principal, the Grinch herself, stealing my Christmas Eve happiness.

"Sorry, kiddos, looks like this is the last one," she declared, her voice a chipper little knife that stabbed my eardrums.

My nostrils flared as I climbed out of the cart and positioned my body directly in front of hers, my weight planted on my back heel. "Good afternoon, Ms. Bragg. I'm sorry, but I don't know if you noticed I was about to grab that."

She swished an over-hair-sprayed curl out of her beady red eyes. "We can't always get what we want."

There were no words to describe the intense anger I felt toward this woman. My blood pressure spiked every time she spoke, and my head spun. She looked and sounded exactly like Umbridge from the Harry Potter movies, and just like the character, it seemed like Ms. Bragg's mission in life was to destroy the happiness of every child she encountered.

I took a step closer to her, closing the distance between us. "You're right; I wanted a country cottage from Kansas to fall on top of you, but alas, the Wicked Witch still stands."

She shuffled the ham to her right arm and grasped her chest with her right hand as she let out an exaggerated gasp. "Young lady, I could expel you for that threat—"

"Young, yes. Lady, no." I grinned. "But if you're going to expel me anyway, I might as well take the ham with me."

I jetted my hands out in front and gripped the cooked pig

locked in her elbow. Ms. Bragg's fingers fumbled on top of mine, and soon, our hands were locked in a fierce tug of war. With each thrust, the tension mounted, our breaths coming in short, ragged gasps. Then, like a moment out of a cartoon, the ham slipped, tumbled to the floor with a resonating thud, and slid across the dusty tile until it smacked into the banana stand.

For a split second, I locked eyes with Ms. Bragg, and in an even shorter one, we both sprang into action, racing to the overcooked pig meat like two Swifties running to buy tickets to Taylor's last concert. I dodged a stray shopping cart as my heart pounded in my chest, and I lunged for the rolling ham. My stomach smacked against the tile floor, and my elbows punched the ground beside me. The force felt like a semi-truck plowing into my chest, but it was all worth it when my fingers brushed against the ham-smooth surface just in time. With a triumphant cry, I swooped it into my arms like a football, cradling it into my chest.

"Ha, I win, bitch!" I screamed at Ms. Bragg as I jumped up and down.

I turned to see Jamie standing nearby, visibly shocked. He held onto the cart, but it seemed more like a way to hold himself up, as he feared our principal more than anyone else. His eyes moved between me and Ms. Bragg, unsure whether he should apologize for my actions or run out of the store as fast as possible. Despite his panic, a hint of admiration flickered in his expression, and suddenly, a proud smile spread across his cheeks. Without hesitation, he pushed the cart he was holding in front of him, blocking the space between Ms. Bragg's path and me.

"Run!" he yelled, and I needed no further prompting. We bolted down the aisle, our feet pounding the ground as we raced towards the exit. I could hear Ms. Bragg's angry shouts behind us, but I didn't dare look back. We burst through the automatic doors and kept running until we practically collided with Jamie's car. Only then did we stop, panting and gasping for breath.

"I cannot believe you just did that." Jamie threw his hands on his knees, bending over to breathe.

"Are you kidding? That was the best Christmas present I could have ever asked for!" I was practically wheezing my words as I gasped for air.

"We are so getting detention when we go back to school."

"Can you honestly tell me it wasn't worth it, though?"

He furrowed his brow in thought. After a few moments, a small smile formed on his lips. "Okay, fine, maybe it was a little worth it."

His breath found its pace, and his eyes met mine. He took a small step forward, his face was only inches from me.

He isn't.

Is he?

He is.

He kissed me.

He ran his hands through my hair, sending shivers cascading from my cheeks to my toes as light wisps of rain began falling from the sky. He pulled me so close I could feel the heat radiating from his skin and the rapid pulse of his heart. Every tug of his lip was an electric shock fusing my touch to his. Every pull of his fingers beneath my hair was like hot water bathing icy skin. And every small gasp of air was like a drug addicting me to its pleasure. It was a feeling I never wanted to end, and one I will forever wish never did.

# CHAPTER 13

*December 24th, 2014: Part 2*

Love is a lifesaving drug
With too many side effects

**December 24, 2014: PART 2**

We drove back to the house in silence, but it wasn't awkward; instead, it quietly echoed with the possibility that maybe we had finally broken some boundary that needed demolishing. Maybe, just maybe, this could work for us. But the universe had a funny way of shattering plans.

As the tires squealed into the driveway, my heart fell to my feet. There, parked beside us, was a black car with a white stripe and three red lights resting on the roof.

"Jason and Rich steal two cases of beer from the 7-Eleven and get a warning. We steal a ham, and they send the cops to my house!" I smashed my finger into my seat belt buckle to free myself from its restraints.

Jamie's tan skin suddenly turned an eerie shade of bluish white. "I don't think they're here for the ham."

I narrowed my eyes at him. "What did you do?"

His jaw dropped. "Why do you assume it was me?"

"Because the worst thing Lucas has ever done is drive four miles over the speed limit, and Kayla's too diabolical to get caught. That only leaves two other options: me or you."

He forcibly shoved his arms over his chest, crinkling his jacket. "I haven't done anything ... this week." He muffled the last two words under his breath as his eyes darted to the steering wheel.

I slumped in my seat and stared ahead. "Then we have one of two choices. Go inside and watch you get handcuffed on Christmas Eve, or we could pull a Bonnie and Clyde." I turned my face to him, expecting to see at least a half-smile on his lips, but instead, I was greeted with his serious face, the deep expression that only etched across his eyebrows when he was working on a math equation.

His eyes flickered to the gas gauge. "We could probably make it to Boston."

"I was joking! We are way too young to become fugitives."

"So next year, then?"

"Ha, ha, very funny." There it was, the smile I wanted to see. "Let's just get inside and see what's going on. Maybe it's nothing."

"We both know neither of us is that lucky."

True.

I took a deep breath as my fingers circled the doorknob

and pushed it forward. The house felt ... heavy, like it was holding its breath, waiting for the inevitable to crash down. Jamie walked beside me, his hand brushing mine. Neither of us said anything, but we didn't need to. The silence in the room was thick enough to drown in.

Two cops stood in the hallway, but they weren't stern-looking; they lowered their heads. Glancing around the room, I saw Lucas holding Kayla tightly on the couch, her face buried in his chest. Julian stood off to the side, but his face was pale. My mom stood next to him, gripping the back of a chair, her lips pressed together like she was trying to keep herself from sobbing.

Something horrible was coming, and we were walking right into it.

Jamie took a hesitant step forward. "What's going on?"

Lucas's eyes shifted upward, meeting Jamie's. His lips parted, but a shadow passed over his face, and he looked away, swallowing hard as if the words he planned to speak physically hurt his throat.

The officer suddenly cleared his throat, exchanging an anxious glance with his partner before starting his sentence. "Jamie," he began carefully, "there's been an incident."

That word hit like a punch in the gut. Incident. What incident? And why was this conversation directed at Jamie? My stomach twisted as I glanced at my best friend's white face. He was staring at the officer, waiting, his every muscle still, his every breath halted.

The other officer stepped forward, his voice quieter but more forceful. "Jamie, it's about your mother."

I saw the realization flicker in Jamie's eyes. His body stiffened as if he were trying to brace for the impact, but there was no bracing for something like this.

"Where is she?" Jamie stepped toward the officers, his voice shaky but insistent. "What happened?"

The first officer sighed, his shoulders sagging. "Your mother ... she passed away earlier this evening. We believe it was an overdose."

Jamie's entire body buckled as if someone had physically hit him. I grabbed his arm before he could fall, pulling him against me. He didn't resist, but he didn't respond either. He was gone, lost somewhere inside his mind, ensnared in the terrifying nightmare he had always dreaded, a nightmare from which he could now never break free.

I held onto him as tightly as I could, but I could feel him slipping away. I felt his breath hitch, felt the tremor in his chest as he tried to hold back the sobs. "No," he whispered, barely audible. "No, no, no …"

One moment, Jamie was stiff in my arms, clinging to the last thread of control, and then he just ... collapsed. His entire body became dead weight, like every ounce of strength drained from him in an instant. His knees buckled, and before I knew it, we sank to the floor. The ground felt cold beneath us, and the room around us blurred, every sound muted except for Jamie's gasps and the harsh, wet sobs that tore from his chest. His grief was so heavy, so overwhelming, I could feel it radiating through my skin.

His chest slammed into mine, his head dropping against

my shoulder with a hard thud. Jamie pressed deep into me, as if he could somehow bury himself deep enough in my arms, and the world around him would disappear.

His trembling fingers clawed at the back of my shirt. His breath was ragged; each exhale came out in short, jagged bursts that hit my neck, hot and fast, like he was drowning. I wrapped my arms tighter around him, feeling his grief crashing down like a tidal wave, pulling us both under.

He was shaking so violently that I thought he might break apart in my hands. His sobs started low, almost like he was choking, and then they erupted from him, deep and guttural, the kind of sound that tears through you and leaves you raw. His whole body curled into mine, his forehead pressing hard into my collarbone, his breath hitching as if he couldn't breathe, couldn't find the air to fill his lungs.

I squeezed him tighter as if that could somehow hold him together. But the truth was, I was barely holding on myself.

The room was cold. It felt as though all the warmth had been sucked out, leaving only an unbearable weight pressing down on us. I could hear Kayla sobbing quietly, her breath shaky, but it was distant, like it was happening in a different world.

"She's gone," he whispered, his voice broken. "I should have been at home with her."

I swallowed hard, my throat tightening. I didn't have any words. Nothing I said would have made this better. And that killed me.

The first officer knelt beside us, his voice low but direct. "Jamie, we need to ask you a few questions about your mother's last few days. Would you like to talk at the station, or do you feel more comfortable here, son?"

They just told him that his mom died. Did they think right now is the best time for an interrogation?

Jamie tried to hold back his sobs. He removed his head from my shoulder and let out a deep breath as if his mind was trying to bury his emotions just long enough for him to get through this conversation. "Here's fine." He acknowledged the police officers, and then our eyes met. I nodded at him, understanding precisely what he needed. He needed me to hold it together so that he didn't fall apart, so I did. I stood up, offered my hand to him, helped him off the floor, and guided him over to the couch.

We sat on the cushions, the plush material a momentary comfort. The police officer sat on the adjacent sofa, and my mother took her position on the other side of Jamie, with her hand resting on his knee for support. Julian walked over. He didn't sit; he stood stern and tall, like a statue guarding the room in case he was needed. Next to him, Lucas copied his expression, the same tough soldier stance as his father. Kayla, however, was a wreck. She had quieted her crying, but the tears still flowed from her eyes and painted her cheeks. She locked her fingers with Lucas, his body acting as a pillar to keep her standing.

The cop on the right spoke first. "There were signs of a struggle at the scene, and we're treating this as a possible homicide."

Jamie's breath hitched. "A homicide?" His voice was barely more than a whisper.

The second officer nodded. "There were signs that

someone else was in the house with her before she overdosed. We found Jack Donahue's wallet at the scene. Do you know him?"

Jamie's eyes darkened. "Jack … yeah, I know him."

The officers exchanged glances. The officer on the left spoke, "Jamie, we need to understand Jack's relationship with your mother."

"Jack and Jamie's dad work together. That's all." I felt oddly defensive. I didn't want these officers to fabricate stories about Jamie's mom because of the reputation people like them had created for her.

Jamie's hand moved to my thigh, and his head shook slightly as if to tell me there was no use in defending her. His stare moved back to the officers. "They … they were together."

"Together?" I gasped, and my own heart sank.

"She was trying to get back at my dad. He's been messing around with other women for years, and I guess … I guess she thought if she did it too, it'd hurt him."

The officers were quiet momentarily, letting Jamie's words settle in. Then the one on the right asked, "Where is your dad, Jamie? Does he know about any of this?"

Jamie's face hardened, the anger bubbling up beneath his grief. "My dad?" He spat the words like they were poison. "He took off on one of his 'errand runs' a week ago. I haven't seen him since." His hands curled into fists, his voice shaking with barely contained rage. "He left her to fall apart, just like he always does."

The officer wrote down notes quickly. "We'll need to talk to him when we locate him, but right now, we need to know more about the past few days. Did you notice anything unusual with your mother's behavior?"

Jamie's eyes glazed over like he was trying to go back, trying to piece together the last few days. "She was quieter than usual," he muttered, almost to himself. "I knew something was wrong, but I didn't think … I didn't think it'd come to this."

Jamie's whole body deflated, and he collapsed deeper into the couch, burying his face in his hands. "I should've been there." He choked out, his voice muffled by his hands. "I should've known …"

My mother placed her hand on Jamie's shoulder. "Jamie, listen to me. You couldn't have known. None of this is your fault."

He shook his head violently, tears streaming down his face. "She was all I had left. And now she's gone. I don't have anyone."

My mom reached up, placing her palm on his cheek, gently forcing him to look at her. "That's not true, Jamie. You still have us. You will always have us."

Jamie's lips trembled, "But I've messed up so bad this year," he whispered. "The drinking, the drugs, skipping school … I'm no better than him. I left her like he did."

My mom shook her head firmly. "No, Jamie. You are not your father's mistakes. You've been wandering without direction, but that doesn't mean you're lost. And when you're ready, we'll all be here to help you find your way."

Jamie sobbed into her shoulder, his entire body trembling with the weight of everything—the grief, the guilt, the pain—he had been carrying for so long. I sat there watching as my mom held him together, her strength keeping him from falling apart completely. My tears threatened to spill over, but I held them back.

"Thank you," I whispered to my mother. She always knew exactly what to say and what not to say, a trait I unfortunately did not inherit.

A few weeks after that night, the officers closed the case. It ended up being an accident, but one that ended with Jamie burying his mum six feet under. Jack confessed to the manslaughter of Jamie's mom after the cops detained him, and there was enough physical evidence to tie him to every part of the crime scene. He didn't purposely try to overdose her, but when she started having a seizure, Jack panicked, and instead of helping her or calling the ambulance, he left her unconscious body on the floor alone.

One thought will always haunt me: if she had chosen differently, maybe she'd still be alive. Maybe Jamie wouldn't have had to close the lid of a casket on his mother's lifeless face. Maybe he wouldn't have had to say goodbye to the woman who read him bedtime stories when he was six and afraid of the dark. The woman who made homemade chicken noodle soup every time he pretended to be sick just to stay home from school. The woman who never missed a school play or a single soccer game. The woman who was now icy blue—and forever lost to time.

# CHAPTER 14

A scar is proof
That even healed wounds
Are never erased

**12:00 a.m.**

"I was the one who kept stealing your homework packet from the basket in fifth grade." Truth or dare was starting to get a little too honest ...

"You devil!" Lucas screamed at me.

In the fifth grade, at the end of each class, our teacher, Ms. Wagner, would distribute a homework packet that we were supposed to complete and put in the homework basket the next day. While this may seem simple, my life's motto has always been—and always will be—'work smarter, not harder.'

Every day, when our class shuffled into the room and placed their homework packets into the bin, I would stand behind Lucas in line. As he put his homework in the pile, I pretended to rest my packet on top when, in actuality, I was switching our papers. I quickly stole his off the top, ran to my desk, and frantically erased his name before swiftly writing mine on top, then returning it to the basket without anyone noticing.

My masterful Houdini act worked for four months until Lucas started inspecting the messy handwriting littering his homework, with a low grade of 64% stamped on the front. He frantically bickered with Miss Wagner, screaming that this was not his homework and that someone had to be messing with him. But his tantrum sounded remarkably like a child blaming the dog for eating their homework.

"I was kicked off the honor roll because of you," Lucas huffed, hacking over his words as smoke left his lungs.

The bed rocked as Kayla uncontrollably laughed. She was always the giggly kind of high. Two puffs and she turned into a patient on laughing gas.

I rolled my head on the pillow behind me. "Oh, don't be so dramatic. I stopped once my grade was high enough."

Lucas's face was now turning a stop sign shade of red. He plunged his fingers into his pants pocket and pulled out a decade-old phone. "You are calling Ms. Wagner right now to vindicate me."

I sat up straight, the world lightly spinning as I tried to focus my eyes on my brother's flushed face. "Why do you have her number?"

"Because I knew the day would finally come when you admitted to sabotaging my life." He looked like a proud detective who had just solved the biggest mystery of his career.

Kayla shuffled her wobbly knees to the middle of the bed and put her hands between me and Lucas like a referee at a boxing match. "You two need a truth timeout. Can somebody please pick Dare before the slapping and scratching begin?"

I sat up from my comfortable pillow and slumped into a crossed-leg position. The smell of smoke filled my room, stinging my nose as I took a breath. "Okay, fine, I'll pick Dare."

Kayla tapped her finger on her head for a dramatic thinking effect, "I got it!" she exclaimed, throwing her arms around Lucas' shoulders. She was very touchy when her better judgment was clouded. "I dare you … to make pancakes!"

I scrunched up my face. "That is the worst Dare of all time." I wasn't trying to be rude, but coming from the girl who once dared me to spray paint a cop car pink and staple bows to the seats, this was not one of her best.

Lucas intertwined his arm with Kayla's; the weed was getting to his brain. "And probably the most dangerous one," he shot back at me.

I scoffed. "I know how to make pancakes." I think.

Lucas played with Kayla's fingers as if the five years they were apart were merely a bad dream, and they were two eighteen-year-olds disgustingly in love. "Toaster waffles don't count," he jabbed back.

I was going to argue, but I didn't have the energy to provide a rebuttal between my brain spinning like a mouse caught on a ceiling fan and the dizzying sight of my brother getting handsy with my ex-friend.

"Come on, please! I'm starving!" Kayla whined again.

I gave in. "Let's go make pancakes."

"Yay!" Kayla sprang off the bed with an impressive bounce, like Tigger on his tail.

"I wouldn't be cheering yet." Lucas stretched his arms in the air as he stood up. "We're probably all going to die of salmonella."

He wasn't wrong.

I swung my legs over the bed and slowly rose to my feet. The room seemed to spin slightly as I walked out of my bedroom. I carefully placed each foot on the steps as I descended the stairs. My legs felt shaky, and I shuffled to the kitchen, gripping the counter for support. The cool surface steadied me as I inched toward the fridge and opened the door to peer inside.

"Wait ... what was I doing?" I slowly looked back at Kayla, who was now propped up on the kitchen island, her toes dancing on the concrete counters.

"Pancakes!" Kayla yelled back like a sugar-high six-year-old.

"Oh, right." I grabbed the butter from the top shelf and put it on the counter next to me. I stuck my head in the fridge to find the eggs, knowing my mom had probably hidden them in the back somewhere. A small carton of expensive farm-fresh eggs was in the left corner, nestled against the wall. I retrieved them and opened the carton to inspect how many were left.

What the heck? I fiddled my fingers around rows of shell carcasses. Every time my mom cooked breakfast, she put the shells back in the container until there were no eggs left. The carton would end up in the fridge empty, with nothing left but yoke-covered egg carcasses.

"We're out," I declared.

Lucas snatched the container from my hands. "Why does she always do that?" he bellowed, throwing it into the trash. "Sorry, Kayla. It looks like you're out of luck."

"But I want pancakes!" Still straddling the kitchen island, Kayla pulled Lucas's shirt collar and yanked him close to her. "I need the pancakes!" she begged, her black braids making a swishing sound as she rocked Lucas's body with her grip on his shirt.

I rubbed my two fingers on my temple. Her cries ricochet through my skull like a pinball being smacked too many times. "I'm sorry, Kayla. Let me go break into the market and steal you some eggs."

Lucas yawned greatly and then said, "I thought you were banned from there?"

Did he think I was going to break into the market? It truly hurt my brain to see someone so smart being so dense. "Yes, Mr. Valedictorian, I'm still banned. I was trying out this new thing called sarcasm!"

He crossed his meaty arms at me and clenched his over-sharpened jaw.

Kayla stood straight up on the counter, towering over us like a Pixie-voiced giant. "Your bickering will not help fulfill my need for puffy carbs smothered in sticky sugar!" If I didn't know better, I could have sworn I heard a light bulb click on in Kayla's brain as her eyes widened and her smile grew. "Wait ... doesn't your neighbor have a chicken coop?"

"Yes ... what does Mr. Heckel's yard have to do with this—" Oh. "Yes, yes, he does." I smiled back.

Lucas shoved his palms down on the counter's edge, smacking the space between where Kayla sat and where I stood. "No," he said with more force than when Julian told me I couldn't dye my hair blue when I was fourteen.

It was adorable how he thought his disapproval would prevent Kayla and me from dragging him into one of our moderately illegal plans.

"Stop kicking me in the face with your shoe!" Lucas roared as he lifted me over our neighbor's fence, my heel planted directly in his forehead.

"Stop putting your face under my foot!" I said back as I gripped the fence's edge and pressed my body upward, flinging one leg over at a time. Then, slowly, I lowered myself into my neighbor's yard, which desperately needed to be mowed and sprayed for weeds.

Despite what people in the town said, Mr. Heckle wasn't a bad guy. Everyone liked to spread rumors accusing him of being a monstrous man who never left his house because he was a psychotic murderer. The truth was, he was just lonely. Julian explained to Lucas and me that before Mr. Heckle's wife passed away, he was a jolly older man who baked cookies for the holidays and organized the neighborhood kids' Easter egg hunts. But his wife was everything to him. She was his oxygen, and without her, he couldn't function.

A grunting sound rumbled behind me as Lucas hoisted Kayla onto the top of the fence.

"It's a good thing you always preferred being on the bottom." Kayla winked at him as she threw her legs over.

I felt my stomach revolt into my mouth. "Gross!" I gagged. "I am this close to pulling a Van Gogh because of you two."

Kayla plopped her feet on a patch of weeds and dusted off her palms. "Oh, please, we both know your life has been endlessly boring without me."

"It was certainly less nauseating."

With the ease of a freaking jungle cat, Lucas hopped straight over the fence and landed perfectly on his two feet. "I can't believe you two are going to steal eggs from Mr. Heckle's chicken coop," he blurted out to us in hushed yells.

Kayla and I stood side by side, our eyes meeting with a discerning amount of mischief. Kayla grinned back at Lucas. "Who said anything about us stealing the eggs?"

Lucas glanced at the chicken coop made of old coffee tables Mr. Heckle collected from dumpsters across town. "Never going to happen. I enjoy not having a criminal record."

For the record, those charges never stuck. "Sorry, that's the rule. I dare you to crawl your mammoth shoulders into that death trap of wood and snatch us some farm-to-table breakfast."

"This is not how Truth or Dare works!" He stomped his foot on the muddy ground. "The person who's asked the question gets a choice." Lucas ran his hands through his shiny black hair, smoothing it back down on the sides.

"Yeah, I don't like that. If you get to choose, you'll always pick Truth. It's my job to throw you into the deep end of life. Besides, I got five years of torturing you to make up for."

Lucas opened his mouth to argue back.

"Less talking, more egg stealing!" I interrupted his dispute. "Now, hop to it before Mr. Hackle wakes up and buries us behind the shed.

"Fine," Lucas caved. "But only because I want to get out

of this yard as fast as humanly possible!" He stomped over to the makeshift chicken coop.

He crouched near the ground and carefully unhooked the pin that secured the door shut. A flutter of wings issued from the pile of wood as Lucas crept through the tiny door. He smooshed his shoulders together and forced them through the small gap, his shirt scratching against the door frame.

"Nice chicken. Nice chicken." I heard Lucas' plea. "AHH!!" A loud thud came from inside the coop. "Devil bird!" Lucas screamed as he tried to unwedge his shoulders from the hole.

Kayla hurried to Lucas's aid and squeezed her hands into the narrow spaces between his shoulders and the coop's frame. After several tugs back and forth and a few more screeches from Lucas, he fell backward and landed on the ground, his body collapsing on top of Kayla's.

I ran over to them to inspect the damage. Lucas's cheek had an angry-looking red peck mark, but the key ingredient to our night's sweet victory was clutched in his hands. "You got the eggs!" I cheered, hovering about their tangled mess of limbs.

"I was almost a chicken's dinner!" he screamed in a whisper.

"We eat them, so it's only fair."

Lucas balled his fists, and just as I thought he would lunge toward me, a loud, squawking noise erupted from inside the coop. I turned my head towards the noise, and the sight that greeted me was a blur of feathers and beaks. Three chickens burst out of the coop like race cars out of the chute, quickly scattering in different directions.

As the chickens sought their revenge, Kayla and Lucas sprang to their feet and ran in the opposite direction like rabbits fleeing from a dog.

I was doubled over in laughter as the chickens chased them around the yard, my stomach heaving with each chuckle.

I winced in pain as I felt a sharp object pierce my skin. "Ouch!"

A fourth bird loomed behind me, its beak gaping wide as it charged me like a knight thrusting a sword. I stumbled and wobbled while attempting to run toward Lucas and Kayla, resembling an even drunker version of Captain Jack Sparrow.

"Up here!" Lucas yelled as he grabbed Kayla's waist and lifted her into a giant oak tree that rested about four feet from Mr. Heckle's deck. "Hurry up!" he yelled at me. At this point, I was seeing three of Lucas and wasn't sure which one was shouting at me. I picked the one towards the middle and put my hands on his shoulders. I was correct because he suddenly hoisted me upward. I gripped onto one of the tree branches and pulled myself up for dear life. We climbed up a few branches until we were in the middle of the tree, Lucas hurrying closely behind.

"Death by chickens." Lucas breathed.

"What?" I gasped for air as I clung to the tree branches, feeling increasingly dizzy.

Lucas hugged the trunk. "Just imagining what my tombstone is going to say."

It suddenly dawned on me as we sat here perched on the branches of our neighbor's tree, trying to avoid the murderous chickens that seemed to be closing in on us, that this was the most fun I had experienced in five years. Sure, my head was spinning into the heavens, but with all of us together, it just seemed right.

A sudden burst of blinding light emanated from the base of the towering tree. The yellow rays bounced off the branches and leaves, causing a sharp impact on my retinas.

"The chickens have developed powers!" Kayla screamed.

Lucas peeked through the branches. "It's worse than mutant chickens." He gulped.

"What could be worse than mutant chickens?" I poked my head through the bouquet of leaves in my face. "Oh shit …" My eyes focused on the blue and tan blobs that were now forming into the shapes of two police officers, their flashlights shining up at us. I squinted my eyes harder to zero in on their faces. Unbelievable … UN-FREAKING-BELIEVABLE! I internally screamed as the tallest cop's face came into focus.

"Emmett ...?" My jaw dropped.

"What's going on?" Kayla appeared next to me. When her eyes fixed on Emmett's face, her expression contorted into a mix of anxiety and dread. "We are so screwed."

"Doesn't anybody leave this freaking town!?" I exclaimed. Emmett wasn't just a former classmate; he was my former junior prom date. My date that I left on the dance floor with a broken nose and a missing front tooth ...

# CHAPTER 15

We stay silent when we should speak.
We speak when we should stay silent,
And we hold on when we should let go.

**March 10, 2016**

Prom was something I had always dreamed of. I knew it was uncharacteristic of me to fantasize about wearing a frilly tulle skirt. But what can I say? I watched A Cinderella Story with Hilary Duff and Chad Michael Murray one too many times. However, when Jamie's mom died, the idea of prom or any other adolescent rite of passage no longer felt important.

After the funeral, Jamie shut us all out, even me. My mom offered to let him stay with us, but he declined. I think there was a small part of him that couldn't be around my mom without thinking about his. I knew he didn't want to burden anyone, but I couldn't just leave him to drown in his grief. Even when he told me not to come around, I did. I snuck out night after night, curling up beside him, just being there. He needed someone, and even though neither of us talked about what we were feeling, I believed we had a silent understanding. But the kiss we shared at the supermarket? We never mentioned it again. After everything with his mom, pushing for more felt wrong. So, we just stayed like this—needing each other but afraid to cross that line.

That line turned into a ten-foot wall of iron and razors on the night of Lover's Lake; the kind of night that stays with you like a scar etched on your skin.

It was officially that time of year when girls waited on bated breath for a boy to surprise them with a cheesy note asking them to the junior prom. The who's going with whom conversation had spread through the halls like wildfire, consuming everything in its wake. Lucas desperately wanted to ask Kayla, and Kayla was oblivious to Lucas's feelings. I had a few guys hint at the idea of going to prom together, but I swatted them away like diseased flies. There was only one person I wanted to go with, even if that meant going as just friends.

March 10th at 10:00 p.m. marked the junior bonfire, an extremely illegal high school tradition that often ended with hangovers and handcuffs. Lovers Lake was our town's very own tragic love story landmark. It earned its nickname after a young couple was forbidden to see each other due to family rivalry, which gave the whole tale a rather Romeo and Juliet twist that I found a bit too dramatic for my liking.

According to the story, the couple decided to run away together in the middle of the night. They planned to row across the lake, which crossed the state border, and start a new life in a new city. However, halfway through their journey, a storm flipped their boat, knocking the boy out. Tragically, the girl didn't know how to swim and drowned. In an instant, their happily ever after was replaced by a tragic ending. Now the lake was used as an excuse for teenagers to party and screw in the bed of pickup trucks. It was all very poetic, obviously.

It was 9:00 p.m., and the house was quiet. Too quiet.

I stopped at the top of the stairs, my rubber soles barely making a sound against the wooden steps. The glow from the kitchen light spilled into the hallway, casting long shadows over the living room where my mother paced back and forth.

"I can't just let you walk back in, not after everything."

My mom's voice was low and sharp. A voice she rarely used, but when she did, I always knew who was on the other end of the phone.

My stomach twisted.

I moved down a step, slowly and carefully. The wood creaked beneath me, and I froze, heart hammering. But she didn't hear. She was too caught up in the conversation.

"I'm glad you're doing better," she said, softer this time. "I am. But you can't expect to—" A pause. A shaky breath. "All I want for you is to find whatever it is you've always been searching for." She steadied herself. "But you can't expect to come back and pick up where we left off. That's not how this works. I can't risk you shattering the home I've built from the rubble you caused."

The knot in my chest tightened.

I crept lower, just enough to see her face. She stood with one hand braced against the arm of the couch, shoulders tense, her fingers white knuckling the phone, her face stained by drying tears. The way she held herself wasn't just with anger. It was something heavier. Something painful.

I heard my dad's voice crack on the other end. "Monica. Please. You know I'll always love you."

My mom looked at the ceiling and closed her eyes. "I know." She whispered. "But that's not enough."

"Mon—"

She hung up.

I should have stayed silent, waited, listened, and given my mother some grace. I knew she loved my father. That was never what they were lacking. Trust, honesty, and loyalty were now the missing pieces. I blamed my mom for that when I should have directed my blame at the person who left.

Words shot out of me faster than my feet could carry me down the stairs.

"Why are you doing this?"

She flinched, whipping around to face me. Her expression flickered surprise first, then something harder, unreadable.

"Alex," she said, already shaking her head. "Don't. This isn't the time—"

"Not the time? You just hung up on my father. Mine! And you didn't even let me talk to him." My voice came out sharp, my pulse roaring in my ears. "He called. After all this time, he finally called, and you're—what? Shutting him out again?"

Her lips pressed together, but she didn't answer.

I stepped forward, heat rising to my cheeks. "You never even gave him a chance."

Her breath caught, the slightest hitch in her throat, so quiet I almost missed it. "I did," she murmured. "More than one, you know that."

I swallowed hard. "Then give him one more."

Silence.

She took one long breath. Then, a second.

"No."

One word. One simple word, built of two letters, sliced right through me.

"Because it won't change anything," she said. "He is who he is, Alex. How many times must he show you that for you to understand? How many times are you going to let him hurt you before you realize I'm not the bad guy here?" Her voice wavered between anger and tears.

Something burned at the back of my throat—words I should never have said out loud. "Are you worried about me getting hurt or yourself? Which one of us are you trying to protect? It's my decision if he's going to be in my life."

More silence.

I heard footsteps approaching from the kitchen. Julian and Lucas moved as if they were spies disarming a bomb.

Julian spoke first. "Alex, this situation is more complicated than—"

"Julian. Don't." I snapped. "You're not my dad. This doesn't include you." He looked like I had slapped him. "

He took a step back and bowed his head like a boxer bowing out of a match.

I thought my mother would be the one to defend his honor but she wasn't. Lucas jumped in front of him. "Jesus, what the hell, Alex! How about you show some respect for the man who raised you all these years?" He jabbed a finger at my chest. "The man who checked under your bed for monsters every night because you were scared to sleep. The man who came to your defense every time you got into trouble in school, which, news flash, has been a lot. The man who took you in as his daughter the second you walked through that door, without ever hearing a thank you from you."

He was right. Julian was always there. But I wanted my dad to be the one who cared. Was that so wrong?

I could feel my eyes welling up with tears, but I refused to cry. My mother placed a hand on Lucas's shoulder, pulling him back. "Stop it. Both of you," she said, looking sternly at me. "I hope that once you've cooled down from your little temper tantrum, you will apologize to both of us."

I knew I was wrong. I hated myself for what I had said, but that didn't stop my lips from moving faster than my brain. "I'll apologize once you apologize for keeping my dad away from me."

She just shook her head, clearly disappointed in my response. "You are a junior in high school, and I can count the number of times your dad has bothered to see you." Her expression never faltered. "That man isn't your dad; he's just some guy with matching DNA. I will not apologize for doing what was right for you."

She stopped.

"And for me," she said, looking me up and down. "I threw away so many years trying to fix the man your father became, trying to turn him back into the little boy I grew up with—my best friend. But nothing I ever did worked. I thought, of all people, you would understand that."

What was that supposed to mean? My whole body froze, as if I were an undercover detective caught in a lie.

"Jamie is nothing like him. And I am nothing like you."

She inhaled sharply.

The air between us felt charged and heavy. Then, in the softest, most deliberate voice, she said, "You're right, you're not. I knew when it was time to move on."

The words hung there, suspended in the quiet.

And then—movement.

A shadow near the front doorway shifted.

I turned, and there he was.

Jamie.

He stood just inside the house, with the open door behind him and Kayla inches away. The dim light caught the sharp angles of his face, and his expression was unreadable. However, I didn't need to see his face to know that he had heard everything.

Before I could speak, before I could try to mend the damage, Kayla pushed past Jamie, entering the house. Her eyes darted between me, my mom, and Jamie, her brows furrowing.

"Whoa." She let out a low whistle, tossing her purse onto the couch. "What did we just walk into?"

Nobody answered.

So, I did the only thing I could do.

I pushed past them, past the weight of my mother's words, past my brother's fury, past the way Jamie wouldn't even look at me, and past Kayla's confusion. "Let's just go," I said.

The drive to the party was quiet. A nervous, suffocating void of sound, the kind of silence that felt like the last ten minutes of a horror movie, the sensation of holding your breath until the suspense was over.

Kayla sat in the passenger seat, legs crossed, her fingers

anxiously trying to break the noiselessness with blaring music, flicking through the radio stations as if she could erase the tension with the right song.

Lucas drove, his grip on the wheel tight, his jaw clenched. He was still pissed at me. Rightfully so. I was an ass, I'm aware.

And Jamie—Jamie was next to me, elbow resting on the door, fingers tapping against his knee. He hadn't looked at me since we left the house.

I stared straight ahead, trying to ignore the way my skin still burned with an odd mix of anger, regret, and humiliation.

He heard everything.

My mother's words, the comparison, the finality in her voice.

I stole a glance at him from the corner of my eye, but he was looking out the window, his face unreadable.

Lucas's voice cut through the music's obnoxiously loud bass. "You didn't have to yell at Monica like that."

I stiffened, fingernails curling into the fabric of my jeans. "I didn't yell."

He let out a sharp laugh. "Right. Sure."

I glared at him in the review mirror. "I was just—"

"Just what?" He turned slightly, just enough to shoot me a look. "Being a spoiled brat and acting as if you know everything?"

My stomach twisted. I opened my mouth, ready to fire back, but Kayla cut in.

"Chill, Lucas." She shot him a warning look. "Just because Alex was being a bitch doesn't mean you can be a dick."

Lucas turned his attention back to the road. "Whatever."

I glanced at Jamie again, but he was still staring out at the dark road and passing trees.

I hated this. Hated the tension. Hated the way my mother's voice kept looping in my head.

Hated the fact that Jamie wouldn't even acknowledge me.

So, I pushed him.

"You know, you don't have to ignore me," I said, turning toward him.

For the first time since we got in the car, he looked at me: just a flicker, just a second. But I caught it.

"I'm not ignoring you," he said.

Yes, you are! I wanted to scream. "Fine."

Kayla shifted in her seat, tossing me a look that I knew meant fix this.

But how could I?

The night was already ruined before it even began.

The bonfire crackled, sparks flying up into the dark sky. The lake stretched out beyond it, calm and still. People milled around, talking, laughing, moving in and out of the fire's glow. The scent of burning wood mixed with the salt from the lake, and somewhere in the distance, someone had a speaker blasting music.

I should have been having fun, laughing with Kayla, who was chatting with a girl from our English class. Instead, I found myself sitting on a half-rotted log, gazing at the flames as if they held the answers to all my mistakes. It felt as if I didn't look up, I might disappear. Honestly, it seemed like my plan was working, since Jamie was pretending I didn't exist.

Across the fire, he stood with Lucas, a beer can dangling

from his fingers. He wasn't drinking it; he was holding it, rolling the can between his palms. His expression was unreadable, as always. His black hair swooped slightly over his eyes as he stared into the drink.

"Are you gonna sit here and pout all night?" Kayla dropped onto the log beside me, nudging my knee with hers.

"I'm not pouting," I muttered.

"Uh-huh." She tilted her head, studying me, and then turned her gaze to where Jamie stood. "God, you two are exhausting."

I frowned at her. "We are not." Now I was pouting.

"You are," she said, taking a sip from a plastic cup. "The whole brooding, longing stares, not admitting you want each other—it's getting tragic."

I rolled my eyes. "Well, tragic sounds about right."

Kayla groaned. "You make things so hard for yourself."

Truth. But why? Why did I always find myself in disasters of my own making? Before I could unload my cringeworthy feelings on Kayla about my daddy issues and abandonment problems for a much-needed best friend therapy session, Lucas walked up. Unfortunately, he wasn't alone.

"Wow," he said, dropping onto the log beside me, Jamie lurking behind. "You look almost as bad as I feel."

I sighed. "Did you come over here just to insult me?"

"No," he said, stretching his legs out, eyes flicking between me and Kayla. "I came to see if you'd stopped being dramatic yet."

I shoved him. "Hey, if you're trying to make amends, you're not doing so hot."

Lucas grinned, but then his expression shifted more serious. "I'm sorry. It was wrong of me to get in the middle."

"No, actually, it wasn't," I confessed. "I was the one in the wrong. Your dad has always been there for me." A trembling breath filled my lungs. "But to admit that means I would also have to acknowledge that my dad didn't care to be there, which stings more than I thought it would."

My brother took my hand. "Hey, his decisions don't have anything to do with you and everything to do with himself. Don't take on his baggage. Let him carry it."

"Thanks," I whispered back.

Kayla darted behind Lucas and me, then scooped all four of us—even Jamie—into a massive hug, pulling Jamie down to the ground in the process. "Aww, you guys, you're going to make me cry! I love it when you two are sappy!"

She was squishing my shoulder into Lucas's. "Well, then I'm about to fill your quota of sap." I poked my brother's knee. "Wasn't there something you wanted to ask Kayla Lucas?"

Two weeks ago, I overheard Lucas practicing how to ask Kayla to the dance in the bathroom mirror. Two whole weeks had passed, and he had chickened out at every opportunity, so I figured he needed me to throw him into the deep end of this prom proposal.

He glared at me: a sprinkle of frustration, a pinch of anger, and a dash of terror swimming in his corneas.

Kayla smiled, utterly oblivious to him. "Sure, Lucas, shoot, what's up?"

His palm tightened around his leg. "Umm. Do you have a date for the prom?" He mumbled

Kayla blinked. "Uh … yeah?" Her voice came out as a question, like she wasn't sure where this was going.

Lucas's shoulders hunched forward as if he had been kicked in the chest. "Oh, cool. Good for you."

I frowned, glancing between them. "Wait, what? Who? Why didn't you tell me?"

Kayla stood to her feet. "I didn't think it was a big deal. It's our junior prom; I figured we would all be going with dates."

Lucas stood up, too, meaning that I also had to abandon the damp log I was sitting on to join them. Lucas, still tense, turned to Jamie. "What about you?"

"What about me?" Jamie asked.

"Are you going to prom with someone?"

"Why? You asking me out?" Jamie teased.

Lucas shrugged him off. "Come on, man, I'm serious. Don't tell me I'm the last dude to get a date."

Jamie hesitated. It was quick. Barely there, but long enough for my breath to stop.

And in that half-second pause, I knew.

I knew before he even said it.

"Kind of, yeah," he finally said. "I, uh … I have a date."

The world around me began to blur. The fire, the voices, the music—everything faded into a white noise. I could barely make out Lucas's frustrated, "Damn," and Kayla's incredulous, "Seriously?" All I could hear was the rush of blood pulsing in my ears. Then, in a voice that didn't sound like my own, I heard myself ask, "With who?"

Jamie's eyes darted away from mine, and his legs shifted uncomfortably from where he stood. "Actually … um, you know

Bethany?"

No … No! I was going to kill him if he said what I knew he was going to. "The bitch who butchered my hair? How could I forget?"

Jamie sucked in a breath. "That was a long time ago."

"Demons can't change their scales," I snapped back.

"I think you mean tigers can't change their stripes."

"Nope."

Jamie bit the inside of his mouth. "She and Emmett broke up because she caught him making out with the new girl. To get back at him, she asked me to the prom. When I used to hang out with the Donahues, I keyed his car, and he has held a grudge against me ever since. She thought I would be a good way to get revenge."

My head and heart ached as if my body had fallen from the Empire State Building and landed on silver spikes.

"But if you have a problem with me going with her—"

"Take her."

Why did I say that?

"Really?"

Stop talking, Alex!

"Yeah. Why not?" I paused, hoping he would stop me from pushing him into the arms of another girl. "Unless there's a reason you don't want to go with her…?" Here it was, my only attempt at giving him a 'get out of jail free card.'

He nodded his head as if there was a side conversation chattering in the hollow space between his ears. "… well then you'd be all alone."

The fuck I would! Screw him! Did he think I was so pathetic that I couldn't get a date?

"Emmett Thompson asked me out." My mouth blurted this out before my better judgment could stop me. It was technically accurate. The previous week, Emmett made a distasteful pass at me, joking about taking my fine ass to the prom. Disgusting, I know. I smacked him, which only seemed to turn him on more. It would take some serious groveling, but I was sure that if I explained the situation of Jamie and Bethany being together, he would want just as much retribution as I did.

"Emmett? Bethany's Emmett?"

"Yup, that would be the one." I snarked back.

His nostrils flared as he let out a deep sigh, and his eyes narrowed with seething anger. "Wow, you're so jealous of Bethany that you'd go out with Emmett just to spite her?"

Did he just call me jealous?

I clenched my fists, feeling a surge of heat flush my body from my head to my toes. "You know what? You kissed me." I slowed it down for him. "You. Kissed. Me."

I must have said that really loud because Lucas and Kayla stopped whatever conversation they were having to watch my next move.

"You've kissed me not once. Not twice. But three times." My tone escalated. "And then you pretend like they never happened!" I pushed his chest with both my hands, setting him three inches back. "Why! Why would you do that!"

Jamie's eyes went from anger to pleading as he placed his hand on my shoulders,

"Alex—"

I threw his hand off me. "No, Jamie, tell me!" My voice

was shaking. "Tell me why I'm good enough to kiss but not to date?" I needed an answer; any answer would be better than this aching uncertainty.

His face was frozen. "I don't—I don't know how to answer that."

Somehow, that answer was worse.

"Wow," I took a step back. "She was right." I had no words. Nothing to say except: "You're just like my dad." It came out like a whispered confession.

Jamie said nothing for a complete second. It was surprising how long a second could feel. "You're right."

Police sirens filled the air before I could comprehend what Jamie said. Panic set the bonfire ablaze. Bodies scrambled, moving in every direction. Someone threw their drink into the fire, sending embers shooting into the dark sky. The speaker that had been blasting music moments ago was suddenly silent, replaced by the unmistakable sound of tires crunching over gravel.

I barely had time to process what was happening before Kayla grabbed my wrist.

"Alex, we gotta go. Now."

But my feet wouldn't move.

Kayla tugged harder. "Alex!"

Somewhere behind me, Lucas was shouting something, probably trying to round up the group—but my head was still spinning, my heart still raw.

The blue and red lights flashed against the trees, too close, too fast.

That was enough to snap me out of it.

The adrenaline hit my system all at once, sharp and electric, sending me weaving through bodies, through panicked voices, and slamming car doors. I turned on my heel and ran.

"Come on, come on," Kayla muttered under her breath.

Lucas was ahead of us, yanking open the driver's side door, with Kayla right behind him, sliding into the passenger seat. They barely made it in before a cop's voice cut through the chaos: "Nobody move!"

"Go!" Jamie yelled at Lucas. "Drive."

As they sped off, tires digging up the ground, a blinding flashlight rushed at me and Jamie.

My chest was heaving, and the cold night air was burning my lungs. Jamie cursed under his breath, lifting his hands like he was already surrendering. He turned to look straight at me.

Something passed between us, something sharp, something desperate.

Then, the officer stepped forward, and the moment shattered.

"All right," he said, voice firm. "The party is over."

That night, my heart was broken, and my hands were cuffed. Yet, that was just the beginning of the prom madness.

# CHAPTER 16

They were hopeless romantics
Waiting on fate

That always came too late

**April 17, 2016**

It was officially the big night, and we were all going to the prom with the wrong people.

Kayla was going with Marcus McCormick, Lucas was going with Lilly Sanders and Jamie, and I was stuck with two of the worst people in our high school. It felt like a teenage nightmare.

My fingers trembled as I fumbled with the hot rollers tangled in my brown hair. I was sitting on the floor, my thighs getting a nasty carpet burn, as I looked at my reflection in the floor-length mirror; I barely recognized myself. My red eyes were hazy and itchy from crying all night, my nose was red, and my cheeks were puffy. This cannot be happening …

Kayla's laughter boomed through the room as she twirled in her sapphire blue dress, the excitement dripping off her. "I should never have let you use my makeup. Your moping is ruining my mascara," Kayla stopped spinning and walked over to the closet, searching through my shoes, which were technically my mom's shoes that I had taken over the years.

I turned my head back to her, the hot rollers lightly slipping, causing a distinct hot searing to burn my ear. That's going to leave a mark. "Would it be such an awful thing if I didn't go tonight? The flu is going around anyway. I could call Emmett and tell him I caught that," I murmured, my voice dropping down to almost a whisper.

Kayla walked over and gently sat on the ground beside me, careful not to wrinkle her skin-tight dress; she reached out to touch my arm in support, yet somehow, it made me feel even more pathetic. "You can't let Jamie ruin your night. Look at me; I'm not crying over Lucas going with Lilly. We deserve to have fun with or without those dumb boys tonight."

"I know." I sniffled as more tears threatened to ruin my makeup for the third time. "I just wish it were with them."

I tried to brush the moment off and continued to get ready. Kayla helped me fix my hair and makeup, and I gave her a handful of forced smiles that allowed the minutes to pass by smoother than the previous ones.

I stepped into my dress and zipped up the purple fabric, the silk clinging to my body like a second skin. According to Kayla, this was a good thing, but no matter how much I fiddled with the fabric, everything felt wrong.

I walked over to my closet. "Do you think maybe we should bring jackets?" I asked Kayla as I rummaged through my closet, looking for something to give me more coverage.

"That would defeat the point of wearing a dress you can't breathe in. Have I taught you nothing?" Kayla applied her lipstick, admiring herself in a tiny, purple, rhinestone-covered hand mirror.

"Hurry up! Everyone is going to be here soon." My brother's voice boomed from downstairs.

"We'll be down in a minute!" Kayla yelled back. She sat on my bed and laced up the straps on her sandals.

I slipped my feet into some silver wedges and then walked up to her. "Why did you let my brother say yes to Lilly? You know he's hopelessly in love with you."

Kayla's face fell as if I slapped her over her blushing cheeks. "Lucas isn't in love with me," she muttered. "He likes the idea of me, but he doesn't love me."

My jaw threatened to smack the floor. "Kayla, this is Lucas we're talking about. The same boy who has been following you around like a lost puppy dog since the day he saw you skipping towards him in the cafeteria."

"Everyone wants to date me until they have to deal with me." It wasn't a secret that Kayla had some mood issues. She had extreme highs and extreme lows. One second, she was on top of the world, dancing naked on a table, singing "Party in the USA" at the top of her lungs, and the next, she wouldn't come out of her room for a week, hiding under her covers and wishing that the world would disappear. Kayla didn't like getting close to people because when she did, she risked watching them leave, and after her mom left, she refused to go through that again. But I wish Kayla had understood that, in Lucas's eyes, she wasn't some notch upon a belt or a stop along the way to the next fling. She was his destination.

I was ready to support my brother and convince the girl of his dreams that he was the boy of hers, but then he opened his damn mouth again.

"Alex! Kayla! If you're not down here in three minutes, we're leaving without you, and you'll have to walk!" Even when my brother wasn't in the room, he somehow managed to kick himself in the ass.

Kayla chuckled. "And that's what you're trying to set me up with?" she joked before hopping onto her feet. "Let's go before your brother has an aneurysm."

The earsplitting doorbell announced the arrival of Jamie, Bethany, Lilly, Marcus, and Emmett. My moronic brother thought it would be an excellent idea if we all went together as one big group. Dread twisted in my stomach as I followed Kayla down the stairs. Jamie and Bethany were the first to step inside the front door, her arm looped possessively around his. Jamie's gaze met mine briefly—guilt flickering before he quickly looked away, his attention turning toward my parents, who were already snapping pictures with their disposable cameras like it was the Oscars.

Lucas stared up at Kayla, looking like he had just swallowed his tongue. His eyes flickered over her as if she were some rare artifact he wasn't allowed to touch. Instead of saying anything meaningful, all he managed to choke out was, "Wow ..." It seemed like the guy had forgotten how to speak English.

Kayla began to say something in response, but before she could, she glanced at Lilly standing beside Lucas. She was giving both of them a thin-lipped smile, and it was evident that there wasn't a soul in the room who couldn't sense the attraction between Kayla and Lucas. Except for Marcus. Sweet, clueless

Marcus, standing there grinning like he'd hit the jackpot by being Kayla's date. If he had any idea as to what was going on, it didn't show.

Bethany's voice cut through the air, dripping with her usual fake charm. "Alex," she said, letting my name hang in the air. Her eyes swept over my dress. "You look so ... purple," she said in the manner of complimenting a child's finger painting.

"Thanks," I said, not bothering to mask my sarcasm.

I glanced at the clock on the wall; its swinging hands mocked me. Emmett was late. He was probably admiring himself in a mirror somewhere, lost in the gleam of his own reflection. The only thing worse than being stuck in a room full of these people would be being stood up by Emmett in front of Bethany.

My mind was filled with escape plans. Perhaps I could pretend to have food poisoning. I could make up an excuse to go to the kitchen and hastily gather some leftovers, then spill them all over the floor. Or maybe something miraculous would happen, like a meteor shower striking my house at that very moment. Just as I began praying for world destruction, the doorbell rang.

My mother quickly opened the door and snapped a photo of Emmett as soon as he entered. With a sick feeling in my gut, I braced myself for what was to come. The town's football star strutted into the living room with his usual air of arrogance, sending uncomfortable tremors down my spine.

His eyes scanned me from head to toe. "Dang, girl, who knew you had a body like that?" His voice was loud, and his hands slid around my waist as if we were already in some nauseating slow dance.

I tensed, digging my nails into my palms as I tried not to

recoil visibly.

Before I could respond or before Julian could remove the boy's head from his body, Jamie's voice sliced through the tension. "Hey, watch it," he snarled.

Emmett tightened his grip on me. "You don't run with the Donahues anymore. So, what exactly do I have to be afraid of?

Jamie stood there calmly, a subtle smile on his face, and his eyes gleamed with anticipation as if enjoying his chance to fight Emmett. "Wow, you strung together a whole sentence. Did the principal finally start making you attend classes, or are you just showing off because I'm going to prom with your ex?"

Julian stepped in before the punching could begin. "All right, boys, let's calm down," he said, his voice relaxed but authoritative. "We're all here to have a good time. Let's keep things civil tonight, okay?"

Both boys nodded slightly and backed away from each other, but the conflict still lingered in the air like a heavy fog. Swiftly, my mother gathered us all together, insisting on taking a group photo. I forced a smile for the camera, even as my insides crawled at feeling Emmett's hands on my waist. After six more pictures, my parents finally released us, ushering everyone out the door, their voices filled with well-wishes and reminders to have fun. As the door closed behind them, I couldn't help but want to run back inside and lock the entry, creating a perfect barrier between me and the rest of our group. Still, instead, I walked forward to the stretch limo that Lucas had rented for everyone, knowing that the night ahead would be filled with both headache and heartache.

The thumping pulse of the music reverberated through the gymnasium. Each beat echoed off the walls and vibrated through my body like a slap, reminding me that everyone was having the time of their lives while I sat alone at a round table covered in a cheap blue tablecloth. The blinding, colorful lights flashing around the room mocked me as they bounced off the shiny gym floor. The smell of sweat and thumping music caused my head to pound harder than the DJ's mixing table. I stared at couples swaying in harmony, their whispers and laughter a stark contrast to the somber atmosphere surrounding my solitary table

Jamie's face caught my attention as he twirled his date in the corner of the floor. I had desperately tried to avoid his glances throughout the night, but Jamie's stare caught mine just as I allowed my eyes to venture in his direction.

Shit.

I ripped my eyes from his and glued them to the empty cup in front of me. Before tonight, I thought the worst thing in the world would be going to prom alone while Jamie danced the night away with Bethany. I was wrong. Sitting alone all night while my date got drunk in the locker rooms with his teammates turned out to be the worst fate I could have written for myself.

There was a rough shuffling behind me that grew louder as it approached. I turned to the right to see my so-called date stumbling back to the table. He crashed down on the seat next to mine, his breath reeking of cheap beer and his words slurred beyond comprehension.

"Tommas and Corbin brought 500 Post-it notes!" I had to watch his mouth intensely to understand what he was trying to say, and even then, I was completely lost.

"Okay …?"

He ran his fingers through his sweaty blond hair. "We're gonna tag the coach's car." He nodded and smiled as if genuinely proud of what he just said.

"With Post-it Notes?" My jaw hung low. I swear I could feel my brain cells shriveling from the conversation.

"Yup." He raised his thick eyebrows up and down with a self-assured smile.

I was partly relieved that he was going to ditch me; this meant I wouldn't have to endure the stench of his Mighty Men's cologne mixed with the Bud Light oozing from his breath. But the other part of me wanted to duct tape his naked ass to the flagpole and watch everyone ridicule him until he begged for mercy.

Was I being dramatic?

Yes …

Did I care? No!

A slow song began to play, its haunting melody filling me with a blend of regret, rage, and the desire for blissful retaliation. My heart skipped a beat as I watched from across the room as Jamie cradled Bethany's waist.

"Look." I locked my death stare with Emmett's foggy one. "I don't want to end my junior year sitting at a table alone. So would you please give me one dance before you lower what's left of your IQ?"

Emmett groaned like a child told to clean his room.

"It would make Bethany jealous." I sighed.

His eyes widened, his jaw slackened, and his eyebrows shot up. "Okay, sweet; let's do this!"

Dancing with Emmett to Ed Sheeran's "Thinking Out Loud" in front of Jamie sounded like perfect revenge in my head.

The second Emmett's arms wrapped around me, his touch became increasingly invasive, his hands roaming freely over my body as we danced. I tried to pull slightly away from his grasp without making it too noticeable to anyone else, but he only tightened his hold, his laughter at my discomfort ringing in my ears. Despite my silent protests, Emmett continued to travel his hands down my back, landing on my ass and squeezing it like a freaking stress ball.

"Stop it," I gritted at him, smacking the tips of his fingers.

Just as the words left my mouth, I suddenly saw Jamie tearing through the crowd towards us like a bullet exiting a gun. His eyes narrowed as he took in a scene, his expression shifting from confusion to red-hot fury. Swiftly, he placed himself between Emmett and me as if his body were a boundary wall.

"Back off." Jamie's voice was deep, his tone leaving no room for argument.

Emmett stumbled. "Dude, chill out. We were having some fun." His words were sloppy and dripping with arrogance.

Jamie's jaw twitched. "Fun doesn't mean crossing somebody's boundaries."

Emmett puffed his chest out. "You're just upset that I felt her up before you did. Don't worry; you can have her back when I'm done."

Jamie's fist flew with lightning speed, connecting with Emmett's nose with a very satisfying thud. The force of the blow sent Emmett staggering backward, his hands clutching his bloody face in shock as his ass collided with the floor.

The room fell silent, the music fading into the background as all eyes turned to the unfolding drama.

Jamie glared at Emmett. "Touch her again, and I'll break more than your nose." His voice was a low growl that made me worry his threat wasn't a bluff.

As I stood there, my heart pounding, Jamie cracked his now red and swollen knuckles. I could have thanked Jamie for defending my honor, but the feminist in me was pissed that Jamie didn't think I could protect myself.

"Why did you do that?" I yelled.

Jamie's eyes flipped to mine in confusion. "Because he's an ass, and you weren't doing anything about it!" he shouted back.

I could feel my anger rising in response. I screamed at him, and he yelled at me, both of us completely ignoring Emmett's bleeding face and the principal marching over to us.

Jamie was okay with getting detention and being suspended, but I was one citation from summer school, and I wasn't risking biology for another three months. Without thinking twice, I grabbed Jamie's arm fiercely and pulled him through the gym. We pushed past lurking students, their eyes wide with shock. The sound of my heels striking the floor boomed through the space as we sprinted towards the exit, not slowing down until we burst out into the parking lot, gasping for breath and racing with adrenaline. We practically smacked into the limo, the car's hood acting as our brake.

I glanced at our reflection in the car window. We looked like a complete mess. Panting and heaving, we struggled to catch our breath, our clothes and hair disheveled. I let out a laugh as I shook my tangled hair. I turned to Jamie, who was beaming, his eyes smushed up from his cheeks that rose high on his face. The air was thick with the sweet aroma of the night.

Then, as fast as a shooting star, Jamie reached for me, his hand sliding to the back of my neck, fingers tangling in my hair as he pulled me closer, like he couldn't stand another second apart. It was rough, urgent, and frenzied, as if he were trying to make up for all the time we had lost. It left my heart racing, my lips burning, and my body desperately craving more. My hands frantically moved up and down his chest, like they were trying to map out every detail of his body, and no matter how tightly I pulled myself into him, it simply wasn't close enough. At that moment, everything else seemed to fade away, and all I could feel was the warmth of his embrace and the softness of his lips.

The only times Jamie ever kissed me were when the adrenaline was high and the stakes were even higher. I was like a drug to him, but he was my addiction, too.

I was the Bonnie to his Clyde. His perfect partner in crime.

… but we all know how that story ended.

# CHAPTER 17

Two broken souls
Fallen from grace
Hunted by shadows, they couldn't erase
Their love was a storm, a fiery chase
Two broken souls
Became whole in each other's embrace

**April 17, 2016: PART 2**

We dashed through the misty night, my bare feet smacking against the wet pavement. In hindsight, keeping my heels on would have been the more intelligent decision so that I wouldn't have ended up with little cuts on my toes, but all thought and logic went out the window that night.

Jamie and I abandoned the limo to avoid waking my parents as we returned to my house, completely drenched from the rain. My dress clung to my thighs like duct tape. As we reached the tree that stretched toward my bedroom window, I hurriedly grabbed the branches to pull myself up. Jamie guided me until we reached the top, his fingers pressing lightly into my hips. The gentle touch made it almost unbearable to stand, and my pulse raced so fast that I feared I might collapse at any moment.

I always left my window unlocked in case Jamie needed to make a quick escape from his house, so I typically wasn't the one climbing back into my bedroom. That was Jamie's job.

I reached for my windowsill and tried to stretch my leg over, and that's when I heard a distinct screech run up the fabric of my dress. I looked back to inspect the damage. A slit ran up the back of the purple material. "Kayla is so going to kill me." I grimaced.

Jamie helped steady my waist as I opened my bedroom window and climbed through the opening, practically tumbling on my face as I entered my room. "How have you been doing that for years without dying?"

Jamie gracefully pulled himself through the window and closed it behind him before offering me a hand up off the ground. "I would climb the Empire State Building if it meant being next to you." He moved his hand behind my neck and pulled me in, his lips gripping mine as his free hand roamed down the sides of my waist, resting on the swell of my back.

I gently placed my hands on his chest. His breath stalled slightly, and his eyes slowly opened. His fingertips roamed my body, illuminated only by the soft glow of the moonlight shining in from the window.

"Is this happening?" Jamie whispered.

I couldn't answer him at first; everything inside me went numb. I told myself to take a breath. "I think so."

I tried to resume kissing him, but he stopped me, eyes now falling to the floor. "I'm sorry." He breathed. "About the dance. About taking Bethany. It was stupid."

I stepped back a little, keeping one hand on his arm. "Then why did you do it?" Don't ask that! Don't ruin this! I pleaded with my lips to zip.

Jamie swallowed deeply as if the words were physically painful. "Because you're my best friend." His dark eyes returned to mine, causing my lungs to protest against taking a breath. "I don't think you realize how much I need you. After everything, I couldn't risk losing us."

"Jamie, it was just a dance, not a battlefield."

"For me, it was." He stepped closer. "What if I mess this up? What if I am like your father? If we do this." He paused and rubbed his thumb in circles on the nape of my neck, his lips dangerously close to mine. "If we start this, that's it. There's no going back, and there's no second chance. I would rather be your friend forever than only have you for a moment." He closed his eyes and lowered his head, his forehead resting on mine. "I don't want to ruin us. I don't want to ruin you."

I placed my finger under his chin and lightly lifted his gaze to mine. "Jamie, you're not my dad. Nor are you yours.

"You don't know that." His voice was broken.

"Yes, I do. Because I know you." I moved my hands over his chest and to the back of his hair. "Because … I love you," I whispered those three words like they were a scorpion ready to sting, like pain was the only thing that could come after.

Jamie's eyes widened in surprise, and he tightened his grip on me. My heart raced as I waited for his response. Then, slowly, a smile spread across his cheeks. It was the kind of smile that started small and grew until it lit up his entire face like a match and threatened to burn the world as well.

"I wanted to be the one who said that first." His cheeks rose as he tucked a strand of wet hair out of my eyes with the tips of his fingers.

"You snooze, you lose."

"I guess I'll just have to show you then."

He pulled my hips into him and tugged my mouth with his.

"I want ..." I said, and then I realized that I didn't know how to say it.

Jamie took a few breaths, his eyes shifting from my lips back to my eyes. "Do you want me to leave?" he asked, his tone tentative as if afraid of his own words.

I chuckled at his concern. "Definitely not. I want you to stay." I held the last word, hoping he'd get the hint, but he looked more confused than ever. "All night." There was a moment of pure silence, and I'm pretty sure I didn't breathe the whole time, and neither did he.

"You want me to stay and keep doing this?"

"I want you to do a lot more than this."

Jamie stumbled over his following words. "Seriously? Are you sure?"

"Just kiss me already." I hooked my finger onto the collar of his shirt and pulled him down to me. I gripped the sides of his suit jacket and ripped it off his forearms. I fumbled with the buttons of his black button-down shirt; part of me just wanted to rip them off with my teeth, but I was trying to show a little restraint.

"Who knew you were in such a rush to see me naked?" His voice pressed to my ear.

Screw restraint. I ripped the rest of his shirt off his arms and threw it to the floor, my hands roaming up and down his torso. Damn, you could wash clothes on these abs.

His hands gripped my shoulders and flipped my body around so that my back was facing him. He lightly undid the zipper of my dress and pulled it down my spine; his feathery light touch cascading down my back sent electricity to my toes. He then traveled back up to my shoulders and pushed my straps off, his fingers caressing them down my forearm. Then he gripped the sides of my dress and moved it down my body until I was left in nothing but my underwear and bra.

His mouth moved to my neck, and he started kissing my skin before guiding my waist to the bed. I sat down, and he sat beside me. Neither of us had the faintest idea of what to do next. I moved my body towards the head of the bed frame and pulled him on top of me. His lips traveled from my mouth to my jaw, then attached themselves to my neck. That does it. My body ached for the simplest touch of his skin, and we hadn't even gotten to the X-rated stuff yet. An involuntary moan escaped my lips, and he groaned against my chest, gripping my waist and pushing our bodies together.

"I'm going to rip those pants off if you don't remove them already," I demanded.

Jamie kissed my bare stomach. "Yes, ma'am." He quickly removed the rest of his clothing, but before he threw them off the bed, he reached into his pocket and pulled out a small packet.

Oh shit, this is happening.

I wasn't afraid or nervous, but it was my first time, after all. It was unfamiliar territory, but with Jamie, every move felt as natural as breathing.

Jamie stopped. "Are …?

"Yes, I'm sure. And if you don't hurry up, I'm going to finish without you."

He grinned through his laugh, weaving the condom package between his thumb and forefinger. He quickly tore the packet open and slipped the disc on. Shifting his body, he returned to hovering over me, then lightly parted my legs with his hand and moved his palm higher and higher up the inside of my thigh.

His lips greeted mine slowly. My hands clung to his waist in a desperate attempt to pull him closer. And then everything in my body tightened as he pressed into me; my eyes squeezed shut, and I lightly gasped. The health teacher wasn't lying when she said your first time hurts, but I would take that pain repeatedly if it meant feeling so connected to Jamie in a way that took my mind and body somewhere I never knew existed.

I loved him, and finally, I knew he loved me. The world could end in a ball of flames, and I would die happy knowing that this moment was just ours.

My eyes fluttered open to see sparkling lights entering through my bedroom blinds. It was early in the morning because the sun still had an orange hue. The rays cast tiny shadows over my floors, which were draped with our clothes. I wasn't ready to leave at that moment, so instead, I rested my head on my pillow and turned to watch Jamie as he slept peacefully beside me. His chest rose and fell in a steady rhythm, and his arm was draped over my waist. I could feel the warmth of his body against mine, and his breath tickled my neck. The silence of the morning was only broken by the soft sound of his breathing. I traced the lines of his jaw with my finger, marveling at how handsome he looked even in his sleep. It was hard to believe that we were finally together. It was like a dream that I prayed would never turn into a nightmare. But seeing him lying here, feeling his body pressed into mine, it made even the possibility of heartbreak seem worth it.

"Oh my god!"

I was jolted from my peaceful moment as I heard the loud boom of my mother's voice coming from outside my bedroom door and down the hall. I launched myself into an upright position on my bed. I couldn't tell if I was just disoriented, confused, or possibly still asleep.

But then I heard the unmistakable sound of Lucas's voice, followed by my mother's raised tone. I couldn't listen to what they were arguing about, but I could tell he was panicked, and she was furious. I listened intently for the following words to travel down the hall, but suddenly, there was a pause in the shouting, and that's when I heard Kayla's apologetic voice like a mouse echoing through an air vent.

'Oh my god,' was right.

Did Kayla sleep with Lucas?

Did Kayla sleep with Lucas?!

I pulled my ear forward, straining to hear more, but the voices slipped into the background, leaving me in the dark about whatever soap opera was unfolding this morning. Just as I was itching to know more, my bedroom door swung open with a bang, crashing into the door stopper. My heart leapt into my throat as I saw my mother standing in my doorway, holding a spatula tightly in her hand. Her face was twisted into a mask of fury, and all the veins in her neck and face were pulsing with rage. Her eyes narrowed into a fierce glance, making my mouth tremble to find words that wouldn't escape my lips.

Before I could come up with some plausible deniability, Jamie woke up. He launched from the bed, his face contorted with fear and embarrassment. I probably could have talked my way out of this moment; it wasn't like Jamie hadn't spent the night hundreds of times before—heck, it wasn't even the first time my mother had caught us in bed together—but the fact that he jumped out of my sheets butt-naked with his clothes scattered on my bedroom floor made coming up with an excuse … complicated.

Jamie looked around frantically, searching for his pants, but they were nowhere to be found. He threw on his boxers, barely covering himself up, giving him just enough time before my mom, still clutching the spatula, charged toward Jamie like a deranged murderer. I watched in horror as she chased him out of the room, her voice echoing down the hallway as she shouted at him.

I gripped my comforter and wrapped it around my body as I ran to the door frame, freezing as I reached the hallway, unsure of what to do or say. And that's when my mother turned to Kayla, who was stumbling out of Lucas's Room, her torso only covered by one of his oversized T-shirts.

"You better start running, too, young lady. You're lucky I gave you a head start to get dressed. Or would you prefer to be jogging down the street in your boxers like Jamie right now?" My mother raised this spatula high in the air.

"I'm leaving! I'm leaving!" Kayla squealed as her toes bounced off each step and blasted through the front door.

I locked eyes with Lucas from across the hallway. His torso was completely bare, and his legs were only covered by a pair of wrinkled pajama bottoms. I suddenly burst into a muffled laugh. From across the hall, I shot my brother a thumbs up, a grin tugging at my lips despite my lingering confusion about how in the world Lucas and Kayla had somehow ended up together that night. But it didn't matter; for the first time, it felt like we were all exactly where we were meant to be.

Together.

If only we hadn't fucked it up.

# CHAPTER 18

Is it too much to ask
For one last kiss
For one last touch
For one last night
For one last memory
To last a lifetime

**2:00 a.m.**

Julian tapped his foot on the police station's cement floor. "You're telling me that I'm bailing out my twenty-three-year-old children and their friend because of a Truth or Dare game?"

The three of us were behind a wall of metal bars, hungover and coming down, dressed in our sweats, covered in feathers and eggs.

Here's the thing about a small town: if you screwed someone over in the past, they're going to screw you over in the future. I knew Emmett was going to hand us our ass the second he caught us in Mr. Heckle's tree, and honestly, I couldn't blame him; our prom didn't necessarily end on a happy note … and thus explains my current predicament: stuck in a nine-by-nine cell with my brother and my brother's ex-girlfriend, nursing my worst headache since sophomore year college. Karma had finally caught me and was happily biting me in the ass.

"Yes ..." I said back to Julian, trying to give a pleading smile.

As the words escaped my mouth, a searing pain impaled my brain like a shish kabob, making my face contort and fall into my hands. "Dear God," I grumbled as acid rumbled from my chest to my throat, dangerously threatening to spew out on the floor. When I was seventeen, I could pull three consecutive all-nighters in a row, but now, a few shots of vodka and half a joint made me want to cough up my organs. Getting old is a bitch.

Julian crossed his arms, attempting to play the authoritative father role, but I could see a sneaky little smile of amusement lifting the sides of his cheek. "You kids are lucky Mr. Heckle isn't pressing charges for trespassing and terrorizing his chickens." The laugh escaped Julian's mouth as he uttered the words 'terrorizing chickens.' "I'm sorry, I can't say that with a straight face." His body shook as he gripped the cold cell bars, his laughter bounced off the walls as he doubled over, struggling to catch his breath, his face turning red.

Lucas planted his feet firmly on the ground and pushed himself up from the bench, his massive frame swaying slightly as he regained his balance, the hangover kicking his ass just as hard as it was kicking mine. "I can promise those chickens traumatized me way worse than I traumatized them!" He raised the hem of his sweats. "Here, I have the peck marks to prove it!"

Julian continued to heave with laughter as if our misery was somehow a comedy show, and he had front-row seats.

There was a loud groan from the corner of the cell, where Kayla was sprawled out, blanketing the cold bench with her limp body. "Can you please get us out of here, Mr. D? This place smells like feet and bodily fluids." Her grimace made me worry that our earlier pizza would soon decorate the cell.

"Okay. Okay." Julian turned to Sheriff Kennedy, standing in the archway connecting the cellar room to the hallway leading to the police station's front desk. "Sheriff, I think they've learned their lesson."

Sheriff Kennedy jammed the silver key into the slightly rusted lock. The familiar clatter of metal sent a shiver down my spine. For a moment, I was seventeen again, staring down the barrel of eternal grounding, my partner in crime at my side.

But Jamie wasn't beside me. I wasn't in high school anymore.

A dizzying wave hit as I stared at the empty space where he should've been. In a single breath, the years peeled away, slipping through my fingers without permission. I could see Jamie's guilt-ridden face, the floppy hair he refused to cut, his fidgeting fingers twisting the leather bracelet I'd made him when we were thirteen.

It was like staring at a ghost etched into the walls.

I turned my head away from where I wished Jamie was standing. I smacked my hand on my chest, hoping the quick slap against my skin would lower my spiking pulse. Ever since Jamie knocked on my door in Boston uninvited, it felt like a part of me was malfunctioning. My heart raced uncontrollably, and my cheeks burned as if on fire. My hands felt heavy, and my fingers tingled.

*Stop it*, I commanded myself. But my nervous system

didn't listen.

*Please don't do this. Not right now. You only have a few more hours*, I pleaded, but bargaining with my brain wasn't helping.

Julian noticed my anxiety taking over. "Come on, let's get you guys home. All of you need to rest before tonight."

Lucas and Kayla's eyes locked with mine, and I could feel the weight of their worry. It was as if they were trying to read my mind, searching for the answer to my distress.

I tried to brush it off. "Yeah, let's go. I think the lights in here are giving me vertigo."

Julian's hands gripped the steering wheel as we returned home. The only sounds were the faint humming of the engine and the occasional rustling of clothes as I shifted in my seat. My eyes drifted toward the backseat where Lucas and Kayla sat, practically passed out. I offered to swap seats with Lucas so he could sit in the front, but he refused, saying he wanted to be with Kayla in case she needed him. Despite being hungover and recently released from jail, Lucas always had Kayla's well-being at the forefront of his mind.

The tires made a high-pitched noise as Julian pulled the car into the driveway. He pressed the brake pedal, and the car came to a gentle stop. Lucas, who was dozing off, stirred awake. Meanwhile, Kayla was still sound asleep, her head resting on Lucas's shoulder. After he unbuckled his seat belt and then Kayla's, he gently slid his arms around her and lifted her body out of the seat, cradling her in his arms. He walked toward the house with slow, steady steps. Kayla's long braids swayed gently as he carried her, her face looking so peaceful in his embrace. I longed for that. I wanted someone who would carry me out of a car, hold me close to provide comfort, and set their own needs aside for mine. I craved all of it. I had that once, and I let it go.

As I reached for the seat belt release button, Julian grabbed my hand, halting me in my tracks. His soft eyes met mine in a way they only did when he was about to give me a dad talk. "Do you remember when I picked you and Jamie up from the station after that party at Lover's Lake? The one right before your prom when Bethany asked Jamie to the dance?"

I love how he remembered all the dramatic details. "Kinda. Honestly, most of the details are quite fuzzy after the police broke up the party and took me and Jamie."

His face turned serious, and he adjusted his body to face me better. "You both rode home in silence. I had never heard you so quiet in all your years. Normally, you couldn't resist talking to Jamie, even when you were mad at him."

"I liked hearing his voice," I whispered to my hands, tightly clutched in my lap. "Even when I wanted to punch him in the face." My cheeks cracked with a dry chuckle.

"Jamie went inside, but you hesitated. When I asked what was wrong, you didn't respond but instead asked a question."

I genuinely couldn't remember this conversation, only little fragments. Then again, when it came to emotional meltdowns, I tended to erase those from my thought bank. "What did I ask?"

Julian took a deep breath. "Why does love hurt so much?"

"Oh." My chest aches. It turns out that I was still plagued by the same pain that haunted me at seventeen. "What did you say back to me?" I asked, not allowing my watery eyes to connect with Julian's comforting ones.

"I told you: love hurts so that you know it's real." Julian placed his warm hand in mine, stopping me from picking at my cuticles. "Just because we don't have that love anymore doesn't mean it never happened."

I wanted to believe that, but the faster the years moved, the farther I felt from Jamie. The moments and memories began to mush together like one big dream, sometimes a nightmare.

"That pain." Julian's hand reached out and gently pressed against my chest, over my heart. "The ache you feel right here. It's not a curse. It's a gift. Without it, all the good moments lose their importance, and all the bad moments lose meaning. It's that pain that makes every moment eternal." He intensified his gaze. "Don't lose yourself in trying to escape the pain."

My chest began to heave up and down, and I realized I was crying. Tears streamed down my face, and I couldn't stop them; there was a lump in my throat that I couldn't swallow. I cried for every fight, every kiss, every hello, and every goodbye. I knew that if reliving that pain meant feeling Jamie's arms around me one last time, I would welcome every second of that beautiful torture.

Julian leaned over the car console and wrapped his arms around me, causing my head to rest on his shoulder. I couldn't stop sobbing, and my tears were likely leaving permanent stains on his plaid shirt. I hated crying—I despised it. Yet the moment I returned home, that was all I seemed to do.

"The trick is to accept the pain without letting it bury you," Julian whispered into my ear and rubbed his hand in gentle circles over my back, trying to soothe me. It felt as if I were a five-year-old child again, crying in his arms after scraping my knee while learning to ride a bicycle.

"I know," I mumbled into his shoulder. "But I'm just so mad at him all the time."

Julian lightly shook his head. "You're mad at his decisions, not at him." He lifted my head from his shoulder and moved my face to look at him, "That poor boy's biggest fear was dragging you down with him. Don't let his fear become a reality."

Tears streamed down my face, and I struggled to catch my breath. Julian tried to ease me out of this difficult conversation. He unbuckled his seatbelt and gave me a reassuring pat on the shoulder. "Come on, kiddo, let's get you cleaned up."

As we stepped out of the car, my legs felt a little wobbly, but before we reached the front door, I threw my arms around Julian and squeezed him as tightly as I could, burying my entire body into him. For just a little longer, I wanted to feel like his little girl again, like he could somehow solve all my problems and save me from myself.

"What's this for?" he asked softly, squeezing me back.

"Thank you," I said, my face still buried in his chest. "I've never told you thank you."

"For what?"

"Being my dad."

I had never called him that before. In my heart, I hoped my father would pull himself together. All these years, I reserved the title of 'dad' for him, wishing he might someday earn it. I focused so much on what I lacked that I overlooked the blessings right in front of me. Perhaps that's the curse of human nature; we become so distracted by the “maybe” in the future that we fail to appreciate the love right in front of us.

# CHAPTER 19

Family isn't always blood
And blood isn't always family
Family is the hands that lift you
The arms that hold you steady
And the voices that call you home

**11:40 a.m.**

The blinding light crept through the window, waking me up from my hungover slumber. My eyes peeled open, revealing the morning light as the world around me appeared distorted and overly bright. I squinted and peeked one eye around, my brain still slightly dazed as I shrugged awake. I pulled the comforters high up over my aching body, wrapping them tightly around me like a little cave filled with warmth and comfort. Today was the day. Today was the day I would be forced into a room with people I hadn't seen in five years, people I planned on never seeing again. Maybe I could pretend to have a contagious illness and fake a quarantine for forty-eight hours ...

No, I can't do that.

Can I?

No. No.

Well...

No!

You have to get out of bed, my inner monologue ordered me. I pulled the covers off, but nothing happened. Move. Still nothing. Any time now? I tried to sit up, but a sudden wave of pain knocked me back down.

"Oh God, my head," I grumbled, squeezing my temples as if my head were an orange I was trying to juice. The room spun, and the ceiling refused to stop moving. I closed my eyes and pushed my forehead into my pillow. I didn't know what was worse, being this hungover or the sickening anticipation of the coming day. After 4:00 p.m. today, I could hide away and die, but right now, I needed to grow up before I threw up.

I heaved myself upright on my bed and rested there for a few seconds, trying to force my vision to steady. Then, I allowed my feet to graze the floor beneath me and hoisted myself up to stand before taking a deep breath and moving forward. I tried to focus on putting one foot in front of the other as I approached the door. As I reached the door handle, it emitted a high-pitched, piercing sound.

"I hate these rusty hinges," I cried.

I dragged my lifeless body down the stairs, my hand tightly gripping the railing with each step, my legs wobbling and shaking as if the wood beneath was a surfboard in a thunderstorm. My foot hit the last step, and my nose caught the beautiful aroma of salty pig wafting through the hallway. I followed the smell to find my mom cooking a perfect combination of crispy bacon, juicy sausage, and fluffy pancakes. Lucky for me, my mother cooked when she was angry.

My mom stood over the stove, scooping pancake batter into a steaming pan. Julian was already seated at the dining table, reading his morning newspaper as he did every day. Lucas and Kayla, looking almost as bad as I felt, were drowning their headaches in syrup and gallons of coffee.

"Did a chicken try to murder us last night?" My brain was taking a minute to wake up.

My mother flipped a pancake on the skillet. "Yes, and with just cause." She slapped the pancake onto a plate, drizzled syrup on top, and aggressively threw sausage on the side. "What were you three thinking?" She shoved the plate at me.

I stared at the plate in my hands. "Coincidentally, pancakes had something to do with it." I pulled my eyes back to my mother. "Wait, how did you make pancakes without eggs?"

My mother's nose flared. "There were extra eggs in the garage fridge."

I carried my plate to the dining table, set it down on the surface, and slammed my body into the chair. "We have a fridge in the garage?"

Frustration etched between my mother's wrinkled forehead. "Only since you were ten."

I sheepishly smiled back, but that seemed to irritate my mother further. So, I shifted my attention towards Kayla. "Hey, at least you finally got your pancakes."

"If only I could keep them down," she grumbled, her face tinted green.

Lucas shoved his fork into his stack of syrupy flapjacks. "These would have tasted much better if I hadn't slept on a jail cell floor last night."

I rolled my eyes. "Oh, come on, we were only locked up for a few hours. Don't be such a crybaby."

"Crybaby?! You got me thrown into jail!" He huffed back.

"No," I argued and shoved my finger toward Kayla, pointing at her dramatically. "We got you thrown into jail."

"Why are you dragging me into this?" Kayla pouted.

I raised my brows at her. "You're the one who wanted the pancakes. And you're the one who came up with the brilliant idea to steal the eggs."

Kayla opened her mouth to protest, but stopped. "... yeah, okay, you're right. Mixing weed and vodka was not a good idea."

There was a sudden clamor of clashing pots and pans from the kitchen. The noise jolted me awake and made me sit up straight in my seat. I could hear my mother's sharp intake of breath from the kitchen. She stormed her way into the dining room, the sound of heavy footsteps echoing through the house. In her mitten-covered hand, she held a sizzling pan of perfectly cooked hash browns. Although I should have been worried about my mother's bright red face of fury, all I could focus on was the enticing smell of greasy potatoes that seemed to call out to me.

"You kids got high!" She pointed at us with an accusing finger.

Julian's newspaper dropped from his face to the table, his eyes wide as he stared at Kayla. "I was leaving that part out of the story ..." He uttered each syllable through clenched teeth; panic laced in his voice.

My mother placed her hand on her hip. "After everything

that happened on graduation night, I assumed you kids would have matured, but obviously not."

The thought of graduation sent a shiver down my spine. For most teens, graduation is the best day of their lives, when high school becomes a thing of the past and the future embraces them like a warm hug. For me, however, graduation was not a new beginning. It was the end.

I tried to lighten the mood. "You know, technically, we're not kids anymore. You keep calling us that."

From the look on my mother's face, there was a good chance I was about to be wearing those hashbrowns.

"Until you three stop acting like toddlers, I will call you whatever I damn please." She tossed a hash brown on Julian's plate but snatched it away when I tried to grab one. "I don't think I've ever been so mad at your stupidity."

Lucas squinted. "Really? Not even senior year when she drove the car through the school gym."

"Hey, that was over five years ago!" I pouted. "And it wasn't even that bad."

"Not that bad?" Lucas leaned back in his chair, folding his arms like a judge about to win a case. "You were three feet from running our PE coach over. I'm surprised he didn't sue you for emotional distress."

I looked over at Kayla. "Maybe if someone had set the alarms like they promised, I wouldn't have had to race to the school at ninety miles an hour."

Kayla choked on her orange juice, barely managing to swallow before bursting into laughter. "Don't turn this around on me. You busted through a cinder block wall!"

"Thank God you don't drive in the city," Lucas added. "You're twenty-two years old, and I bet you still drive like an 80-year-old with cataracts."

I paused in mid-bite of my toast, narrowing my eyes at him. "I can drive just fine, thank you very much. I just haven't needed to since senior year."

Julian let out a hacking laugh. He rested his elbows on the table and gave me a smirk that indicated he was about to share some unsolicited dad wisdom. "We could test that theory. How about we all get into the car for a driving lesson? Let's settle this debate once and for all."

I stared at him, the toast halfway out of my mouth. He couldn't be serious.

"It's almost noon. We don't have time." I pointed to the clock hanging to my left as if it were the prince who would save me from this madness. "We have to leave by 2:30."

Julian shrugged as if it were no big deal. "We've got time. And we could all use a little distraction before tonight, right?"

"I'm still in my pajamas. We all are." I tried one last defense.

Mom jumped in. "So? It'll be like when Jamie would come over for sleepovers, and I took you kids to McDonald's in your pajamas in the middle of the night. Remember?"

"Yeah," Lucas chimed in. "I remember you and Jamie getting the same thing every time. He got the Oreo McFlurry, and you got the M&M. Then, halfway through, you guys switched, which was disgusting.

Kayla grimaced. "Gross."

"We were eight," I defended.

Julian chuckled. "I'm pretty sure you two continued that little arrangement throughout senior year."

I let out a long, dramatic sigh. "Fine, I'll go along with this driving lesson if we stop talking about Jamie and me swapping spit, okay? I pushed my plate away and crossed my arms in defeat. "But I'm not responsible for anything that happens in that car."

It wasn't so bad.

The car rolled slowly into the empty school parking lot. My palms clung to the steering wheel like it was a lifeline, but my pulse had slowed down from "impending doom" to "mild anxiety."

"See? You've got this. There's nothing to be scared of," Julian said from the passenger seat, his voice annoyingly calm, like always. I did appreciate him not mentioning the mailbox I almost demolished on the way out of our driveway.

Of course, Lucas wasn't going to let me off that easily. He watched me like a hawk from the back seat, his judgmental eyes glaring at me in the rearview mirror, his grin tugging at the corners of his mouth, waiting for my next disaster.

Kayla leaned lightly forward to speak. "You're doing pretty good, Alex. I mean, you're driving like a grandmother on sedatives, but technically, this is driving."

I shot her a look. "Hey, I'm respecting the speed limit, thank you."

I tried to ignore everyone around me and focused on the lot. Thankfully, the school was empty, with just a few stray cars near the gym. I was driving in a giant circle around the large parking lot with virtually zero chances of danger. I could do this—slow and steady, with no sudden movements. No crashes. No casualties.

Maybe this was all right.

Maybe I overreacted all those years ago.

"Perfect, Alex," Julian encouraged. "Keep it smooth, easy turns."

I nodded, easing the car around the curve of the lot. The wheel moved smoothly under my hands. A slight twinge of confidence was growing inside me, a tiny spark of pride warming my chest.

"Why don't we try parking?" Julian said.

"I don't know about that," Lucas said. "That's how I got whiplash the last time."

I scowled at my brother. "Don't be a backseat driver."

I turned the wheel to the right, aiming for one of the painted parking spots on the far side. My foot was steady on the pedal, my hands precise. Everything felt controlled, the tension in my shoulders easing, and my body relaxing. "I've got this," I muttered under my breath. I pushed my foot slightly down on the gas, and the car responded perfectly, gliding forward with a gentle ease.

Maybe parking wasn't so terrible.

Maybe—

Maybe I should have picked a parking spot that wasn't in front of a light post …

I pressed the brakes, slowing the car to a crawl as I prepared to ease into the space. The wheel turned under my fingers like magic, the post lining up perfectly with the vehicle. I could feel the triumph building, a smug grin creeping onto my face, and then ... I saw it. In the rearview mirror, Kayla's hand moved towards Lucas's. Their fingers intertwined.

My stomach dropped. What the—

I turned my head, curiosity pulling me to look at them, completely forgetting to put the car in park. My stomach dropped as the vehicle began to roll forward. Panic surged through me, and in a moment of sheer terror, I pressed the gas pedal instead of the brake. The car lunged forward violently, a wild beast escaping its restraints.

We charged towards the light post. The car's bumper collided with the metal pole with a loud crunch. The car stopped, but the damage was already done. There was a moment of silence as we tried to process what had happened. To make matters worse, Kayla was still holding hands with my brother. Embarrassment ached in my stomach. Betrayal and anger burned inside my chest. And a bit of terror mixed with panic shook me to my very bones.

No one dared to speak first. I let out a long, slow breath, pried my fingers from the wheel, and sank deep into the seat. My cheeks were burning, and humiliation rolled over me. My breath felt suffocated, and I had to get out of the car. I quickly unbuckled my seat belt and pushed the car door open, my hands shaking as I stepped out, gravel crunching underneath my sneakers. A metallic taste of anxiety laced with anger coated my tongue, a deep acid burning inside my chest that had nothing to do with the car crash. I glanced back to see Kayla and Lucas still sitting in the back seat, their hands untangling slowly like neither of them had realized they were intertwined with each other just seconds ago.

The distant sound of the fire department and police sirens was muffled by the sound of my pulse pounding in my ears. Someone in the school must have seen me plow into their light and called the cops.

Lucas was the first to swing open the car door, fumbling slightly as he climbed out onto the asphalt. Kayla followed closely behind. My mother and Julian chose to remain firmly seated.

Words suddenly escaped from my mouth. "After what she did to you, Lucas, you're just going to take her back? One night of delusion, and you're ready to forgive everything?" The bitterness of the words lingered in my mouth.

They both stood there, frozen. I knew I was overreacting, and I understood that they had every right to be together. But if I couldn't have Jamie, why should they have each other? I realized I was being selfish and bitter, but today, of all days, I couldn't bear to watch them build the life I would never have with Jamie.

"Alex, it's not—" Kayla's voice was soft but scratchy like nails on a chalkboard. I wasn't in the mood for excuses. Not today.

I took a step closer, my arms crossing tightly over my chest. "Not what? Not you playing Lucas again?" My gaze flicked between them.

Kayla glanced at Lucas, desperately searching for backup, but Lucas stood silent. His shoulders were stiff, and his mouth was sealed. "Why can't you let it go? I thought last night may have changed things."

"Because it's not fair!" I screamed.

The distant wail of sirens sliced through the air, their red and blue lights flashing in the corner of my eye. Julian stepped out of the car, leaning against the hood. The fire department, police, and EMTs surrounded us. We stood there awkwardly, silent, as one of the police officers approached.

"All right, folks," he said, stopping in front of Julian. "Mind telling us what happened here?"

Julian rubbed the back of his neck. "I let Alex drive." He pointed toward the fallen light post, now lying pathetically on the ground with wires poking out, still smoking slightly from sparks.

"Again, Alex? You hit the school again?" the police officer said, mouth wide open. Everyone was aware of my driving record.

"It was an accident! And I only hit the light, not the building this time."

"Uh-huh. Sure, that makes it better." He scribbled something down on his notepad. "The fire department needs to check the light, while the EMTs must examine everyone in the car. It's standard procedure to ensure no one is hurt. You know the drill."

Yes, I knew the drill.

"We're fine," I said quickly, but he didn't seem to care.

And that's when I heard a familiar voice.

"You three okay over here?"

The voice was low, familiar in a way that felt like a memory. As I turned my head to look, the intense sun blinded me. Blinking rapidly, I attempted to focus my eyes and adjust to the sudden change in brightness. My mind played a trick on me for a fleeting moment, and I caught sight of Jamie's father. My heart leaped into my throat, and a cold sweat broke out on my forehead. I knew my imagination was running wild, but it still made my body freeze. The last thing I wanted was to see that man anywhere near me.

My eyes widened as I blinked rapidly, and my vision cleared, allowing me to see better.    Not possible.

I rubbed my eyes again.

Why is the image not changing?

I blinked again. What was in those pancakes? I must have been hallucinating.

But I wasn't. No matter how many times I blinked, the person standing before me never changed. Jamie's dad was standing three feet from me, wearing an EMT uniform, hair slicked back, and clutching a first aid kit.

My heart stopped. It didn't race like it usually did when panic settled in; it just stopped. The last time I saw Jamie's dad was when I ran out of his trailer after discovering Kayla in Jamie's bed. That was the last time I saw Jamie in five years, until last month when he knocked on my apartment door in Boston.

A wave of vertigo washed over me, and the air spun. I had to steady myself against the car door to avoid losing my balance. Everything blurred and swirled as the world faded into darkness. My vision turned black, and my mind shut off, leaving me with nothing but the cold, sweet embrace of nothingness.

# CHAPTER 20

The moment you find the one
Your life becomes undone

**August 29, 2016**

Life can change quicker than the snap of a finger. Bad can turn to good, and good can turn to bad. Life after our junior year was much the same. Before prom, life was bad, but afterward, it became good. If only we had known the ruin that would soon impel our future.

The summer before my senior year, life felt like a storybook. Every day, the sun shone, the birds sang, and all was right with our little world. Lucas and Kayla, who had been flirting for what felt like an eternity, had finally made their relationship official. Their love story often resembled something straight out of a cheesy romantic comedy. Meanwhile, Jamie and I were that couple who always seemed inseparable, going on dates every weekend and being sweet to each other to the point of being nauseating. All was right in our little world, that was until the Scholastic Aptitude Test—the SATs—and the question about our college futures came looming.

August 29, 2016, was the night before the test, a weird, late-summer SAT the district decided to squeeze in at the last minute. A dozen textbooks were scattered around my room like depressing decorations. I blinked, the action releasing a disturbing squeaking sound from my dry, rubber-like eyeballs. Glancing up, I saw Kayla lying upside down on my bed with her legs resting high in the air on the headboard, flipping through the SAT guidebook as if it were a magazine. Lucas was sitting cross-legged on the floor, surrounded by perfectly aligned, color-coded notes that resembled an art project more than a syllabus. Meanwhile, Jamie was lying flat on the floor with a book on top of his face, acting like a tent, and the sound of his snoring was rumbling through its pages.

"I don't know why we're still doing this. Can we please go to bed, Lucas?" I muttered, dropping my highlighter on the floor and stretching my arms behind me.

Kayla sighed dramatically, "If I have to read one more thing about prime numbers, I'm dropping out of school and joining the circus."

Lucas barely looked up from his note cards. "Maybe if we had started studying this afternoon like I suggested, we wouldn't have to stay up all night," he said. It was true that Lucas had the better idea of studying in the afternoon instead of at midnight the night before the exam. But I couldn't help but watch the Twilight movie marathon on HBO that morning.

I folded my arms over my Scooby-Doo graphic sweatshirt. "Excuse me, Mr. Organized, but if my memory serves, I'm pretty sure I'm the one who suggested that we study last week.

but you wouldn't stop sucking face with Kayla long enough for anyone to study," I shot back.

Kayla rolled over onto her stomach. "I'm going to miss your bickering when we all go off to college."

I chuckled, but a hollowness in my chest made it difficult to breathe. College was the exact conversation I was trying to avoid.

Kayla shuffled forward on the bed, resting her head lightly next to Lucas, who was below her. "Hey, I found this super cute apartment right next to Stanford. It's only a five-minute walk to the campus café. How great is that?"

Tension tightened in my chest. I knew it was coming, but hearing her talk about it as if it were a done deal made everything feel real. My entire life, the only thing I had focused on was escaping this tiny town. Don't get me wrong, I had a great childhood, all things considered, and this place would always be home, but I didn't want it to be my final destination, as it was for many of the people who graduated from high school here. Yet, when the opportunity to escape was right within my grasp, I surprisingly no longer wanted to seize it. For once, everything was perfect.

Someone tucked a piece of hair behind my ear, and a body pressed into my shoulder. "Hey, beautiful," Jamie said softly, still groggy from his nap.

I shifted my body deeper into his, allowing his arm to wrap around me and pull me to the side of him. "Hey," I said, hoping the conversation about college would end.

Jamie looked up at Lucas. "So, is Stanford a done deal?"

Ugh, why does Jamie have to keep talking?

Before Lucas could answer, Kayla jumped in, her smile

stretching from ear to ear. "Definitely! I've been planning it for months. Just need to crush this test tomorrow, and the rest is history."

Jamie nodded lightly, his body sinking a little bit. My eyes flicked up to him, but his gaze was locked on Kayla and Lucas. There was something dark in his expression, something quiet and restrained, a look that I, too, was mirroring.

Kayla was oblivious to our discomfort. "What about you guys? Have you figured anything out yet? You two never talk about the future; the times are ticking."

Yeah, I know.

I gulped and looked down at my textbook. "We haven't discussed it yet."

Jamie took my textbook away from me. "Maybe we should …"

"Now?"

"Can you think of a better time?"

"At my funeral, preferably."

"Not funny."

A shift in his tone silenced the room, and even Kayla set up, her highlighter rolling off the bed. I swallowed hard, feeling the weight of unspoken words. His gaze was locked on mine, something profound and urgent shimmering beneath the surface.

"I think you should apply for Emerson," he said.

I shrugged. "Why?"

His eyes narrowed. "Because you've been talking about that program since we were fifteen."

I felt my face flush. "So? Things change. I don't want to go that far away from home."

Jamie's eyes widened, and he quickly pulled his arm away from me, his body tensing with surprise. "Since when? That's been your only dream since you were like six."

Now, I was getting irritated. "Why do you keep using the past like an equation to calculate the future?"

Jamie's jaw clenched as he stared at me. "Why do you keep pretending it's not?"

I dropped my gaze to my hands and picked at the cuticles of my nails. "I don't want to go somewhere you're not."

He took my hand in his. "Who says I won't be there?"

"What do you mean?"

A smirk tugged at his lips. "Boston's got other schools. State schools and community colleges. I'll get in somewhere."

My heart stuttered. "You'd ... go to Boston?" My voice came out quieter than I intended.

He shrugged like it was the easiest decision in the world. "Where you go, I go. I'd follow you anywhere."

I was speechless at his words. Without hesitating or talking myself out of agreeing to this plan, I grabbed the front of his shirt, pulled him into me, and pressed my lips to his. In that instant, nothing else mattered. Our lips said more than words ever could.

Kayla groaned. "And we've officially hit rom com territory. Someone get me popcorn for this chick flick."

Lucas chuckled, but he didn't interrupt. Jamie and I didn't move; we were locked in our little bubble of romantic bliss. It was sappy, but I couldn't help but feel a little hope for the future.

Jamie wasn't just saying it; he meant it. Jamie would follow me to Boston, to the ends of the earth. He would always be by my side.

"Just think about it," he added, leaning deeper into me. "You're meant for something bigger than this town, Alex. Don't settle. Not even for me."

I bit my lip. Honestly, I hadn't even planned on applying. I wasn't sure if it was the fear of rejection or the possibility of getting in that held me back from filling out the application. But the way Jamie was looking at me now made me reconsider everything.

"I'll think about it," I whispered.

Three loud knocks pounded my bedroom door, rattling the knob.

"Hey! Why are you kids still here?" Julian's voice boomed, the urgency in his tone snapping me awake.

Still here? I rubbed my eyes and glared at my alarm clock.

Oh shit! It was 8:30 a.m.!

A bolt of panic surged through my chest. "Oh my God!" I launched my feet off the floor like a rocket shooting to the moon.

I twisted my neck, feeling a sharp crack and pop as I looked around. Jamie and Lucas were crumpled up next to me, snoring softly, their limbs entangled in a mess of scattered papers and textbooks, a sticky note with Lucas's elegant cursive writing plastered directly on his forehead. Meanwhile, Kayla sprawled out on my bed like a princess under a sleeping spell.

"Get up! Get up! We overslept!"

Jamie mumbled from the floor. "Five more minutes, Mom."

"Wake up!" I yelled so loudly that I was surprised my windows didn't break.

Kayla rolled off the bed, landing with a loud thud. She squinted as the morning sun hit her face. "No … no! Why did no one set an alarm?"

I balled my fists up at her. "Because you said you would set an alarm." I snapped.

"… oh." She guiltily smiled back.

Lucas scrambled to his feet, frantically searching for his phone. "The test starts in ten minutes. We'll never make it in time."

"We will if I'm driving," I announced, throwing my hair into a bun that looked worse than a bird's nest.

Lucas shoved a calculator into his backpack. "Absolutely not! If you drive, we will all die before we get there. And mark my words; I will haunt you in the afterlife."

I slipped on mismatched socks and stuffed them into my Converse. "How would that work exactly? You'd be hunting another ghost. I think there's a flaw in your reasoning." Even though we were late for the most crucial test of our lives, I wasn't about to miss the chance to tease Lucas.

A blue vein throbbed on his forehead as he threw a sweatshirt over his white T-shirt. "Maybe if I hadn't slept on the floor and hadn't been woken up by my sister screaming at me, my brain would have had more time to process logic!"

"Touché …" I tripped over Jamie's knees as I tried to reach the door. "Jamie, get up!" "No," he whimpered.

"Lucas, can you please handle him?" I asked.

"I've got this." Lucas bent down and lifted Jamie off the

floor as if he were a bag of bones. "Come on, man."

Jamie's black hair fell over his face like a curtain. "I hate both of you," he grumbled at us as we pushed him through the door. Kayla trailed behind, applying a thick coat of gloss to her lips.

I gripped the wheel of Lucas's car tightly, my knuckles turning white and my foot pressing the gas pedal harder than a block of iron. My stomach turned with nausea as we screeched into the school parking lot. We had sixty seconds before the test would start—sixty seconds before they would lock the doors and keep us from our college dreams. Sixty seconds before, I felt like I would hurl all over the school's front lawn.

"Park here," Lucas directed; his voice annoyingly calm for someone who should be panicking.

I pulled the car into the spot, our bodies flinging forward as I stepped on the brake. By some stroke of luck, we had secured the best parking spot in the whole lot, ten steps away from the gym's open double doors.

Jamie, who was in the passenger seat, clutched the car's handle like it was the last life jacket on the Titanic. He looked at me in horror and said, "Are we alive? I saw a white light after you ran the third stop sign."

"I prefer to look at those as suggestions," I argued.

Lucas poked his head between me and Jamie. "You're not in the lines," he pointed out.

"Does that matter right now?" I barked at him, unbuckling my seat belt.

"Yes, it matters!" Lucas insisted, "Rules are essential; without them, society descends into chaos."

I didn't have the time or energy to argue against Lucas's OCD, so I shot him a withering look to save us both the headache before putting my car in reverse. "Fine. I'll straighten it. Happy?"

Except I didn't put the car in reverse.

The car surged forward, bouncing over the sidewalk and shooting into the grass. Adrenaline flooded my brain, and I did the only thing I could think of: I slammed on the brakes.

Only I didn't hit the brake.

I slammed my foot onto the gas instead of the brake. The car lurched forward, smacking into the cinderblock wall of the gym with a sickening crunch. The impact sent a deep crack, splintering across the blocks, knocking a piece loose. A hole opened up in the wall, just big enough to see through.

I sat there, begging for a rewind button to reset the last two minutes of my life. Then, after a beat, a face appeared in the newly formed hole—our gym teacher. They peered at me through the rubble, raised an eyebrow, and opened their mouths to speak, but no words came out. Kayla inched forward from the back seat. "At least we're not late."

# CHAPTER 21

Not all goodbyes are final
And not all hellos
Are meant to last

**May 15, 2017**

Today was the day I had been eagerly anticipating throughout my educational journey: graduation day.

I stood in front of the mirror, my fingers fidgeting with the tassel of my graduation cap as the clips my mom used to secure the blue fabric into my head were digging into my scalp. The bathroom was dimly lit, and I could hear the distant chatter of my fellow about-to-be graduates right outside. I put my hands under the cold water that ran from the faucet. I was ecstatic to be graduating, but I couldn't help but feel a little pang of sadness hit me more frigid than the water running over my skin; this would be the last time I'd ever be in this bathroom. It was the last time I would walk down these halls as a student, and it was the last time I'd sit in the school auditorium. It was simply a day of endings. I should have been filled with hope for the future. I mean, I was about to go to college! Jamie and I were moving to Boston together, and Lucas and Kayla got into Stanford! We were about to start the lives we had dreamed about, but that also meant losing the only world I knew.

I looked around, taking in the graffiti-covered walls, the scribbled profanities, and the inappropriate drawings etched into the paint of the stall doors. It was a strange sort of comfort, knowing that this place would always be the same, even as everything else changed. I took a black pin out of the pocket of my blue gown. I found a blank spot on the cinder block wall and wrote the four of our initials in big, bold letters. Below, I wrote, "Forever and always." The smell of alcohol from the pen filled the air as I wrote the last word. Part of me felt a little bit better knowing that we were now a part of this messy wall.

Kayla's head poked through the bathroom door, and I turned to face her. "Come on, Alex," she hurried me, "everyone's starting to line up."

I took one last look at our names, then roamed my eyes over the bathroom one last time before following Kayla out into the brightly lit hallway that led to the school auditorium. I hurried over with Kayla and squeezed in line next to Jamie, our fingers immediately intertwining as his lips kissed my cheek. Early in the day, I tried to bribe Mr. Madison, our senior PE coach, to let Jamie and me sit together for the ceremony. Still, sadly, due to our last names being nowhere near each other in the alphabet, we were going to be separated, but at least I could steal a few moments with him in line.

I gazed up at him as we stood there, his eyes flashing back at me in cheerful confusion. "What? Do I have something on my face?" he questioned, still wearing a smile.

"Just your normal goofy grin," I teased back.

We're graduating! Jamie is graduating! The thought continued to hit me harder and deeper every second we stood there. I couldn't believe that we all finally made it to this moment. The air around me felt warm, like a giant hug, as we waited for the ceremony to begin.

I looked beside me at Lucas, who towered over everyone and everything as he draped his arms around Kayla. Despite Kayla being fairly tall, she seemed positively tiny in comparison to Lucas, as if he were a giant and she was a Smurf.

"We did it, guys," Lucas spoke in a sentimental tone that made me want to mock him, but I was feeling just as sappy as he was.

Jamie chuckled. "I'm not sure if my diploma counts. Ninety percent of those grades are due to sitting next to Alex in every class." Jamie wrapped his arm around me. "We're just lucky I sat next to Colin. I swear that dude is freaking Urkel."

Mr. Madison threw open the auditorium doors and gestured for us to enter. He began calling our names out to assign us to our seats. My heart was pounding hard in my chest. Something about the idea of climbing up a set of stairs to walk across the stage without tripping over my ridiculously long gown was shooting anxiety into my brain. Once we were all seated, the outside doors swung open, and parents began to take their seats. Once everyone was settled, Ms. Bragg took center stage; there's no doubt in my mind that her speech was stolen from some overpriced self-help book, but it filled me with joy, knowing it would be the last speech I would ever have to hear her give.

The names of my classmates were called out one by one, and they quickly raced onto the stage, giving big smiles and bows as they took their diplomas from Ms. Bragg's hand. Then, the best sound I've ever heard boomed through the auditorium: "Jamie Angeles."

My heart immediately swelled with pride and joy as I watched him walk up the steps to accept his diploma. Jamie was neither a straight-A student nor would he ever be accused of having school spirit, but that didn't matter. He made it to graduation day! He was the first in his entire family to earn a high school diploma; as far as I was concerned, that diploma was worth more than gold.

I wish Jamie's mom could have been here to witness this. She would have been so proud, like one of those crazy parents who bring a giant sign and a bullhorn to cheer him on. But I'm sure she was there in spirit, or however all that works.

As I was scanning the crowd, I caught sight of Jamie's dad sitting in the very back row of seats. I blinked my eyelids open and shut multiple times. I'm pretty sure I let out a gasp because the person sitting next to me smacked my arm. Jamie's dad's eyes were slightly red from the tears welling up in them, and he was smiling from ear to ear. I turned my head to look back at Jamie. He tightly gripped the diploma in his hand, and his eyes looked like a deer caught in the headlights as they focused on his dad. The two men exchanged a slight nod and a barely perceptible smile. It wasn't much, but it was probably all Jamie needed.

After the graduation ceremony, our parents gathered around us, taking countless photos. My mother was determined to capture every possible angle of all four of us in our caps and gowns. She had an endless amount of energy and enthusiasm for milestone events. She directed us to stand in different positions and forced us to smile in unison like we were plastic mannequins at her disposal. Finally, after what felt like hours, she let us go, allowing us to take a deep sigh of relief and quickly change out of our hot and heavy graduation attire. Julian and Kayla's dad were smart and promptly found a cozy corner to hang out in with the other dads, keeping far away from the chaos.

The teachers moved everybody into the gym, which was decorated with picture boards set up to showcase every student's life. It was like walking through a giant time capsule, one made of bad haircuts and braces. I found myself standing in front of Kayla's display, which was possibly the most vibrant one in the room—actually, no, scratch that—it was the most vibrant one in the room. I'm pretty sure my eyes still haven't recovered from the jarring neon pink and fairy lights scattered around the photos framed in purple jewels.

Lucas stood to my right, wearing the suit Mom had picked out for him. "Leave it to Kayla to show everyone up." He chuckled as his gaze roamed over Kayla's display.

"Wouldn't have it any other way."

Jamie approached from my left, his hand wrapping around mine. Meanwhile, his other hand shoved a handful of cookies from the dessert table into his mouth. "Damn, this thing is like an art project. Maybe I should have done more to mine." Jamie glanced at his display board, which consisted of only a few photos stapled to a cardboard poster.

Lucas's expression turned serious as he leaned in to examine the photos of the four of us doing reckless and stupid stuff.

"I hope life is always like this." He sighed.

Jamie playfully punched Lucas's shoulder. "Of course it's always going to be like this! It always has, and it always will."

I heard Jamie's words, and I wanted them to be true, but just like Lucas, a part of me knew it wasn't going to be. It's funny, when I was in high school, I desperately wanted it to end, but when it did, I desperately wanted to go back.

Kayla bounded up next to Lucas, appearing virtually out of nowhere. She had pulled a stellar change in costume and was now clothed in a blinding pink sequin mini dress with oversized puffy sleeves. If Kayla's personality had to be summed up in fabric, this outfit was it. "Corbin says the after party at his house; we're going, right?"

Jamie moved his hand from mine and placed it on my waist, holding me from behind like he always did. I felt the warmth of his embrace as his arms crisscrossed around me. "Do we have to?" he grumbled, his breath lightly smelling of chocolate chip cookies.

Kayla stomped her hot pink stiletto on the gym floor. "Yes! I can't believe you thought I was asking. This was our last night as stupid, careless high schoolers. Tomorrow, we will wake up as soon-to-be college freshmen looking down at the barrel of four years caged in another educational prison! We must take advantage of our last night as reckless teenagers!"

I grumbled back at her, "Come on, Kayla. We have our whole college career to party. Can we just go to my house and watch a movie tonight? I'm exhausted, and all I want is to burrow into fuzzy pajamas and slip into a sugar coma of licorice and jellybeans."

Kayla's ebony skin was now turning an eerie shade of red. "We are not ordering pizza and watching a movie! We are dressed for a fabulous night filled with stupidity and possibly stomach-pumping."

Lucas shook his head. "You do know how to sell an idea, babe."

I always gagged a little when Lucas called Kayla 'babe.'

Kayla was just about to deliver her subsequent plea when Jamie chimed in, "You know what? I'm with Kayla. Let's do the party." I turned my head up at him and opened my mouth to protest, but he stopped me. "She's right. We don't have many nights altogether left."

I tugged on his arm, which was still wrapped around me. "Hey, don't talk like that." I turned my head back to Kayla and Lucas. "No one is allowed to talk like that for the rest of the night." I huffed at everyone. "I'll go to the stupid party as long as nobody says anything else that's depressing tonight."

Lucas hacked a laugh. "Interesting." He snorted.

"What?!" I squinted my eyes at my brother, pouting my lips at him.

He shrugged his big shoulders. "Nothing. Nothing." He raised his hands in defense. "It's just normally we're the ones telling you not to be depressing."

I gasped. "I'm offended."

Kayla twirled a skinny pink braid that cascaded to her waist. "That's because the truth hurts." Her face crinkled with uncontainable laughter, and then suddenly, all three of them were laughing at me as I stood there, mouth gaping at their accusation. It may have been accurate, but it was still rude.

"You know what, fine! You'll see I'm going to be the life of this freaking party. And we are going to have the best night of our lives, mark my words!" I shot back at everyone. This party was now becoming a weird challenge, and I was determined to win, regardless of the slight lump I felt in my stomach at the idea of going.

Everyone has a built-in alarm, a siren that goes off when danger is near. I could feel that alarm going off in me when Kayla asked to go to the party, blaring in my ears, causing my stomach to turn and my throat to fill with acid. Something about going didn't feel right. Sometimes, gut feeling is more than anxiety or nerves. Sometimes, this is the universe physically screaming into our nervous system not to do something. But I could count on two fingers when I listened to this alarm, and graduation night was not one of them.

At exactly 11:00 p.m., we reached the party. Corbin's house was incredible. It was a beautiful, historic 1920s mansion situated atop a small hill. I genuinely believed it was the most stunning house in our small neighborhood, and it blew my mind to know that this magnificent place was soon going to be torn down.

Corbin's parents moved to Aspen during his junior year, leaving him living alone until he finished high school. Corbin was, without a doubt, a prep, and thus, like any good rich kid, he hung with the popular crowd, but honestly, he was pretty far from the stereotypical snob. He was compassionate and approachable, going out of his way to help others. In fact, tonight, he designated himself the party DD, offering anyone a personal taxi service to ensure everybody got home safely.

Corbin was a good guy, but his parents sucked. When he turned eighteen, they put his childhood house up for sale and sold it without even telling him. The new owners didn't want to spend the money it would take to restore the house, so instead, they planned to demolish it with a wrecking ball. Corbin saw this tragedy as the perfect occasion to throw a massive kegger in which we were allowed to spray paint the walls, break the furniture, and sledgehammer the floors.

We parked a few houses down and walked hand in hand towards the mansion like the gushy, lovesick teenagers we were. Kayla and Lucas staggered a few paces behind Jamie and me as they tried to simultaneously suck faces and move their feet at the same time.

As we entered the foyer, the floors vibrated due to the volume of the music blasting through every room and hallway. Bodies were piled on top of bodies, and I'm pretty sure the house was 100 degrees. The loud thump of the stereo was almost deafening as we navigated our way through the sea of newly graduated students, bouncing up and down with their red Solo cups.

Of course, we followed suit and weaved our way to the kitchen, where a crystal bowl sat on the massive marble island filled with a murky purple liquid. Lucas used the plastic ladle and poured three extra-large glasses for the three of us. Since he was driving, he would have to stick with water tonight. I took an enormous sip and immediately regretted my decision. The liquid burned my esophagus and eroded my stomach, leaving me with the aftertaste of a moldy Jolly Rancher.

"Why can't they just serve tequila shots? It's simple. To the point, now my tongue is going to taste like the Jolly Green Giant for a week." I grimaced.

Kayla held her nose and swallowed her liquid down in one gulp. "It's better if you plug your nose and down it," she said, smacking her red cup onto the counter and shaking her head. Come on, let's dance!" She gripped Lucas's arm and pulled him into the living room.

I copied Kayla and chugged the green acid. "I think we should dance," I told Jamie.

Jamie gave me a little smirk as if he found my actions amusing. "Only for you." He begrudgingly took my hands, which stretched far in front of me, waiting to pull him into the crowd of sweaty bodies grinding up against one another, scattered everywhere. We pushed through the crowd before stopping in the middle of all the flying and shaking limbs. I moved my body up and down Jamie's as his arms wrapped around my torso. His fingers traveled from my shoulder blades to the swell of my back, then pulled my hips directly onto his. We certainly weren't allowed to dance like this at school ... I turned my body around and pushed myself against his chest, his hands moving to the front of my hip bones, continuing to drive my body up and down his.

We lost track of time in the swirling haze. My intoxicated brain, mixed with loud music, high adrenaline, warm bodies, and Jamie's hands running up and down me, quickly made the seconds disappear and the minutes vanish into hours. It truly was a fantastic night, the picture-perfect way to celebrate the end of an era and the beginning of our new lives.

But here's the lesson: nothing good happens after 2:00

a.m.

So, when that clock strikes, go home.

My body started to crash, and my limbs trembled from all the dancing. "Come on, let's go sit down." I gripped the back of my tangled hair and lifted it slightly to get some air on my skin. I grabbed Jamie's hand and pulled him over to the couches, which were draped with an obscene number of bodies, causing me to wonder about the couch's structural integrity. I found Lucas and Kayla pretty much horizontal on top of each other in the far-right corner of the large sectional.

I smacked Kayla's leg. "Move it, love birds; if I don't sit, my knees are going to snap. Scoot over." We crashed our bodies onto the pillows, Jamie's arm draping over my shoulder. "I think I've had my fair share of fun. Can we please go home so I can change into my sweats and let the comforters consume me?"

Lucas leaned forward to look at me. "What happened to being the life of the party?" he teased me, his words slurring as his body lightly swayed.

I crooked my head at him. "Are you drunk?" I accused him, my jaw almost smacking my knees. If there was one thing I could count on in this world, it was that Lucas was the most responsible person to bestow the title of designated driver; he was like the drunk-driving safety net of the friend group.

"Maybe ..." Lucas slumped a little further into the couch cushions.

Jamie slapped my brother's leg. "Dude, you're supposed to DD tonight!"

"It's fine, man. Corbin said he'll drive anyone who needs a lift home."

Jamie clenched his jaw and planted his palm on his forehead. "But who's going to drive my truck back?"

Lucas's face was blank, as if Jamie's words were taking the long route to Lucas's brain. "Alex and I can swing by and pick up your truck tomorrow."

I glanced at the almost empty red Solo cup in his hand. "You mean after the headaches wore off?" Lucas's body did not handle alcohol well, and thus, the odds of his doing anything tomorrow were slim to none. "Has anyone seen Corbin?"

Kayla whined at me, placing her hands on my shoulders and shaking them. "Come on now, Alex. Let's stay for another thirty minutes, and then we can go. Please!"

Naturally, I gave in to the madness because even though we were officially out of high school, I was certainly not above good old-fashioned peer pressure. Besides, it was harmless fun. I was with my three best friends in the world, and we were at a party filled with everyone we've known since we were in kindergarten—what could go wrong?

"Look what we have here," a familiar deep voice said from the crowd.

Aiden and Dallas Donahue moved with a particular purpose. Their footsteps boomed in the room as they circled the couch, positioning themselves in front of us. Their presence loomed large, casting a shadow that seemed to engulf the entire space.

Dallas spoke first. "The snitch," he spat at Jamie.

After everything that happened with Jamie's mom and their dad, Jamie didn't go near the Donahue brothers and had skillfully avoided them until about a week before graduation. Jack was up for his parole meeting, and Jamie's lawyer advised him to make a statement about Jack and his business dealings. To keep Jack in jail, Jamie had to snitch on everything he knew about the Donahue family. After that day, Aiden and Dallas circled Jamie like hyenas, ready to feast on their prey.

Jamie launched from the couch and dashed to the fireplace where they stood, narrowing his eyes at the two of them. "Come on, guys, let's not do this here."

Dallas got close to Jamie's face. "You know the rule, Jamie. Snitches get stitches."

My heart raced and pounded against my ribs as I watched Jamie raise his hands, palms out, trying to offer a peace treaty. "Let's not be like our parents, Dallas. I don't owe you anything, and you don't owe your dad either. Let's just all move on."

Aiden stepped forward, the Donahues effectively blocked Jamie in, using their bodies as a wall. "Your family takes orders from us, not the other way around."

Jamie's hand clenched into a fist, so without thinking, I immediately shot up from my seat and grabbed his arm, pulling him. "Just walk away," I begged. "They're not worth it, and you know it."

Jamie loosened his fist.

"Yeah, be a good little boy and listen to your bitch," Dallas hissed at Jamie.

And just like that, our happily ever after was erased. Life is comprised of a series of decisions, some we make, and some people make for us, but how we react to those decisions determines how our story will end. Jamie responded by throwing a right hook.

Aiden quickly defended his brother, delivering a jab to Jamie's chin. Lucas leaped from the couch and shoved Aiden, sending him flying across the room. Dallas retaliated with a hit to Lucas's jaw, and Jamie protected Lucas by grabbing a picture frame off the fireplace and smashing it across Dallas's head. Dallas, a thick trail of blood running from his ear, shook his head back and forth multiple times, trying to steady himself, but suddenly, his body hunched over, and he fell onto the floor, passing out. To protect his brother, Aiden lunged back at Jamie, but this time, I could see a small silver object in his hand.

I always said I would walk through hell for Jamie, but it only became true when I placed my body in front of his like a shield.

The knife tore through my skin and ripped a hole in my stomach. Warm blood began to ooze around the metal. I watched Aiden's eyes widen when he realized what he'd done, and I watched as he bolted out of the house, leaving his brother passed out and bleeding on the floor.

Everything slowed down significantly at that point, and the sound became muffled, as if I were watching a movie underwater. I think I heard Kayla screaming in the back and Lucas dialing 911. I remember my body slouching to the floor and Jamie's arms wrapping firmly around me as he pressed his hands to the surface where the knife still stuck out in my upper stomach. Just before breath abandoned me, I heard the faint sobs of Jamie begging me to stay awake. Then there was nothing. It was like falling asleep after too much cough syrup, groggy and slow, but then all at once. Quiet darkness took over and dragged me into its somber night.

If it's after 2:00 a.m.,
Just go home.

# CHAPTER 22

We yell when we care
We care when we shouldn't
We stay when we should leave
And we leave when we should stay

**May 31, 2017**

After four days of unconsciousness, I woke up to discover that I had suffered severe internal bleeding and punctured my spleen like a pincushion. At least, that's how the nurse described it when she was changing my IV. I felt confused and disoriented for a couple of days.

It took a week before anyone explained to me why Jamie hadn't visited. Lying in the room next to mine was an unconscious Dallas. Jamie had hit him over the head with a picture frame, which caused his brain to bleed. Even though Dallas instigated the fight, he wasn't the one who threw the first punch. So, while I was in the surgical room, fighting for my life, Jamie was behind bars, wondering if he was going to have one.

It took Jamie's dad twelve days to come up with the money for his bail. During those days, Jamie woke up every morning with the fear that he would spend the rest of his life trapped in a windowless room like a caged animal. Even after Jamie was released, he didn't visit me. I understood his absence at first, but my concern for him turned into pure rage as the second week passed.

On the day I was discharged from the hospital, Dallas emerged from his coma. If I believed in miracles, I would consider this one a miracle. Had Dallas not recovered, Jamie would have faced manslaughter charges; instead, his sentence was reduced to assault. While this was positive news, it still meant Jamie would spend six months in jail and would carry a criminal record.

The sentence was bullshit, and everyone knew it. Perhaps Jamie would have received a fair trial if we hadn't lived in a small town where everyone knew each other and if the judge hadn't already decided Jamie's fate before the case reached the court. Perhaps the judge would have considered Jamie an eighteen-year-old who had graduated high school, an eighteen-year-old about to start college, a young boy with a bright future ahead of him—one that was now stripped away.

May 31, 2017, was my first day back home, and my mother was extremely overprotective. She wouldn't let me do anything, not even tie my shoes. After several hours of her constantly watching over me, I was finally able to persuade her to let me go upstairs and sleep by myself.

Was I tired?

Absolutely not.

Was I desperate for some alone time without being asked if I was okay every twelve seconds?

Yes.

I crawled under my comforter and closed my eyes, winching slightly as one of my stitches pulled at the bandage on my stomach. As I was settling in, I heard the unmistakable rumble of Jamie's truck pulling into the driveway. I got up as quickly as someone who had just undergone surgery could and hobbled down the stairs, my mom calling out to me to be careful as I stepped outside.

Something was wrong. Jamie stood there, looking down at the ground, his hands tucked slightly into his jeans' pockets. He was chewing on his lip, a habit he only did when he was nervous or agitated. I ran up to him, unsure if I was excited to finally see his face after all these weeks or furious at him for not coming by sooner. Any argument I had with myself quickly melted away when I tried to grab his hand, and he pulled away, refusing to meet my eyes.

Finally, after what seemed like an eternity, he spoke. "Are you okay? Lucas …" he stammered. "Lucas said you were okay, and the doctors fixed everything."

He still wouldn't look me in the eyes as he spoke. I wish I had told him I was alright and everything was fine. I wish I had given him the support he so desperately needed at that moment, but I was so caught up in rage that I couldn't see past my feelings of hurt and betrayal.

"You know you wouldn't have had to ask Lucas how I was doing if you had just come to the hospital," I shot back at him, crossing my arms over my chest. I flinched when my arm brushed the bandages.

Jamie's hand grabbed my arm, and his eyes went as wide as if I had screamed in pain. "Does it hurt?" His face was contorted with fear and concern.

I narrowed my eyes. "I was stabbed in the stomach. It doesn't feel like rose petals and cotton candy."

It was as if my words had teeth and bit him. His hand slowly descended to his side, and he took a step back, leaning against the solid frame of his truck. "I think we need to talk."

"Really? What about?" My tongue was dry and sliced like everything else I had said. God, why didn't I just shut up?

"We can't do this anymore."

"Do what?" His words baffled my mind, but then it clicked. He was talking about us.

My breath caught in my throat, and my knees started to shake. I felt like the entire world around me was crumbling down and burying me alive. Sure, I was furious at Jamie, but I never envisioned him wanting to break up. I assumed we'd fight, pout, and then make up, like we always did.

"What?" The word didn't sound like my voice. It was high-pitched and raspy as if those four letters got stuck on my vocal cords, trying to escape my lips. "What are you talking about?"

"We can't keep doing this.

"Doing what? Being together? This is stupid, Jamie. We have a plan. We're moving to Boston in August. We're going to live together, and we're going to go to college. That's the plan!"

"Plans change."

"No!" I cried back.

Jamie moved from his truck and inched closer to me, putting both his arms on my shoulders, trying to steady me as my cries came in chest-heaving sobs. "You're leaving for college, and I'm going to be stuck here." I tried to argue back, but he cut me off with his thumb, wiping a tear from my lashes. "I'm going to jail, Alex. They're not going to let me into college."

"Then we'll do the long-distance thing until you're out, and we can save up enough money to live together. You can get a job in Boston. We'll make it work. We always make it work—"

"Not this time." His eyes began to well up, and his words became rough and enforced. "I can't keep holding you back. I won't."

"Jamie, please don't," I begged through flowing tears. "Why won't you at least try?"

He took a long look at me, his eyes skimming my face as if he were memorizing every feature of me. I could see the pain and regret in his eyes, and I knew this was hurting him just as much as it was killing me. There was a fleeting second where I thought he might change his mind when his face softened, and his touch grabbed me a little closer, but then, as if physically restraining himself, he lightly pushed my shoulders back and released me. "Call me when you get to Boston." His voice was barely audible as he strained to speak.

I could feel my heart breaking in my chest—no, not breaking, shattering. You can mend a break with time, but at that moment, I knew I was destroyed: my heart was crushed and forever turned to sand.

With those last words, he turned away, leaving me standing alone. I should have chased down his truck, pounded on the hood, jumped into the bed, and ridden to his house. I should have done anything to make him stay, but I couldn't move; my legs felt heavier than cement.

The saddest part of growing up was learning I had to let

go of things I wanted to hold on to forever. I just never thought one of those things would be Jamie.

**June 7, 2017**

A week later, I hadn't heard anything from Jamie. I had called him a dozen times, but he never answered. Maybe it would have been better if I had left for Boston without seeing him, started my summer job, and allowed us time to discover who we were apart and possibly find our way back to each other. But I didn't. I couldn't, so I went to his place.

The trailer park looked nicer than usual. Jamie's neighbor had planted a bunch of flowers to make the place feel a little happier for the summer. Those flowers filled me with a false sense of hope that maybe, just maybe, I could break through to Jamie, and we would ride into some imaginary sunset together. I wanted him to know that no matter what he did, he could never hold me back. Without him, I would always feel frozen in time—an incomplete puzzle, half a soul, never able to become whole.

I knocked on the silver door of Jamie's trailer, but there was no response. I waited for a while, hoping he was sleeping, but still, there was no answer. Knowing that his bedroom was at the back of the trailer, I walked around and looked up at the small window that overlooked his bed. Unfortunately, it was too high for me to see inside, so I looked around and found some old wooden boxes lying in the yard. I decided to stack them up to create a makeshift stool to reach the window. As I climbed the boxes, I hoped they were sturdier than they looked. The boxes were old and rickety, and I was pretty sure I was going to get a concussion and probably rip my stitches open, but it seemed like a small price to pay.

Once I reached the top of the boxes, I peered through the dusty and cloudy window. The room was quite dark, with only the outside sunlight illuminating it. Despite this, I noticed some movement in Jamie's bed and tried to get a better look by squinting my eyes. My heart sank as I realized that Jamie wasn't lying there, but instead, I saw long limbs peeking through his bed sheets. Before I could take a breath, the girl rolled over. I gasped so hard that my body physically rocked backward.

Oh shit.

I knew it was coming before it happened. My body arched backward, and the boxes collapsed beneath me, sending me hurling toward the ground. I slammed into the dead grass, a jolt of pain ripping through me. My stomach recoiled like it had been punched from the inside, and my stitches stretched to their limit as a rock jabbed into my back.

"Who's out here?" Jamie's dad yelled as he swung open the trailer door and rushed out. He came blasting around with a bat in his hand, ready to pummel anybody who was breaking into his home. Then he saw my motionless body lying on the ground. "Alex ...?"

"Yep, it's just me." I groaned, not wanting to get up, partly because it felt like my entire body was broken and partly because I was humiliated. I glanced down to see a small bit of blood seeping through my shirt.

He rushed over to me and swiftly helped me onto my feet as gently as possible until my body was back on my two feet. I have to admit I kind of wish I were still lying on the ground. My head was pounding, and my ears were ringing. My knees felt like something had grabbed them and twisted them around a hundred eighty degrees, and my back was twitching like it was hooked up to an electric chair.

"Why are you trying to break into Jamie's room?" His tone was a mix of concern and frustration.

"You didn't answer your door," I said, trying to come up with a defense.

Jamie's dad looked at me like I had just reinvented stupidity. "So instead of calling, you tried to shimmy through a window half your size."

My defense was getting weaker by the second. "Technically, I wasn't trying to get through the window; I was just trying to look through the window …"

I don't think I've ever seen Jamie's dad dumbfounded. I mean, truly at a loss for words. "My bad, that makes complete sense." He was mocking me, genuinely mocking me. This was the lowest point of my life.

There was a rustling noise coming from around the trailer. Thank God, somebody saved me from this embarrassment. The person poked their head around and quickly dashed to us when they saw the scene.

It was Jamie. This really can't get any worse.

"Alex, what are you doing here?" He looked down at my stomach, which must have been oozing more blood than I thought. "My God, you're bleeding!" He threw his hands to my stomach, which I immediately pushed away.

"Why is Kayla in your bed?" I shot back at him.

"What?" He shook his head and squinted his eyes.

"Why is Kayla naked in your bed?!" My sentence came out as an accusation more than a question.

Jamie's expression turned from shock to fear and then from fear to guilt. He opened his mouth to speak, but said nothing. He closed his mouth and stepped back, as if examining the situation before him. Then, like a computer screen switching off, his face went blank.

"I think you should go," he said, his voice void of emotion.

I clenched my fist so hard I could feel my nails sinking into my palms. "You want me to go?" I stepped forward, closing the space that he had created. "You want me to go after I find my brother's girlfriend rolling around in your bed sheets?" I tried to calm my breathing, but nothing worked; I was hyperventilating with fury. "If I go right now and you don't tell me what the hell is going on, I'm not coming back."

No, don't say that!

You don't mean that!

"I mean it."

Jamie took three breaths. I distinctly remember those three slow breaths. "Go home, Alex."

When I was stabbed, I thought I knew what it felt like to die, to have your body betray you, to have your breath abandon you. I thought I knew what agony was, but I was wrong. At that moment, I officially understood what death truly meant. It wasn't about physical pain; it was about feeling speechless, motionless, and hopeless.

# CHAPTER 23

Redemption isn't just about repenting
It's about carrying the weight of your failures
And learning to move forward

**1:00 p.m.**

The throbbing in my head made it hard to focus. The world around me felt unsteady, like I was caught between reality and a dream. The harsh sunlight made my vision blur, turning the figures around me into shifting silhouettes. My body felt sluggish, weighed down, and it took me a second to process the firm surface beneath the gurney.

I didn't remember getting on here. Didn't remember much of anything. But the steady murmur of voices grounded me.

Lucas stood closest, his mouth moving, but the words were nothing more than a muffled noise in my ringing ears. I shifted my gaze, and Julian came into focus beside him, his expression tense, his hand braced lightly on my shoulder.

Then I saw him—Jamie's dad.

Crouched in front of me, silent. Watching.

A strange kind of dizziness swept over me—not from accident, not from exhaustion, but from something more profound. Something I wasn't ready to name.

I tried to sit up straight, but I was wobbly. Julian's voice broke through the fog. "Easy there, kiddo," he murmured, his palm steady against my back. He only let go once he was sure I wasn't about to fall apart.

Jamie's dad's face revealed a mix of emotions—concern, shock, and uncertainty. He stammered an apology, his eyes darting from person to person as he searched for the right words. "I'm sorry I startled you," he finally said. "I had no idea it would be you when I got the call."

"No, it's my fault." I shrugged him off, trying not to show how embarrassed I felt. "I'm the one who ran into a light post." I couldn't help but stare at him. Seeing Jamie's dad was like encountering a ghost from my past—like a literal ghost standing at the foot of my bed and yelling "Boo!" at 2:00 a.m.

My mother approached from my right, the loud popping and smacking of her yellow flip-flops drumming as she walked. "It's nice to see you, Tim. I wish it were under better circumstances." It always felt strange to hear him referred to by his first name. I had rarely called him anything other than Jamie's dad.

As I looked at him now, he didn't seem like his usual self. He was well-groomed, with clean-shaven cheeks, gelled hair, and ironed clothes. It felt as if I had been thrown into a parallel universe where everything was upside down and backward.

"Nice to see you as well, Monica," he answered my mom before looking down at me. "I have something for you. I was going to drop it off at your house before tonight, but since you're here …" Not waiting for my response, he turned the corner and vanished around the side of the ambulance.

He returned a few seconds later, holding a medium-sized brown package. "It's from Jamie," he said, maintaining eye contact for so long that it felt like we were in a staring contest. He extended the package toward me, waiting for me to take it from him. "It arrived yesterday. I had planned to drop it off at your house before this afternoon, but I guess now is as good a time as any. I know things didn't end well with Jamie, but you deserve to have this."

My hand didn't reach for the brown package; my arm felt as if it were glued to my side. Lucas noticed my paralyzed gaze and quickly took the package from Jamie's dad. "Thank you, that was very thoughtful," Lucas replied.

Jamie's dad nodded at Lucas and gently lifted me off the gurney, guiding me back to my feet. As he pushed the gurney into the ambulance and closed the double doors, an unsettling silence hung in the air.

He began to walk back to the passenger seat, but when he opened the door, he locked sorrow-filled eyes with my parents. "I've never thanked you both," he said, gripping the door handle as if the words about to leave his mouth might push him over the edge. "I was never able to give Jamie the home he deserved. But you did." He glanced at Lucas, then at me, and finally at Kayla. "You all did. I'll never be able to fully express my gratitude for the impact you've had on his life."

As he started to get into the car, Lucas stepped forward, a deep sincerity in his eyes. "Jamie told me you're sober now, and he couldn't stop raving about how proud he is of you." He reached out, extending his hand to Tim. "Thank you for finally being the dad Jamie always deserved." His voice trembled slightly.

Jamie's dad stood there, his brow furrowed and his eyes shimmering with unshed tears. He opened his mouth, but the words seemed to falter in his throat, lost in a tide of unexpressed feelings. After a moment, he gave a slight nod, reaching out to shake Lucas's hand. His grip was firm yet trembling, and his face was a canvas painted with gratitude, relief, and an ache of sadness.

He cast one last lingering look at us, a flicker of a smile breaking through the heaviness before he quietly closed the car door. The soft click bellowed in the stillness, and then he drove away, the taillights fading into the distance.

After giving me a hefty ticket for reckless driving, the cops and firefighters left. The air was so quiet that I could hear butterflies flapping their wings. It was just the five of us standing in an empty parking lot next to a banged-up car and a scuffed light post. Everyone's eyes were glued to me, waiting for my next move, as if I were a fragile porcelain doll about to fall and break.

"Why is everyone looking at me?"

My mom intertwined her hand around Julian's arm for comfort. "Do you want to go home so you can open the package in private?" she spoke softly to me as if I were a child who had just broken an arm.

I shoved my hands into my pockets and shifted my weight to my back leg, closing my body off to everyone as if my defensive posture would protect me from their questions. "I'm not opening it," I said firmly.

Lucas pushed the package toward me as if he were passing off a football. "Yes, you are," he demanded.

Kayla tiptoed forward next to him. "Alex, you have to see what's inside." She made that statement as if she had a say in what I did.

My cheeks were suddenly burning, and my insides were shaking. I took two steps toward her. "Why?" I shoved my question at Kayla, egging her to say something I could throw back. "Why would I want to see what's inside? It's not going to change anything unless it's a time machine that can teleport me back to last month when Jamie knocked on my door. Or maybe a genie that could grant me the wish of erasing the day you slept with my boyfriend."

I was desperate for her rebuttal, ready to pounce. I yearned for her to defend her actions that night, so I could unleash the full force of my anger and tell her just how terrible I believed she was. I wanted to blame her for everything that had happened, so I didn't have to acknowledge the truth: I was responsible for setting my world on fire.

I moved closer to her face. "You screwed my life when you screwed Jamie."

"I didn't," Kayla whispered through stinging tears.

I pulled my body back slightly. "What?" My question was barely audible.

"I didn't sleep with Jamie." She spoke as if giving a eulogy to the past.

No …

She was lying, trying to redeem herself and change the narrative so she wouldn't be the villain in this story. I desperately wanted to know the truth, yet I was reluctant to let go of the lie.

Lucas pulled away from her, and his towering figure

seemed to shrink as his broad shoulders sagged. "What do you mean you didn't sleep with him?" His eyes searched hers as if pleading with fate to write a better ending.

Kayla's breaths were coming in short gasps, almost hiccups, as she tried to suck in her tears. "A couple of weeks after graduation, my mom called to tell me she was getting married and wouldn't be able to help with my tuition." She looked at Lucas. "I didn't receive a scholarship to Stanford like you did. Without my mom's assistance, there was no way I could make my dad shoulder that responsibility."

The light that usually sparkled in Lucas's eyes had dimmed, replaced by a hollow emptiness. He clenched his fists at his sides, the knuckles white, and drew in a shaky breath. "Why didn't you tell me?"

Kayla gave him a soft smile, tears flowing over her cheeks and lips. "Because I knew you wouldn't go without me."

I gripped the back of my neck, feeling the tension coil like a tightly wound spring. This conversation felt like assembling a puzzle made of sand. "This doesn't make any sense. If you didn't sleep with Jamie, then why were you in his bed?"

Kayla steadied her breath before confessing the truth she couldn't take back. "That day, I went to Jamie's house and told him what happened with my mom. I asked for his help in telling Lucas." She placed her hand on Lucas's shoulder. "I didn't want you to give up your dream for me." Her gaze shifted to me. "While I was there, you texted me saying you were headed to Jamie's place to confront him. That's when Jamie came up with the plan. He knew neither of you would leave us behind unless you thought there was nothing left to save. So, we made it look like we had slept together. I undressed in Jamie's room and climbed into his bed. He was supposed to open the door and let you catch me inside. But at the last second, he changed his mind. He got in his car and tried to find you before you arrived." Kayla paused as if the story could somehow get worse. "But you didn't take your usual route to his house that day …"

There was a lump in my throat, pressing against my words as I tried to speak. "No, it … it was flooded …" My chest tightened, and my breathing became shallow. "I went the back way around the school." One decision, one moment, one wrong turn had changed everything.

Kayla's eyes pleaded for mercy as she placed her arms on my shoulders. "He tried to call it off; he truly did. But you had already seen me. We promised each other we would never speak of it again because the truth was too unbearable to say out loud."

Lucas's knees trembled as he leaned heavily against a car tire. The cool rubber provided a grounding sensation as he slid down to the gritty pavement. His breath hitched, and he pressed his palms against his face as if trying to stifle the overwhelming torrent of emotions crushing him.

This wide-open parking lot somehow felt suffocating, the air thick with unspoken words. A fire surged in my veins—was it anger, sorrow, or just a raw need to scream? My hands trembled, itching to claw at anything nearby to release the tension coiling in every cell.

With a shaky sigh, I slid down the car, my shoulder crashing into my brother's. I drew my knees to my chest, resting my head against the cool fabric of my sweats. Silent tears slipped down my cheeks, pooling in the creases of my shirt.

Kayla's body trembled as waves of sobs, muffled by her hands that were pressed against her face, her breath hitching with every cry. Lucas extended his arms toward her, his expression tender. He gently reached up for her waist and guided her softly to the ground, where we were mournfully huddled together.

There we sat, silent, sorrowful, and somber, trying to figure out how to move on.

With a gentle motion, Lucas picked up the package and placed it in front of me. "We can't go back, but maybe we can go forward."

# CHAPTER 24

Forever isn't always an option
But right now is

**April 4, 2022**

I hadn't seen Jamie in five years until a month ago, when a knock on my door obliterated the life I had built and the life I thought I was going to have.

Before that day, I was doing great. I had graduated from college with an English degree, although I had no idea what to do with it. I got a job as an assistant at a law firm, where I spent eleven hours a day making coffee for wealthy lawyers who were destroying the world. And I had a sexy-ass boyfriend named Mark … who was also sort of my boss and was sleeping with a girl in HR.

But really, I was doing great.

I was sitting on my uncomfortable bed, trying to take off a pair of red stilettos that matched the red blood dripping from the blister on my toes. My injuries were caused by spending four hours on my feet at a mind-numbing wedding rehearsal for Mark's sister, even though he ditched me at the last minute.

With numb, stinging feet, I hobbled to the kitchen to eat the leftovers I stole from the hors d'oeuvres table. As I stared down at my plate covered with food that may or may not have led to a nasty case of food poisoning, I'd be lying if I said my life was looking promising. But everyone struggles in their twenties, right? Everyone receives a text from their boyfriend saying he has to work late with Karen, the HR manager, on a case over wine and pasta at 9:00 p.m. And everyone lives with no lights, A/C, and a fridge containing two apples and half a sandwich they stole from someone's desk, right?

Please tell me I'm right …

Just as I was about to flip a coin to decide whether to eat a piece of cheese that twenty other people had touched, there was a tap at my door. The knock started with some force, but then it abruptly stopped, as if the person's knuckles hitting the wood had scared them into silence.

I stretched my arms behind me, contemplating whether to answer or to pretend not to be home and hide. The person knocked again, but this time with an even more confident pounding. I huffed at the intrusion and shuffled my bare feet to the door, reaching my hand out to turn the cold brass door handle. "If that's you, Mark, you better be here to apologize—" It wasn't Mark.

My words stuck in my throat as my eyes were shocked by the sight of Jamie's face. He looked older. Good. Sexy. He was all grown up. His chiseled features and tanned complexion gave him a more refined and confident look. His hair, now shorter on the sides, was still long and tousled on top. His shoulders had broadened considerably, and the fabric of his shirt stretched taut over his well-defined arms; he certainly wasn't the same wiry teenager he had been in high school. Despite all these changes, he still retained his sweet, captivating smile that always left me mesmerized.

Snap out of it! I yelled at my champaign-soaked brain, regretting the third glass right now.

"Hey, Alex." I'm sure it was my imagination, but even his voice seemed older, as if it had grown rougher. He just stood there, his hands in his pockets, waiting for my lips to move and for my voice to string out a sentence. The boy who had once been my everything was now a stranger standing before me, a ghost of the past I begged my soul to banish.

"Jamie." The word slipped out of my mouth in a single breath. I blinked hard and gripped the door frame to steady myself. "What are you doing here?"

He lightly stepped forward as if testing the waters and the tension between us. When I didn't make a move, his gaze fluttered for a moment, a quick flicker of vulnerability betraying the light smirk he wore just a few seconds ago. "I wanted to see you," he admitted, his words hanging fragile in the air like a string made of glass. "I needed to see you." His voice was barely above a whisper.

Every cell upon my skin begged me to reach out and touch him, to prove he was real, that this wasn't some cruel trick of my longing-starved mind. To rejoin the shards of our past, to make myself whole again with the warmth of his arms around me. But the ghost of what we once had kept me frozen. Instead, I wrapped my arms around myself, creating a shield against the flood of emotions that threatened to crumble the cage I had built for Jamie's memory.

"Well, you've seen me," I replied. "Was there something else you wanted?"

Jamie's jaw tightened, and his gaze flickered with a mix of hurt and acceptance. He took a small step back, his shoulders stiff like he had braced himself for this conversation 100 times in his head. My heart hammered in my chest as I watched him retreat, a slight pang of regret gnawing at my insides like a feral cat.

"Do you want me to leave?" he asked, like a promise. If I wanted him to walk away and never return, he would respect my wishes and vanish again.

"… no." My whisper was so desperate that it made my chest shudder. "Come in." I moved back, allowing Jamie to pass through the threshold and into my combined kitchen, living room, and bedroom.

Jamie moved about five feet in, his eyes roaming the walls as if they would tell the story of my life these past years. "So, how have you been?" This was awkward as hell, but at least it was better than asking about the weather.

"I've been …" I tried to think of something borderline braggy to say, something that would show Jamie how well I was doing on my own, but that would mean I needed something actually to brag about, and with just one look at my apartment, anyone would know I didn't have anything to be boastful of. "Great. I've been great. Got a job at this cool law office." I thought that adding the word "cool" would make "law office" sound less depressing.

Jamie looked puzzled. "Do you want to be a lawyer?" This earth-shattering idea was about to knock Jamie off his feet.

"No!" I spoke louder and faster than I intended. "I mean,

there's nothing wrong with being a lawyer, but four more years of college just isn't for me." Nice recovery. "I'm working there until writing starts paying the bills."

Jamie stood a bit closer to me. "And how long has that been?"

"A few years ..." I know where he was going with this.

"And what have you written during that time?" He quizzed me like one of my old English professors.

I shot my hands to my hips. "Hey, you don't get to show up at my doorstep with your cute smart-ass grin and accusatory tone and assume I'm going to answer your questions," I jabbed back at him.

He stepped forward. His face was so close to mine that I could feel the steam of his breath on my cheeks. "You still think I'm cute." His smile was dripping with arrogance, making my blood boil and my skin shiver.

I was practically panting as my eyes lingered on his lips. "Maybe. But I also think you're a smart-ass."

He swiftly placed his hands on my hips and pulled me into him, our bodies connecting like two magnets. "So, nothing changed."

Those three words made the last shred of my restraint shatter like glass. Without a word or a witty comeback, I crashed my lips into his. It was anything but gentle: it was raw, angry, passionate, and filled with an urgency that bordered on desperation. Our lips moved hungrily against each other as if trying to consume every ounce of longing and regret that had lingered between us since we parted.

My fingers tangled in the back of Jamie's hair as I pulled

him closer, desperately trying to get my body to melt deeper into his. My movements were erratic, burning with a fever, veering into madness. We gripped each other so tightly, our hands moving desperately over every inch of skin, that I feared we would leave a trail of bruises in our wake. We were two halves of the same broken soul, finally reunited after years of wandering in the darkness.

Suddenly, Jamie stopped. His breath hovered above my lips. "Alex," his voice was breathy and low as if he feared the thoughts about to slip out of his mouth.

I didn't want to talk anymore. I didn't want to think anymore. I wanted to forget and feel his body on top of mine. I didn't wish for the past or the future. I wanted now.

I grabbed the collar of his shirt, yanking him down to my level. "Just fuck me already."

Jamie's teeth grazed his lower lip as the corners of his mouth curled in a grin that sent quivers down my already wet thighs. "Yes, ma'am," he smirked.

Our lips crashed together hard in a desperate kiss that tasted like anger, passion, and need. Fuck, I need him. I needed every inch of him.

He slid his hand from my arms to my waist, pulling me closer. I felt the cool edge of the counter push against my back, but I didn't care. All that mattered was the feeling of Jamie's body pressed into mine, the way his hands moved over my figure as if he couldn't get enough; they roamed up and down my thighs, gripping my ass, his nails almost tearing the fabric of my dress.

There was a deep groan from Jamie's chest, then his hands moved to my hips and thrust me effortlessly onto the counter. The cold surface sent a shiver down my torso to my cheeks, but the heat of his touch quickly extinguished it as he gripped the hem of my dress and yanked it upwards until my bare thighs were exposed. His thumbs suddenly trailed down my inner legs; just the damn anticipation of his fingers dancing toward my clit made my body quiver with a begging pulse.

"I'd tell you to beg, but it looks like your body already is." He snickered against my lips, his breath hot and heavy.

"Screw you." I tugged on the base of his hair and bit his bottom lip.

"You're about to," he whispered into my neck. I could feel his smile on my skin.

His fingers slid beneath the smooth satin of my underwear, two of them easing inside, stretching me gently as they pressed against my sides, while his lips traced a path down from my throat to my chest. His hand ran through my hair and clawed down my skin as if we were two starved animals finally devouring our first full meal in weeks. I gasped as he explored deeper and deeper, his thumb rubbing in circles, keeping perfect harmony with his two fingers as they found their ideal spot inside me, a move he had mastered since we were teenagers fooling around. I moaned, leaning into him, my hands springing back and slapping against the counter for stability. His hand tangled in my hair, pulling my head back slightly to give him better access to my neck. His lips attacked my skin as if he might bite, nipping at me as his fingers moved in and out with a relentless rhythm. Each forceful touch, each deliberate stroke, sent jolts of hot pleasure through me, igniting a fire in every atom, threatening to consume my every movement.

"God, I've missed this," I said in a moaning yelp.

"I've missed you," he whispered back.

I released my grip on the counter and thrust my palms onto his shoulders, my nails digging into his skin as the pressure inside me coiled tighter and tighter. Incoherent pleas and moans slip past my lips as my knees try to close, my body begging to feel every last aching sensation building in my core.

"Faster." I whimpered.

"As you wish." And just like that, my wish was his command.

His fingers moved faster, pushing me closer to the edge. I felt my body tense, a wave of ecstasy crashing over me as I cried out his name. Every nerve in my body shakes until my eyes roll into my head, and my back arches tightly. Suddenly, the spasming stopped, and my limbs collapsed on my kitchen counter.

I gasped for air, needing a moment to regain my composure, but Jamie didn't give me a moment to recover. He captured my lips and gave a fierce kiss, his hands moving to my hips again and lifting me off the counter. I wrapped my legs around his waist, and we stumbled towards the bed, his hands keeping me straddled on his body until we tumbled onto the bed, the sheets cool against our heated skin. He tore my dress off, physically tore the seams apart, and threw it aside as if it were nothing but a piece of paper in his way. I repaid the favor by ripping off his clothes as fast as my fingers could fumble with the fabric and tossing them across the room.

I paused, letting my eyes linger over Jamie's exposed torso as he hovered above me. His body had changed since high school; he was no longer the scrawny teen I remembered. His shoulders had broadened, each muscle defined under his skin, and his chest was so solid that I bet I could bounce quarters off it.

I'm so screwed.

He leaned down and pressed two lips on my neck, then my chest, and danced his mouth over my bare breast. I gasped softly, arching into him as he slid in and out of me, my fingernails clawing down his back from his neck to his waist, leaving red scratch marks in their wake. His lean body fit perfectly between my legs, and his hot skin felt heavenly on top of mine. He lifted my thigh to wrap around his waist, his fingers digging into my leg as he pushed harder and deeper into me. My toes curled, and every muscle in my calves tightened and quivered around his back as I screamed his name repeatedly in rough, moaning breaths. Then, as fast as it struck, the sensation released and left me breathless and motionless, buried in my bed sheets.

Jamie rolled to my side, his arm gripping my waist and pulling my limp body on top of his, forcefully stealing my lips as if he were sure that if he released me, this moment would disappear.

My phone buzzed on the counter. Its ring snapped Jamie and me back to reality. Our lips parted from each other so fast that it was as if a scorpion had stung us. Our chests heaved, and our eyes were startled, partly from the continuing ring of my phone and partly because I don't think either of us planned for our bodies to silence our brains.

I sat up and pulled the blanket at the foot of my bed over me, wrapping it around my body. "Let me—let me just answer that." My cheeks were red and pulsing, and my breath still did not return to its normal pace as I hopped out of bed, leaving Jamie speechless and alone on my comforter.

I picked up my phone to see who the intruder was. Damn, it's Mark. "Hey, I'm busy. Can I call you back?"

He seemed frustrated in his response, as if somehow my lack of time for him insulted his fragile ego. After enduring a few backhanded remarks and angry sentences, I hung up, fully anticipating an argument that would come later.

I smacked the back of my phone case on the counter before turning around to face Jamie, who had reclothed his body and was now walking over to me. I ran a hand through my hair, trying to cool down and begging my brain to reboot and refocus on the situation at hand. I kissed Jamie. What was I thinking? What am I doing? And what do I want to do? This was all too much. He was too much. But no matter how many times I told myself these past years to stay away from him, I knew we would end up right here. He was fire, and I was ice. Two halves of perfect balance, forever destined to be each other's destruction.

"Who was that?" Jamie interrogated me.

"My boss," I tried to deflect.

Jamie squinted. "Does your boss always call you at 10:00 p.m., sounding like a bitchy boyfriend?"

"He's not bitchy," I defended, gripping the blanket tighter around my body, suddenly realizing I was still very much naked. "Not all the time, anyway."

Jamie huffed. "Sounds like a real keeper."

Jamie was right; Mark was the worst. Honestly, I was only with him so that my job wouldn't vanish before my eyes; it was a job that was also the worst. But Jamie had no right to come into my house and judge my life, not after he chose to throw away the one we could have had together.

"You don't get to act like a jealous boyfriend anymore, Jamie. You're the one who cheated on me, remember?" I pointed my finger at his chest and jabbed it at him with every word I said. "You broke me. Not the other way around."

His face softened, and his shoulders hunched in. "You're right."

I was? Yes, I was!

He tucked the piece of wild hair out of my face and placed it behind my ear. "I wasn't ready back then, but I'm ready now."

"Ready for what?"

"Ready for you."

I couldn't believe what I was hearing. How could he come here after all these years and expect me to fall back in line, fall back into his arms, and allow my heart to fall for him again? It wasn't right; it wasn't fair. I wanted to be the one to walk away this time.

I pushed his arms off me. "No, you can't do this. You can't do this to me again!" I gripped my head as it spun and pounded with his words. "What are you even doing here? How did you even know where I live?"

His eyes were begging me to give in to his pleas. "Your mom told me." He paused for a moment, his chest rising as he drew in a long, deep breath. His eyes flickered with momentary hesitation as if he was about to reveal a long-held secret. "She told me you're a mess. That you're dating some douchey lawyer, living without power, and that one of your old professors nominated you for the chance to get a book published through the university press, but you never sent anything in."

I could feel every nerve in my body exploding with fury as I screamed back, "And?! So?! What does any of that have to do with you?"

As he leaned in towards me, his eyes locked onto mine with an intensity that made my body ache. "Because I gave you up so you could have the life you deserve." He shook his head. "Not this." He gestured around my apartment.

There was a deep pain in my chest, and I genuinely was concerned I was having a heart attack. "I'm sorry I didn't live up to your expectations." I could feel the corners of my eyes puddling with water; I held my breath, begging for the tears to retreat.

Jamie immediately reached out his hands and put them on my shoulders, his thumbs rubbing little circles on my neck. "Alex, you're everything to me. Everything." His voice broke with each word as if the letters were daggers piercing his skin. "I couldn't give you the life you deserved back then, but I can now." He rested his forehead against mine and closed his eyes. "Please let me give you that life. Let me fix what I broke."

That did it. Hot streams of tears flowed down my cheeks, past my lips, and down my neck. "I can't—I just can't" I cried into him.

He lightly released me, his hands trailing down my arms. Then, reaching into his coat pocket, he pulled out an object and handed me a small, velvet box. "Think about it." My lungs had abandoned me as all forms of breath evaporated, and I was left there standing, staring motionless at the little jewelry box in my hand. "I'll be back in fourteen days. Think about it and tell me then," he said, walking back towards the door without me even speaking a word, without giving me time to comprehend what was happening. His hand was on the doorknob, twisting it open. "I let you go once, and it was the biggest mistake of my life. I will spend the rest of my time trying to make that up to you. I'm going to give you the life of your dreams. You'll see."

He opened the door, his body halfway between the hallway and my apartment.

"I love you," he said.

"Forever and always," I whispered.

With those last words, he walked out the door, closed it behind him, and left me with the weight of the world smothering me until I was lying on my kitchen floor, gripping an engagement ring in my palm.

# CHAPTER 25

Nothing starts impossible
But it becomes so when you cease to try

**1:40 p.m.**

I climbed into the backseat with Lucas and Kayla, my fingers curled tightly around the package from Jamie's dad. Its textured surface was cold against my skin. It felt daunting. I wasn't ready to open it just yet. I promised Lucas I would, but only after we got home. After Kayla dropped the information bomb of the century, I needed a moment to catch my breath.

My dad turned the key, and the engine coughed to life. Honestly, I was shocked it still ran. When we finally arrived home, the house towered above us—an unspoken heaviness hanging over everything.

"Maybe I should go home and change. There's not much time left," Kayla suggested, her voice barely cutting through the silence.

"You can wear some of my clothes if you want. There are

a bunch of my old dresses in the closet. They're probably yours anyway," I tried to keep my tone softer than usual—my attempt at offering an olive branch.

Kayla flashed me a grateful smile, and for a moment, it felt like a fragile truce was forming.

My steps felt like lead as I climbed out of the car. I could hear Kayla's footsteps behind me as I walked inside and traveled up the stairs. Lucas … well, he disappeared to his room to get ready. My mother's voice drifted from the bottom of the stairs, faint and far away. She said something about "forty minutes," but the words barely registered. Time didn't feel real anymore. Nothing did.

I reached my room and set the package down on my bed. The muted thud sounded louder than it should have. My hands felt numb, like they weren't even my own, as I walked to the bathroom. Mechanically, I splashed water on my face, the icy water barely registering on my pale skin. My reflection stared back at me in the mirror, unblinking, as I put on makeup and curled my hair. There was no life in the motions—only routine.

Kayla moved to the closet after what felt like hours of silence, pulling out a dress. I followed her as if on autopilot, my fingers grazing the soft fabrics hanging inside, each item of clothing etched with a piece of my childhood. I lingered, my fingers pausing when they touched my graduation dress. It felt significant, somehow. That day was about goodbyes. Today was no different.

I slipped into the dress, the fabric foreign against my skin, like it no longer belonged to me. Maybe nothing did. I walked to my bed and picked up the package again. Somehow, it felt heavier than before.

A soft knock at the door shattered the fragile silence. Lucas stepped inside, and the sight of him in that black suit nearly knocked me over. His eyes were red, swollen; he'd been crying. "You ready to see what's inside?" he asked gently, nodding to the package. He stepped closer, but I could hardly move.

"No," I said back. "But I never will be." My fingers shook as I fumbled with the package. The air between us grew thick, every breath heavier than the last. But there was no turning back. There, all three of us stood, looming over the package as if it were a snake about to bite.

We huddled together, and our heartbeats seemed to sync in the shared rhythm of anticipation and dread. My hands were cold and trembling as I peeled the tape away slowly; the sound of the cardboard tearing cut the air like a knife. My breath caught in my throat as I pulled the sides of the box apart, terrified of what lay inside. My heart raced, pounding in my chest as if trying to escape this moment.

I hesitated, feeling the weight of everything pressing down on me. Then, with a shaky breath, I peeked inside. Inside the box lay a neatly stacked manuscript, the pages slightly curled at the edges as if they had been handled before. Resting on top was a single envelope, its crisp white paper standing out against the yellowed pages beneath it.

Curious, I reached for the envelope first, my hands trembling slightly as I slid a finger under the flap and pulled out the letter inside. The sight of the official letterhead made my stomach tighten, but it was the bolded words in the first few lines that sent a jolt through me:

"We are pleased to inform you that your submission to

the Creative Fiction Contest has been selected as the winning entry. Please contact us at your earliest convenience to discuss next steps for publication."

I blinked, rereading the words, my mind scrambling. I had never submitted anything.

Heart pounding, I set the letter aside and reached for the manuscript. I gasped as I took in the title printed on the first page: The Enemy of Time. Below it, in sharp, precise type, was my name.

"Is everyone ready? We need to leave soon," my mother called out as she stepped into the room. I barely registered her words, my mind consumed by the letter before me. Suddenly, I felt a rush of air as my mother gasped.

In an instant, she was hovering over me, her eyes wide with astonishment. The sun's rays filtered through the window, casting a warm glow that illuminated her face as she took in the words etched on the pages. "He did it," she whispered, a radiant smile breaking across her lips.

"Did what?" My voice quivered. I couldn't believe what I was seeing. How was this even possible? My mind was racing with questions and doubts. Maybe I was still asleep, and this was all a hallucination from the five-year-old moldy weed. Maybe I was lying in a hospital, hooked up to IVs, in a coma after falling out of Mr. Heckle's tree. Anything would make more sense than what was happening in front of me.

My mother's eyes softened as she spoke. "Jamie came over after he saw you in Boston and asked to go into your room." She placed a comforting hand on my weak arm. "He said if you wouldn't reach for the stars, he would grab them for you." She took the manuscript out of the box and opened it up. "He wrote down all those little poems from your high school journal and submitted them to that contest you refused to enter."

My mom held the manuscript to me, gesturing gently as she passed it back. I took it from her and flipped through the pages, each decorated with the words of my childhood and teenage years. It was like uncovering a time capsule, memories long forgotten suddenly brought back to life and printed on the page for anyone to see.

"He submitted my journal," I said, my voice barely above a whisper.

"He said you always did your best work when you thought no one was looking," my mom replied.

He was right.

My fingers continued to move through the pages until I hit the last one. My breath caught in my chest as I read the final words:

*To: Bonnie*
*From: Clyde*
*-Forever and Always.*

I knew Jamie would be my future—that we would be eternally linked, written in the stars, and forever intertwined. But I never imagined it would be like this. Jamie fulfilled his promise like he said he would; he gave me the future I desperately wanted but was too fearful to grasp. I just always thought that the future would be with him, not because of him.

And in that instant, reality crashed down on me. It wasn't just the book or the day—it was everything. The walls I'd built, the lies I'd told myself, the numbness I'd clung to—it all shattered.

It was real. Today was real.

# CHAPTER 26

You don't have to love to be loved.
You don't have to live to be alive.
You don't have to die to be a ghost.
Life is made of flickering moments.
Hold on to each and every one tight
Before The Enemy of Time says goodnight.

**2:30 p.m.**

We drove in silence, none of us knowing what to say or wanting to speak. The clock had run out of seconds. Time was forcing me to face the events of today: the life I lost and the future Jamie had offered me. But a future without him—without his goofy smile that illuminated even the darkest days, without his warm touch that melted my cold heart, and without his laughter that made every moment feel magical—seemed unbearable.

How does one live without the heart that made theirs beat? I twirled Jamie's engagement ring around my finger, the one he gave me that night in Boston. I spent all night waiting for him on that fourteenth day. I spent hours doing my hair and even longer doing my makeup. I bought the most expensive dress I have ever owned, and I wore ridiculous strappy pink sandals to match. I was planning to say yes to him. I was going to confess my feelings and tell him that I wanted him to hold me and never let me go. I waited all night on the fourteenth day, only to receive a call on the fifteenth informing me that moment would never come.

I had five more minutes left before I had to confront the stark reality that awaited. We passed the old playground where Jamie became my white knight, the open field where the Carnival was held every year, and where Jamie kissed me for the first time. We passed the high school where we dashed out of prom and spent our first night together, truly together. We passed all the places that would forever hold the memory of Jamie and me, but now everything looked gray. Without Jamie sitting next to me, the town was void of all happiness.

My stomach hurt from the memory as we drew near to our destination. Julian turned off the car, and my mom slowly unbuckled her seatbelt. I was sitting in the middle between Kayla and Lucas, all of us dressed in black and gray. None of us was in a hurry to get out of the car. We sat there, hoping that by remaining still, the day would vanish and erase itself from the present. Lucas broke the silence by suggesting that we go inside the building before it was too late. He opened the car door and stepped out, and we followed him. His movement gave us the strength to exit the car and walk towards the large double doors that stood between us, and the truth I could no longer deny. Lucas was just about to open the door, just about to open Pandora's box and unleash all the horrors that came with it.

"Wait! I placed my hand on top of his, stopping him. I

peered down at my finger, the shiny diamond sparkling in the sun like a little star of hope. My story with Jamie was written, and the book was now closed, but Lucas and Kayla's story wasn't over, or at least I wasn't going to let it be that way.

I looked into my brother's mournful eyes. "I let my past erase my future. Don't make the same mistake." I took the ring off my finger and gently placed Jamie's final gift in Lucas's palm.

He fixed his gaze on me with a mixture of disbelief and astonishment. "Alex—"

I stopped him from trying to play the big brother role. "Not every love story needs a happy ending. But yours deserves one." I lightly nodded my head to Kayla, who stood behind us, her eyes glued to the ring like it was a wish fallen from the heavens. "Go get her," I whispered. Small tears trickled down my cheeks, but they weren't tears of sadness. I was crying because I knew this was precisely what Jamie would have wanted.

As Lucas's eyes met Kayla's, a big, goofy grin spread across his face. His eyes sparkled with a mixture of indescribable joy and immense nervousness. His lips parted, and he was about to say the four words that would forever bind the two of them together—

"Yes!" Kayla blurted out before Lucas could get down on one knee.

"Yes?" Lucas asked back in shock.

"Yes." She declared repeatedly until he slipped the ring on her finger and sealed their fate with a kiss.

My mom and dad were standing behind us, speechless, and their eyes were welling up just as badly as mine. In one minute, my world would shatter, but at this moment, I could hold onto the little bit of light shining through the darkness.

Kayla broke away from Lucas's embrace and put her hand on my shoulder. She didn't need to say anything. I knew it was coming, but at least now I wasn't facing it alone.

I gripped the handle of the large double door and pushed it open. I walked into the cold building and looked around to see everyone I had gone to school with sitting in rows of chairs lined up to form a walkway. I moved past them to see Jamie at the front of the room. I don't even remember moving, but suddenly, I was standing right in front of him, looking at his beautiful, messy black hair and sun-freckled nose. I wanted to talk to him. I wanted his arms wrapped around me one last time. I tried to tell him I was sorry for not reaching out again and for not trying harder. But I couldn't and would never get the chance because I wasn't standing in front of my Jamie. I was standing in front of a lifeless body. Jamie's body.

The noise from the funeral parlor was muffled by the sound of my heart thumping in my ears as oxygen left my lungs. I officially couldn't lie to myself any longer.

I wasn't at a reunion. I was at my best friend's funeral.

For a moment, I couldn't believe breathing was even possible. Maybe I was the one who had died, and all of this was some kind of illusion.

I inhaled sharply. My heart was still beating. Air still filled my lungs. I was alive.

But I couldn't comprehend that the person in front of me wasn't. I stared down at Jamie—Jamie, the kid from the wrong side of the tracks, who could never shake his reputation. Jamie, who stole candy bars from the grocery store and sold them at school. Jamie, who copied my tests just so he wouldn't look dumb. My Jamie. My other half. The person I would never be whole without. The person who was now lying in a casket with his head slightly elevated on a small white pillow.

His hair was pushed back, and his face was void of expression. His skin was pale, with no flush in his cheeks like when he was angry or embarrassed, no dark circles under his eyes, and no bruises along his jaw from school fights. I told myself to look away, but I couldn't. Maybe if I could stare at his face long enough, memorize his features, map out the lines and marks on his skin, count his every eyelash, every freckle, I could pretend that he wasn't dead. Pretend that he was still alive and we were both simply living separate lives. I could pretend that he found a nice girl, got married, and had two kids, just as he always wanted. I could pretend that he was growing old and happy, instead of frozen in time, about to be laid to rest beneath the earth.

Jamie was gone, taken from this world at 7:42 p.m., killed by a drunk driver on the wrong side of the road—the night he was driving to hear my answer to his question I'd never get to answer. I never had the chance to say goodbye—I never had the opportunity to make it right. Why didn't I call him? Why didn't I put away my pride? Could this day have been avoided? I prayed for an answer to an unknown question. I prayed for more time—time that I would never get back and time I would never have again. But that's the thing about time; it isn't kind. It passes while you're too busy to notice, too busy to care, until one day, the hourglass is shattered, and the enemy of time strikes, and death steals your final breath.

# Epilogue
## The End?

The backyard looked nothing like the battlefield it had been when we were kids. No abandoned bikes, no half-crushed juice boxes, no siblings screaming about who cheated in tag. Tonight, the grass stood trimmed and polite, fairy lights dripping from the maple tree like someone had shaken the Milky Way loose right over our heads.

Kayla stood at the top of the makeshift aisle, a trail of wildflowers curling around her feet, and exhaled the kind of breath reserved for brides in movies who finally get their happily ever after. My brother waited beneath the arch he'd built from branches and flowers gathered around town, tapping his foot like he fully expected her to bolt at the last second.

When she reached him, my brother brushed his thumb over her hand with a tenderness that made the whole backyard fall quiet, as if the air itself were holding its breath. Our dad stood behind them, chest puffed with pride, delivering the ceremony with a seriousness so earnest it nearly made me laugh.

I caught myself glancing at the empty chair beside me, and a small smile tugged at my lips. I'd kept it open for him—for Jamie—because even if he wasn't physically here, I knew he wouldn't miss this day. The hurting would never fully go away, but it had shifted into something softer, something that wasn't pain anymore.

Their vows were simple. Honest. Awkward in the sweetest possible way, the kind you only get from two people who survived adolescence side by side and still chose each other anyway.

And then my brother slid the ring onto her finger.

Jamie's ring.

Once part of my story.

Now part of theirs.

It's strange how the past can slip so gracefully into the future when you're not fighting it anymore. How something that once felt like the end of my world could become the beginning of theirs.

When they kissed, the whole yard erupted like fireworks, loud, warm, and just chaotic enough to feel like home. And then, in true small-town fashion, everyone sprinted toward the reception the moment the promise of cake and booze became real. The canopy over the tables looked exactly like the backyard forts we used to build, if you swapped out blankets and stolen bed sheets for twinkle lights and linen. Same cramped chaos, same dim glow, same absolute disregard for personal space. Some things really don't change.

Then someone tapped a glass.

My name rose into the air like a question I'd forgotten to study for.

Of course. Maid of honor. Sister of the groom.

A doomed combination.

It was practically guaranteed I'd be giving a speech; I'd just hoped I could sneak away before the glass-clinking brigade got organized. No such luck.

I stood from my seat and brushed off my terrible puffy pink dress, the one I'd been forced to wear because of "the color scheme" and some horrific Pinterest board none of us had the courage to protest. When I looked around, the yard felt smaller somehow, like all our childhood memories had squeezed in around us, watching, waiting to see if I'd trip over my own feet.

"I'm not the best with words; ironic, being a writer and all," I said, already hearing the wobble in my voice. "So, I apologize in advance for whatever mess I'm about to unleash."

I fumbled with a tiny stack of note cards, the speech I'd spent weeks drafting, scribbling out, rewriting, hating, rewriting again, and still somehow despising in this moment.

I looked at Kayla and Lucas, their faces glowing, their cheeks lifted so high it was a miracle they could still see, their arms wrapped around each other like they'd been knitted together. Then my eyes drifted to my purse hanging off the back of my chair. Inside was the first copy of my book. The words Jamie believed in more than I did.

I set the note cards down on the table. They made a soft, defeated flutter. Then I reached into my bag and pulled out the soft-spined book, holding it the way you hold something fragile that somehow survived a storm.

"A friend of ours couldn't be here tonight," I said, my voice steadier now. "So, I thought I'd bring a part of him to us."

I opened the book.

The last page waited for me like a familiar doorway, one I'd been afraid to walk through, until now.

"For Jamie," I said.

And I read:

## THE ENEMY OF TIME

Time has a way
of pulling us forward,
not gently,
not always kindly,
but steadily,
like gravity teaching the tide
when to rise again.

And we hold on to the moments
that make us,
the ones that break us,
the ones that mend us,
the ones that remind us
that love is still a risk
worth taking.

Some chapters arrive early,
some too late,
and some end
before we realize
we were meant
to hold onto them;

But love doesn't slip away
when the clock stops ticking.
It lingers,
in the corners of memory,
in the soft ache it leaves behind,

in the gentle proof
that true love,
when it chooses you,
always finds a way to stay.

And maybe time,
in its quiet mercy,
shows us this:
love outlives every ending.
The last page
is never truly goodbye,
just the moment you breathe
before the next story starts.

When I closed the book, the backyard held its breath. Fireflies drifted between the chairs like slow-moving sparks.

I looked at my brother. "It turns out the past doesn't trap us," I said, my voice steady. "It shapes us. And the future isn't something we wait for, it's something love helps us walk toward. So here's to the two of you… to every moment that brought you here, and every tomorrow waiting to unfold."

Applause rose like a warm tide. I stepped back, letting the night settle around me, the chilled air, the old maple trees, the ghost of the boy who breathed life back into me, and brought my brother back to his greatest love.

Love had opened their forever.

Love had softened my yesterday.

And love was offering all of us a brand-new tomorrow.

# About the Author

Haley-Grace McCormick holds a Bachelor's degree in Creative Writing with a concentration in Screenwriting, along with minors in Art History and Psychology. She has lived across the United States, from California to Florida, gaining a deep appreciation for diverse cultures and landscapes. This exposure has fueled her passionate interest in exploration and travel. Growing up with a father in the hotel industry and a mother who runs nonprofit organizations, Haley-Grace has been immersed in business and philanthropy from a young age, fostering a love for entrepreneurship and a desire to contribute to societal good.

Diagnosed early with dyslexia, dyscalculia, and dysgraphia—the perfect love triangle of learning challenges—she views these conditions as unique gifts. Dyslexia, in particular, has shaped her distinctive approach to thinking and problem-solving, enhancing her creativity and resilience.

Haley-Grace is also a board member and ambassador for Nature's Negotiators, a nonprofit founded by Clare and Max Donovan, where she advocates for environmental awareness and youth engagement. She describes herself as a forever traveling, dyslexic writer and artist on a mission to do good, create wildly, and live passionately.